A HOT DAY IN MAY

Recent Titles by Julian Jay Savarin from Severn House

HORSEMEN IN THE SHADOWS
MACALLISTER'S TASK
NORWEGIAN FIRE
THE QUEENSLAND FILE
STARFIRE
STRIKE EAGLE
VILLIGER

The Berlin Series

A COLD RAIN IN BERLIN
ROMEO SUMMER
WINTER AND THE GENERAL
A HOT DAY IN MAY

A HOT
DAY IN MAY

Julian Jay Savarin

severn
House

This first world edition published in Great Britain 2004 by
SEVERN HOUSE PUBLISHERS LTD of
9–15 High Street, Sutton, Surrey SM1 1DF.
This first world edition published in the USA 2004 by
SEVERN HOUSE PUBLISHERS INC of
595 Madison Avenue, New York, N.Y. 10022.

British Library Cataloguing in Publication Data

Savarin, Julian Jay
    A hot day in May
    1.   Muller, Hauptkommissar (Fictitious character) - Fiction
    2.   Police - Germany - Berlin - Fiction
    3.   Suspense fiction
    I.   Title
    823.9'14 [F]

    ISBN 0-7278-6069-0

Typeset by Palimpsest Book Production Ltd.,
Polmont, Stirlingshire, Scotland.
Printed and bound in Great Britain by
MPG Books Ltd., Bodmin, Cornwall.

This one for PB

One

'*They're trying to kill us!*' he screamed.

They were both pulling hard at each of the control yokes. The small private jet, in an almost vertical dive, howled earthwards. Twenty thousand feet below, the jagged peaks of the Alps, white smears of snow giving a camouflaged pattern to their dark rock surfaces, waited in unforgiving solidity.

'*It won't . . . move!*' she cried, all hope gone.

Her hands, white-knuckled, had a powerful grip on the right-hand yoke, straining to haul it back towards her.

'*Keep trying!*' he urged. '*Keep trying!*'

But the yokes remained stubbornly immovable; and the peaks were fast approaching. Soon they had grown massively, blotting out the daylight.

'Oh God!' he cried softly.

'Jens!' she said.

That was all they had time for as the glistening rampart of a mountainside appeared to slam at the jet, squashing it like a fragile insect. The aircraft burst into a fireball that spilled its way down the mountain, trailing flaming debris and shards of avalanching rock.

'*Aaarrgh!*'

Müller jerked awake to sit bolt upright in bed, breath rasping, eyes straining open in the darkness. The nightmare still mirrored itself before him, the gloom serving as an eerie screen upon which it was displayed. Then, gradually, taking its time about it, it faded.

1

'Jesus,' he muttered softly, fighting to control his breathing. 'It was just a dream.'

His entire body was damp, and he could almost smell the singeing of his flesh in the flames of his nightmare.

As the image in the surreal mirror finally left him alone, his eyes focused upon the lights of Berlin-Wilmersdorf.

The vast bedroom in the four-bedroom, penthouse apartment atop the building he owned, was not truly dark. Beyond the foot of the bed, a full third of the wall, which ran the length of the building, was taken up by huge, triple-glazed windows that were almost floor-to-ceiling in height. Not overlooked, he tended to sleep with the heavy curtains open, leaving only the secondary, translucent Romans drawn. On this occasion, the Romans were also open, and the night teased him with its secretive beauty. The windows, partially open, let in a faint breeze from the unusually warm night.

Müller did not turn on any lights. Fully naked, he got out of bed and walked to the window, to stare out at the lights of the city.

'What do you know?' he said to them.

Nearly five months had gone by since he had heard the shocking news from the dying Rachko: that his parents had not died accidentally in an aircrash, as he'd been led to believe since the age of twelve. Twenty-two years later, he had received the first strand of what might be the truth: they had been killed.

To order.

Struggling with the turmoil of his emotions, he had sat on that terrible knowledge for all those months, confiding in no one; not even in Pappenheim. Only Carey Bloomfield knew – because she had been there to hear it. Now, Müller felt, he was at last ready to start digging. The nightmare – in all its graphic detail – had given him the signal; for the woman sitting next to him at the aircraft controls had been his mother. It was as if his parents were themselves telling him that, finally, it was time to begin to hunt out the truth of what had really happened all those years ago.

Müller felt a shiver go through him as he continued to stare out at the city.

'What do you know?' he repeated to the urban nightscape. 'Nothing,' he added after a pause.

Müller, police *Hauptkommissar*, returned to bed and fell soundly asleep.

It was 0300 hours.

At exactly the same moment in time, but in another country and time zone, a man picked up his phone.

'It's been five months,' he said in reply to a question. 'It's obvious he doesn't know. He would have reacted quite, quite savagely upon receiving such information. Revenge is always sweet, even to a paragon of virtue like the noble *Hauptkommissar*.' This was said with an icy contempt. 'Rachko did not have the time to tell him anything. Everything's under control . . . just as it was twenty-two years ago.'

The man grimaced as he hung up.

'Moron,' he said of his caller.

The gleaming, seal-grey Porsche 911 Turbo burbled into its allotted parking bay in the underground police garage. The building was one of the many glass palaces that had sprung up all over Berlin since the fall of the Wall, and the nation's subsequent unification. That building, comprehensively rigged with unobtrusive security systems, housed the special unit to which Müller belonged.

It was considered by its admirers to be staffed by highly motivated people, members of a police unit whose status was somewhere between the intelligence services and the police proper, its function to take on the sensitive cases that no one wanted to touch; even with someone else's barge pole. Its detractors – who were many – considered it to be yet another tier of politically created bureaucrats with guns, upon whom tax payers' money was squandered to give them expensive,

3

high-tech toys to play with. The truth, as always, was very different; but the motivation was real . . . as was the ongoing hostility. This was particularly strong even among some of their colleagues from other forces, who hated their perceived autonomy, but none of whom really wanted, if pushed to admit it, the responsibility of working there.

Müller switched off the engine and sat in the car for a few moments, listening to the sounds it made. One particular sound gave the impression it had sighed with pleasure as its engine cooled.

Müller climbed out, squeezed the remote to lock the vehicle, then made his way to one of the lifts that would take him up to his top-floor office. The lift hissed open before he reached it. Someone was already inside.

'Saw you arrive,' Hedi Meyer greeted. 'Thought I'd wait.'

He gave her the briefest of smiles. 'Thank you, Miss Meyer,' he said as he entered.

Hedi Meyer, a sergeant, was a tall and elegant young woman in her mid-twenties. Raven-black hair framing her face and startling blue eyes, with blue eye shadow. Pale, almost ghostly complexion. Her paleness, and apparent fragility, were a good front. She was one of the healthiest people around. She wore a long, sleeveless black dress of a material that just managed to hide the body beneath. Black was her favourite colour. Everyone called her the goth, and she was considered the best electronics expert in the building; which put her ahead of the man who was her boss, Herman Spyros, a *Kommissar*. Her nails were a bright red.

The lift was a large stainless-steel cubicle with a control panel that looked as if it belonged in a spaceship. Müller leaned against one of the sides as she touched the control screen to select their floors.

As the doors hissed shut, Müller glanced at her nails. 'You're a violent red today. Last winter, you had green on one hand and blue on the other.'

The lift accelerated smoothly upwards.

She gave him a vaguely arch look. 'I'm feeling danger-ous today.'

'Ah.'

Her eyebrows furrowed as she studied him. 'You're not your usual self.'

'What do you mean?'

'You look . . . preoccupied.'

'I'm still asleep.'

'I doubt that's the reason . . . sir.' She added that as an afterthought.

'Are you also a clairvoyant, Miss Meyer?'

The lift arrived at its first stop with its familiar silence, and braked with a powerful decelerative force.

'One of these days,' Müller grumbled, 'I'll bring up my breakfast. A lift that thinks it's a jet fighter.'

She gave him a steady speculative look. 'Yes. Something is definitely eating at you.'

The doors sighed open.

She started to leave, then paused. 'Are you sure you're alright?'

'Miss Meyer, I am perfectly OK. Trust me.'

'You're not a doctor,' she countered, and walked out.

The doors sighed themselves shut.

'I really needed that,' Müller said as the lift shot upwards at suicidal speed, homesick for the top floor.

When it had come to its high-negative-g stop, Müller got out thankfully and began walking along the polished corridor that led to his office. The walls of the corridor were festooned with no-smoking logos. As he passed Pappenheim's office Müller paused, then decided to continue.

By the time he had got to his door, he could hear one of his phones ringing. He entered. It was the direct line to Pappenheim.

He went to his uncluttered desk and picked up the phone. 'Yes, Pappi.'

'There you are,' came the cheerful voice. 'Someone's worried about you.'

'Let me guess. The goth called you.'

'You're so telepathic it hurts. She said you looked . . . well . . . strange.'

'Her words?'

'All hers, except the last one. That's mine.'

'She has fiery red nails.'

'That's an explanation?' A chuckle came down the line. 'It's going to be a hot day, the weather doxy said. So perhaps she's come prepared.'

'Early for the jokes, Pappi.'

'I remember last winter,' Pappenheim steamed on, 'she had green and blue. Green for fertile, she said, then, looking at you . . .'

'Are you grinning, Pappi?'

A loud suck came down the line. 'That's not grinning you hear.'

'First of the killer sticks for the day?'

'As if. Number four, at least. And don't change the subject.'

'If you go on about the goth and me, I'll go on about Berger.'

'Ouch. The man's ruthless. So? What's on your mind?'

'What makes you think—'

'This is me, Jens. Pappi. I've been listening to your voice as we've been talking. Something definitely on your mind. Give.'

Müller was silent for long moments.

'I can wait,' came Pappenheim's voice. He did not hang up.

'My parents,' Müller began at last, 'did not die accidentally. They were ordered killed.'

This time, the silence was Pappenheim's. Then he hung up.

Müller slowly replaced the phone and leaned against the desk to wait.

About a minute or so later, Pappenheim barged into the office, scrupulously bereft of cigarette. He stopped uncertainly, then shut the door behind him, studying Müller as he would a suspect.

Müller remained where he was.

Pappenheim – without jacket – came forward, and stopped before him.

Pappenheim was a big round man with a cuddly exterior. His eyes, baby-blue, exuded an innocence that effectively hid the worldly-wise individual beneath. His rumpled clothing, ash-speckled, helped promote that impression. His choice of ties was an apparent anomaly: they were always well chosen. His fingers, unexpectedly for a man who smoked so compulsively, were scrupulously clean. There was also something of the predator in him that came to the fore when he was on the hunt. His prey were criminals; and information, which he could ferret out of the unlikeliest of sources.

He never smoked in Müller's office.

'Where did you hear that?' he now asked, eyes fixed upon Müller's.

'*When* would be more to the point. Last winter . . . from Rachko.'

Pappenheim stared at him. '*Last* . . .' Pappenheim paused. 'You've been sitting on this for nearly *six* months?'

Müller eased himself off the desk and walked over to the huge panoramic window that overlooked the Friedrichstrasse, several storeys below.

Pappenheim turned, an antenna tracking. He did not follow.

'I needed the time, Pappi,' Müller said, 'to collect my thoughts, to come to terms, and to decide what I was going to do; and to tell you. I had to do that within myself first. Learning that your parents – whom you believed since you were twelve died accidentally – had in fact been murdered, takes some getting used to. It means I was lied to.'

Müller's voice had grown cold. In the already increasing warmth of the day, it brought a chill into the room.

Behind Müller's back, a fleeting expression of guilt lived briefly upon Pappenheim's face.

'Rachko was dying,' Pappenheim began.

'All the more reason for him not to lie.'

'That does not always follow.'

'I know. But what he said had the ring of truth. There is a file somewhere, with the details. KGB file, Stasi file. I don't know. He never had the chance to tell me. And he knew about Neubauer . . .'

Pappenheim was startled. '*Neubauer?*' He joined Müller at the window. '*The* Neubauer?'

Müller nodded without looking at him. 'The late and unlamented *Polizeidirektor* Neubauer. If he hadn't been shot by his own driver last winter, I'd feel like doing it myself. The bastard came to my home, just before my parents went off on their last flight. He had something to do with it.'

'Jesus.' Pappenheim seemed to have been made irresolute by the news. 'I think . . . I need a cigarette.'

Müller kept staring out at the city. 'Not in here you don't.'

'I'm not suicidal.'

Despite himself, Müller gave a tight smile. 'I had a dream last night,' he continued. 'Nightmare, really. I was in the plane, and it was falling out of the sky. I saw my mother. That was when I knew the time had come to do something. Time for closure, as the Americans would say.'

Pappenheim thrust his hands into his trouser pockets, to stop them twitching for the cigarette he wished he had. 'What are you going to do?'

'I'm a policeman. Investigate.'

'Ah, yes. I can just see the Great White Shark going for it. If what Rachko told you is true, this will reach into places the GW will not want you to poke at.'

8

'What our wonderful superior Kaltendorf thinks, or wants, is of little consequence to me.'

'That's a good one. *Hauptkommissar* takes on political animal of a *Polizeidirektor* (probationary), who hates his guts, and actually *wins*. Something about fairy tales always appeals,' Pappenheim continued. 'Must be the child in me.'

'I won't do it in official time. I've got plenty of unused holidays. Time to take them.'

'And he'll really agree to that.' Pappenheim was scepticism itself.

'That . . . is irrelevant.'

'So you'll go off, unauthorized. What a smart way to send your career into freefall. Never thought I'd see the day when you'd want to make him so happy. But . . .' Pappenheim went on, leaning forward slightly to peer down at the traffic. 'God. Look at those people. Put them behind the wheel . . .' He paused, shaking his head slowly, then, turning to look at Müller, went on, 'As you seem determined to commit professional suicide, you'll need someone to watch your back.'

'Pappi, I'm not going to ask you to—'

'You're not asking anything . . .'

'—ruin your career . . .'

'I'm making a decision. And the last time I looked, I was fully compos mentis and therefore fully capable of making my own—'

The door banged open. A fully suited Kaltendorf stood there. The inevitable thin file was tucked beneath an arm. He strode on loud heels into the room, almost halting to attention before them. Baleful eyes raked Pappenheim, pausing with contemptuous deliberation as he studied the *Oberkommissar*'s attire.

'You're not in your office, Pappenheim . . .'

'No, sir. I'm not in my office.'

The baleful eyes glared. 'Is that a joke, *Oberkommissar*?' Kaltendorf snapped, taking refuge in rank.

'No, sir. Statement of fact.' Pappenheim allowed his eyes to linger briefly on Kaltendorf's choice of tie for the day.

Kaltendorf noticed the look, and colour rose to his cheeks. Kaltendorf's choice of ties was a cause for hilarity among the unit's personnel, tie-wearers and non-tie-wearers alike. And Kaltendorf knew it.

He bit back what he really wanted to say and looked at both subordinates in turn. 'As you're both here . . .' He paused.

They waited.

'As you're both here,' he repeated. 'We have been asked to provide cover for a visiting dignitary . . . from the Middle East.'

Neither Müller nor Pappenheim said *shit*; but their expressions mimed it eloquently.

Kaltendorf waited with barely concealed pleasure for the objections he knew would be coming.

Pappenheim was first. 'We're not the diplomatic protection crowd, sir. Our job—'

'Happens to be what I say it is.' Kaltendorf looked at Müller. 'And what are *your* objections, Müller?'

His eyes strayed towards Müller's ponytail and the tiny single earring Müller wore. He could not have helped himself. Both earring and ponytail drove him to distraction.

'I was about to put in a request for some holiday, sir,' Müller replied. 'It's a relatively quiet time, and I haven't taken a holiday for—'

'Firstly,' Kaltendorf interrupted, 'it is *never* a quiet time; and secondly, request denied. You can't be spared.'

Pappenheim gave Müller a surreptitious glance, as if to say, *I told you*.

Kaltendorf had caught the look. 'Do I need your approval, *Oberkommissar*?'

'Of course not, sir.'

'*Of course not, sir!*' Kaltendorf mimicked savagely. He shoved the buff-coloured file at Müller. 'Study it, then let me have your comments.'

Without waiting for a response, he wheeled and marched out of the room. He did not close the door.

'Ah,' Pappenheim said, going up to the door to push it shut. 'Those exits. And did you *see* that tie?' he continued, as he returned. 'It's the worst he's ever threatened us in. Yellow and *purple*! Fashion victim? Or fashion victim? But, more to the point, see how happy he was about your holiday request? What now, oh smart one?'

Müller went over to his desk and dropped the file without looking at it. 'I'm taking my time off.'

'You'll make him a very, very happy man. He'll be delirious with happiness. You'll be suspended, then sacked . . . without pause for an inquiry.'

Müller idly touched the file. 'He needs me. He needs something to hate. Gives his life meaning. And besides, Neubauer was a crony of his.' Müller's eyes were cold. 'I'd like to know what our unloved chief knows.'

'Not much of a crony,' Pappenheim said, reminding Müller. 'When Neubauer came here last winter, it looked more like the GW being glad to have such an important colleague. Neubauer didn't give a shit about him.'

'Perhaps. But Neubauer was implicated in the deaths of my parents, and Kaltendorf knew him . . . no matter how tenuously. Given what happened to Neubauer, I don't think it's a connection Kaltendorf would enjoy being reminded about.'

'A little blackmail?' Pappenheim was dryness itself. 'That's more my line of work. I'm impressed.'

'Your bad habits are rubbing off on me.'

Pappenheim grinned. 'Always gladdens the teacher's heart when the pupil learns.' He joined Müller at the desk and opened the file, spreading it flat. 'As you won't look at it . . . might as well.'

Müller still did not look.

Pappenheim studied the full-length shot of the subject. Full head of dark, wavy hair, tinted glasses through which the eyes could be seen. White suit.

'Seems pleasant enough,' Pappenheim said. 'Obligatory moustache, of course. Daood Hassan.'

'Christian Arab,' Müller said. 'Interesting.'

'How do you know he's Christian?'

'Daood means David. Many people don't realize that Arabs use Christian, as well as Jewish, names. Sulieman, for example, is Solomon.'

'It's that Oxford education that the GW hates so much . . . as well as the Porsche, your money, your title, Herr Graf, your hair, your earring, your insubordination, your Armani suits, your—'

'Finished?'

'Just getting into my stride.'

'And what about you?'

'Take away the Porsche, the title, the money, the hair, the suits, the earring, and we're the same . . .'

'Insubordinate bastards,' they said together.

This time, despite himself, Müller's smile was an open one.

'Still doesn't solve your problem,' Pappenheim reminded him.

Müller glanced at the file. 'What else?'

Pappenheim continued his scrutiny. 'He's a peace activist.'

'Just what we need,' Müller grumbled. 'A peace activist from the Middle East.'

'Is that an oxymoron? See? I'm picking up your big words.'

'It's something. Daood Hassan must either be very brave . . .'

'Or a hopeless idealist. You still have a problem.'

'Give it to Berger and Reimer. They can look after our man from the east. They're our best . . .'

One of the phones on Müller's desk rang. 'Our master's voice?' he said to Pappenheim.

'I'd bet on it.'

Müller picked up the phone at the fourth ring. 'Müller.'

'I know you, Müller!' Kaltendorf's voice barked. 'Don't pass this to Reimer and Berger! You and Pappenheim. This is an order!'

The line clicked dead.

Müller replaced the receiver slowly. 'Could you hear?'

'I heard. I think the people in Flensburg heard. No. Make that North Cape.'

Müller went back to the window. 'When is Hassan due to arrive?'

Pappenheim turned a page. 'Two days from now. We pick him up at his hotel.'

'The diplomatic protection boys must be taking him there from wherever he enters the country. So why don't they just stay with it and leave us out of their business?'

'Perhaps he's meeting some of the GW's political friends and the GW, looking for kudos, volunteered us. "I've got just the people you need,"' Pappenheim went on in a spookily accurate imitation of Kaltendorf. '"One is rich and lounges around in Armani . . ."'

' *"Lounges"?*'

'Don't stop me when I'm in full flow.'

'Be my guest.'

'". . . and the other's a smoke-pit of a slob. Insubordinate, both of them. But they are good, worse luck . . ."'

'I don't think he'd say worse luck . . .'

'I'm not finished!'

'Sorry.'

'"But if something goes wrong . . ."' Pappenheim continued, 'And here's where it gets good. He gives a pregnant pause.'

'Pregnant pause.'

'As in shit hitting the fan.'

'We get it in the face, and he continues to smell sweet.'

'Send the man to the top of the class. How does that sound?'

'It sounds exactly like our dear leader,' Müller answered.

'Just so you know. Now that he has blocked Berger and Reimer . . .'

'Give it to them. They're under my command. I delegate.'

'Oh, we do like living dangerously.'

'What is he going to do? Suspend us? How would that look to his political friends?'

'Face to save?'

'Exactly. I thought you were dying for a cigarette,' Müller added, after a pause.

'Thanks for reminding me,' Pappenheim said quickly. 'On my way.' At the door, he paused to look back. 'Sorry about your parents, Jens. Rough thing to hear. Rachko could still have been wrong . . . but anything I can do . . .'

Müller nodded slowly but did not look round.

Pappenheim shut the door quietly as he went out.

Pappenheim's office was indeed a smoke-pit. Despite the relative newness of the building, the large window already possessed a nicotine-applied opacity. It was as if it belonged to an office that had existed for decades. His summer-weight jacket, crumpled and looking sorry for itself, hung limply from a hook on one wall. Beneath that was his shoulder rig, with a huge automatic pistol in its holster.

In sharp contrast to the immaculate layout of Müller's office, Pappenheim's could have been charitably described as a dump. This would not have upset Pappenheim, who revelled in watching the expressions on the faces of his visitors. Even a suspect who had once been brought to him had stared in horror.

'My God!' the man – an illegal weapons dealer – had exclaimed in shock. 'You *work* in here?'

'You're in no position to criticize my workplace,' Pappenheim had snapped back.

Pappenheim's desk looked as if papers and files were there just to see how high they could be piled without falling to the floor. The only other chair in the room, apart from the one behind the desk, was itself stacked with its own pile of papers. The large ashtray fighting for space on the desk seemed permanently overfilled, despite regular emptying by the security-vetted, civilian cleaning woman, who had long given up trying to make the place tidy. She had once made the mistake of tidying the desk, only to be taken to task for doing so.

'You'll ruin my system,' he'd scolded her.

She now only emptied the ashtray, barely cleaned the floor, and was always in a hurry to get out of there. She couldn't breathe, she would insist.

Pappenheim had lungs of steel.

'Aah!' he said as he entered, and breathed deeply of the tobacco-impregnated air. 'That's more like it.'

He made a beeline for the packet of Gauloises Blondes lying next to the ashtray, took out a cigarette, lit it, stuck it between his lips and drew happily upon it.

'Aah!' he said again. 'I needed that. I *needed* that.'

Instead of taking his seat behind the big desk, he picked up one of the phones and tapped in a number.

'This is Pappi,' he said when the other person had answered. 'I'd like a look at a Stasi file or two.'

'Lots of people want to do that these days.'

'Lots of people are not me.'

'Tell me about it. So? Who's got your interest this time?'

'Neubauer, for one.'

'The *Polizeidirektor* who got shot by his driver?'

'The very same.'

'That could be difficult.'

'I hate that word.'

'I'll see what I can do.'

'I like that better.'

'And the other?'

'The Graf von Röhnen.'

'Is this a joke?'

Pappenheim blew a perfect circle at the ceiling. 'What do you mean?'

'He's your superior. *Hauptkommissar* Müller . . .'

'I don't mean him. I'm talking about his father . . .'

The line went dead.

Pappenheim stared at the phone. 'Something I said?' He took another deep pull at the cigarette before dialling the same number. 'Did someone pull the plug?' he began as soon as the person had answered. 'Or did you just hang up on me?'

'I was exercising prudence. As should you.'

'My little request worry you? You sound worried. Not like you at all.'

'Look. Let me think about this. I'll call you.'

The line went dead for a second time.

Pappenheim replaced the receiver. 'So, there is a Stasi file, after all.'

He lifted the receiver once more and dialled a new set of numbers. A female voice answered.

'Pappi,' he said cheerfully into the phone. 'I want you to find a number for me.'

'Whose?'

Pappenheim told her.

There was a long silence.

'Hello?' he called. 'Still there? Or have you fallen off your chair?'

'What are you up to, Pappi?'

'I've no idea. I'm floundering.'

'You do a lot of things. Floundering isn't one of them. This person's number will be highly secure.'

'But I know you can get it.'

'One of these days, you'll cost me my neck . . . and yours will be with it.'

'Don't be ridiculous. Mine has already long been mort-gaged.'

'Then I don't want to join it . . . but I'll see what I can do.'

'You're an angel.'

'On my way to Hell, perhaps. Today is certainly going to be hot enough.'

'You see? You're in a good mood already.'

'Piss off, Pappi.' But the voice had a smile in it.

'Your wish, as ever, is my command.'

They hung up together.

Pappenheim was at his desk when the direct phone to Müller rang.

'Happier now?' came Müller's voice as he picked it up.

Pappenheim blew three smoke rings at the laden chair. 'Much. To what do I owe the pleasure?'

'Since you're determined to put your neck into the noose with mine . . . those connections of yours that I don't want to know about.'

'Ah,'

'Files on Neubauer, and the Great White.'

'Ah,' Pappenheim said again.

'You're short on the vocabulary all of a sudden.'

'That could be because I've already been there. Chasing one on Neubauer, but didn't consider the GW. Sailing close to the wind, aren't you?'

'I'll sail close to the Devil himself to find the people who ordered the death of my parents. If I have to stomp all over Kaltendorf to get to the truth, I'll stomp.'

Pappenheim frowned. 'You worry me. Never forget you're a policeman, not a vigilante.'

'I won't forget. I also want to know,' Müller went on, 'how often those two met, and where.'

'There's a Stasi file on Neubauer – perhaps several files – and there's bound to be one on the GW, given his run-in with your late cousin, Colonel of the DDR police, Dahlberg, made late by your good self – with some help from a certain lady . . .' Pappenheim paused.

'I'm not losing any sleep. He deserved it.'

'No argument from me. Alright,' Pappenheim continued. 'I'll get on with it. See what I can find.'

'Thanks, Pappi. And don't forget to warn Berger and Reimer about their babysitting.'

'I won't.'

As with the second of Pappenheim's contacts, they hung up together.

Pappenheim stared at the phone. 'I know it's eating at you. But watch your step.'

In his office, Müller looked at his own phone. 'I know you're worried I might go off the edge, Pappi,' he said to it. 'But I've been preparing myself for months. I know what I'm doing.'

Two

Schlosshotel **Derrenberg, near Saalfeld, Thuringia.**

Aunt Isolde had been inspecting a luxuriant rose bed in the vast hotel grounds. Now, she was lying next to it, out cold. A man in a white suit and a wide-brimmed hat was stooped anxiously next to her.

'*Hey!*' a voice shouted. '*You! What are you doing?*'

The owner of the voice, a bare-headed young man in an approximation of a hussar's uniform, was racing towards the couple, face hostile. He was one of the hotel staff.

The man in the white suit did not turn to look. He appeared to be trying to help.

'*Don't touch her!*' came another shout.

Still the man in the suit did not turn to look. It was as if he had not heard.

The hussar arrived. He grabbed at the man and forcibly hauled him up. 'I said leave her alone!'

The man in the suit looked at the hussar calmly. 'Take your hands off me. There's a good chap.' He spoke German hesitantly, but grammatically correctly.

Something in the voice, and the demeanour of the man, made the hussar let go.

'Thank you,' the man said with unnerving politeness. 'I was trying to help.'

'What did you do to her?'

'I think you are a little hard of hearing. Why should I be trying to help if I had done something to her? Instead of facing each other like a pair of stags ready to do battle over a female

19

of the species, shouldn't we do something about helping her? She's fainted.'

'Why?'

'I think she was surprised,' the mild voice replied. 'Any more questions?'

'I'm calling the police!' The hussar unclipped the mobile phone at his belt.

'Ah. I see. You look at my complexion, and you see terrorist, perhaps. Thirty-odd years of very hot sun tends to do that; the complexion, I mean. Very well. Do call the police . . . and *Hauptkommissar* Müller while you're at it.'

The hussar's eyes twitched. 'The Herr Graf?' He was astonished. The mobile was held a little away from his body. But he made no attempt to use it. 'How . . . how do you . . . ?'

'Know him? I've known him for years, dear chap. Of course, he was not a *Hauptkommissar* then. Unlikely, given he was a child at the time.'

The hussar frowned. 'Are you pissing with me?'

'I very much doubt I would want to go to the toilet with you . . .'

'You're not funny!'

'Not trying to be. Look. We can't leave dear Isolde . . .'

'*Baronin*, to you! And how do you know her name anyway?'

'Oh that. That's easy enough. I'm her husband, you see.'

The hussar was stunned. His mouth gaped open.

'Close that,' the man in the suit advised. 'Get a fly in it on a hot morning like this.'

The hussar clamped his mouth shut, then opened it again to speak. 'The *Baronin*'s husband is dead.' There was a look of triumph in his eyes.

'Ah, yes. Of course he is. But that wasn't me. I'm the first husband. I can see I'm confusing you. Let's leave all explanations till later, shall we? Now let me get on with reviving her. And do call the police, if you must. I would suggest the *Hauptkommissar* first.'

Without waiting for a reaction, the man squatted on his heels and began to attend to Aunt Isolde.

Müller picked up the phone at the first ring. 'Müller.'

'Herr Graf,' he heard an agitated voice say, 'it's Christian.'

Müller was suddenly still. 'You sound very odd, Christian. What's wrong?'

'It . . . it's your aunt, Herr Graf.'

'What has happened to her?'

'She fainted . . . but she's awake now.'

'Is she hurt?'

'No . . . but . . . her husband is here!' The words came in a rush, as if Christian doubted what he was saying.

'Her husband is dead, Christian. Calm yourself.'

'It's . . . it's her *first* husband, Herr Graf.'

'*What?*' Müller exclaimed softly. 'He's supposed to be dead too!'

'He asked me to call you. He said he knew you when you were a child.'

'If he really is the person he claims to be, he would have known me then. Although how come he knows I am a policeman . . .' Müller paused. 'Alright, Christian. Don't worry. I'm coming down.'

'Yes, Herr Graf.'

As soon as he had ended the conversation, Müller picked up the phone to Pappenheim.

'You again?' Pappenheim began.

'I'm going out.'

'Far? Should I tell the GW? Do you want to be found?'

'Not far enough, no, and no.'

'Well that's clear. Do I get more information? Or is it a national secret?'

'I'm going to my aunt's. It seems she has a visitor who's

come back from the dead after thirty years. Her first husband.'

'This is turning out to be some day,' Pappenheim said, after a long pause.

'I'm going down to check him out. Could be some con merchant looking for a rich widow. If all's well, I should be back by late afternoon.'

'Six hours' round trip if you take it easy, four hours' if you don't, even with heavy traffic. In that machine of yours, I know you won't be having a Sunday afternoon crawl.'

'I expect to be there by midday. Sooner, if I'm lucky with the traffic.'

'What do I tell the GW?'

'Anything you like. Use your unassailable inventiveness.'

'Two big words. What a day.'

'Pappi!'

'Got it. You're out, dunno where, situation with Daood Hassan under full control. How does that sound?'

'Knew you'd come up with something. Any news on the other, don't hesitate to call me.'

'I never hesitate. Hate getting lost.'

'Keep it up,' Müller said with a definite grin, and hung up.

He did not leave his office at a run, but he was not strolling either. He hoped he would make it to the first lift without running into Kaltendorf, who was known to prowl the corridors when in the building, instead of staying in his office like any high-ranking policeman should. Kaltendorf was one of those people who believed hands-on command meant looking over his subordinates' shoulders at every opportunity, when he was around. Some openly grumbled that he tended to treat them – highly skilled professionals – like recalcitrant children. This from a man who was once known to have been among the best of the best.

Everyone in the unit hated him for it, including the senior officers under his command; Müller and Pappenheim most of all.

The lift arrived just as he got there. The doors slid open to reveal Berger, carrying a thin file. She wore a sleeveless olive T-shirt, beige jeans and soft-soled trainers. She also wore a full shoulder harness, with a regulation automatic tucked in its holster.

'Morning, sir,' she greeted Müller as she got out. She did not look happy.

'Good morning, Lene. Sorry about the babysitting.'

'Why am I in the kitchen if I can't stand the heat?'

'That's one way of putting it.'

'Do you know who it is, sir?'

'I do . . . but I think it best to let Pappi give you the whole works.'

'That bad?'

'It could be a pushover.'

'Hah!' she said, experience trouncing hope.

'Oh,' Müller went on.

Berger paused.

'Anyone asks for me . . .' Müller began.

'I never saw you,' she finished, her sudden grin shameless.

'My faith in human nature is restored,' Müller said as he entered the lift.

The doors closed and the lift hissed into its stomach-churning descent.

A bare second later, Kaltendorf turned a corner and into the corridor. Berger did not break her stride, but continued purposefully towards Pappenheim's office.

'*Obermeisterin* Berger,' Kaltendorf began as they were about to pass each other. He stopped, forcing her to do the same. 'Did I just hear you talking to yourself?'

'Yes, Herr *Direktor*,' she admitted without hesitation. 'Boyfriend trouble. I was just telling myself how difficult it is to be a police officer when you've got a jealous man. Take this morning . . .'

'Yes, yes, *Obermeisterin*. We all have crosses to bear.' Kaltendorf nodded at the file. 'Who's that for?'

'Er . . . *Oberkommissar* Pappenheim, sir. He wants to check the pay scales . . .'

'*Pay* scales? That's what we have a financial department for. Why would he want to check . . . ?' Kaltendorf stopped and held out his hand. 'Let me see.'

Berger handed over the file without hesitation.

Kaltendorf looked as if he thought there was something hidden behind her unhesitating compliance.

He thumbed through the file, then handed it back.

'He's up to something,' Kaltendorf said, staring hard at her.

Her eyes, as she held his gaze, were mirrors of innocence.

Pappenheim suddenly appeared in his doorway. 'Ah! Berger! There you are at last. I've been waiting . . .'

Kaltendorf's head snapped round. 'Why do you need to see the pay scales, today of all days, *Oberkommissar*?'

'Never a bad day on which to check the pay scales, sir,' Pappenheim replied, expression totally devoid of guile. 'Things change all the time. Never know when a small rise might appear.'

'If it does, you will be notified in the usual manner.'

'You know me, Herr *Direktor*. Always like to check up on things.'

'I know you, Pappenheim!' Kaltendorf snapped, and walked on.

They waited until he had gone out of sight before Pappenheim said to Berger, 'In!'

She entered, and as he shut the door, said, 'How did you know he would be in the corridor?' She handed him the file.

He took it, and on his way back to his desk, chucked the file on the laden chair. A trail of smoke followed him.

'I didn't,' he replied. 'But a wise man takes all precautions.'

She gave a sniff of derision. 'Pay scales. What next?'

'If the occasion demands it, the fuel allocations for the month.'

'One of these fine days, Chief . . .'

'He'll catch me? He'll have to get up very early. And you didn't hear me say that.'

'Did you say something, Chief?'

Pappenheim grinned as he returned to his seat behind the desk. 'Take a seat.'

She gave the laden chair a dubious glance and decided to remain standing. 'I'm alright. So who's the baby?'

Pappenheim told her.

'Shit!' she said.

'Our thoughts exactly.'

'He brought it to you, you gave it to us.'

'That's the beauty of being an *Oberkommissar*, or a *Hauptkommissar*, for that matter. You can do things like that.'

'Thanks!'

'And don't be rude to your superior. Bad for the complexion.'

Müller made it to his car without running into Kaltendorf. It would not have surprised him if the police director had suddenly turned up in the garage.

He quickly entered the car, started it, eased his way out of his parking slot to drive to the start of the exit slope, where he paused. The armoured door began to roll itself upwards. As soon as it was high enough to allow clearance for the Porsche, he quickly drove up the ramp and into the street.

Müller considered that Kaltendorf might choose that very moment to peer out of an overlooking window and spot his exit; but that could not be helped. He decided it was an acceptable risk, and accelerated smoothly away.

Unfortunately, he was right. Kaltendorf, in conversation with a *Kommissarin* from the finance department, had chosen that precise moment to take an idle glance out of the window; and spotted the departing Porsche.

'*Müller!*' he snarled. He turned to his subordinate. 'I'll talk with you later!'

'Yes, sir,' she said, and watched expressionlessly as he stalked out.

When she was certain it was safe to do so, she grabbed her phone and rapidly dialled an extension.

'Margit,' she announced as soon as Pappenheim had answered. 'He's spotted Jens leaving and stomped out of here looking as if he has a bad case of trapped wind. He could be headed your way.'

'Thanks for the warning.'

'Any time.'

But Kaltendorf did not immediately storm his way to Pappenheim's office. He went instead to the large office shared by Berger, Reimer, and three other sergeants, two of whom were senior. The office was empty.

He glared about him in frustration and was about to leave when Klemp, one of the senior sergeants, entered.

Klemp, a shortish man with a bodybuilder's frame, was taken by surprise; but before he could speak, Kaltendorf got there first.

'*Obermeister* Klemp, have you seen Berger and Reimer?'

'Er . . . no, Herr *Direktor.*'

'Have they already been in?'

'Yes, sir.'

'But you did not see them leave.'

'No, sir. I left them here when I went out to get—'

'Thank you, *Obermeister.*'

Kaltendorf went out, leaving Klemp staring after him.

'Fart,' Klemp muttered when he was certain Kaltendorf would not hear. He went to the nearest phone and dialled Pappenheim's extension. 'Trouble on the way,' he said as soon as he heard Pappenheim answer. 'He's been here looking for Berger and Reimer.'

Pappenheim needed no further explanation. 'Thanks, Udo.'

In his office, Pappenheim put down the phone, and hummed to himself.

*   *   *

Kaltendorf, however, did not go directly to Pappenheim from the sergeants' office. Instead he returned to his own, where a message was waiting on the answering machine linked to his direct outside line.

'Call me,' the message said. That was all.

He knew the caller, and quickly dialled the person's number.

'Have you done it?' was the immediate response.

'I've ordered them.'

'Those two are notorious for disobeying orders. In the normal scheme of things, they are excellent policemen; exceptional, even. But this is not the normal scheme of things. Their prying into places they should not has caused a lot of important people a lot of grief. I am not partial to that kind of grief, Heinz.'

'Then this duty will keep them out of everyone's hair. A simple cover job.'

'I hope you're right. Nothing is ever simple where those two are concerned.' There was a pause, then the person at the other end continued, 'Policemen have been known to fall in the line of duty. Even very senior ones. Remember Neubauer.'

The line went dead.

The distance from Berlin to Aunt Isolde's *Schlosshotel* was just over 300 kilometres.

It took Müller less than thirty minutes to get to the Autobahn A9 junction near Potsdam. The increasing warmth of the bright day seemed to have affected the traffic at that point, for there was less of it than expected. This enabled him to let the car have its head and soon the engine at the back was howling its pleasure along the virtually empty stretch of road.

Normally, he would have turned on the CD player to let a given choice of music flood the car. But he was not in the mood for it. Instead, he preferred the accompaniment of the mechanical sounds of the turbocharged Porsche as it sped towards Saalfeld.

Ever on his mind was the strange fate of his parents. Who had ordered them killed? And why?

Over the months, this had eaten at him. He had not wanted to rush blindly about, and so give any warning to whoever the people behind it all might be. He wanted those unseen to remain unknowing; until he was quite ready to face them.

Eyes cold, Müller felt his lips tighten and his hands gripped the steering wheel more firmly than usual.

The car began to twitch at high speed. Müller relaxed his grip and the car settled once more, hurtling towards its destination.

In his office, Pappenheim wondered what had happened to Kaltendorf.

'What's keeping you?' he murmured at the ceiling, peering at the smoke rings he'd just blown towards it.

Four perfect circles in neat trail formation hung suspended, weaving imperceptibly. He sent another four, which collided in sequence against the first group, pushing them upwards. They began to collapse about each other, shifting shape as they did so, turning into a spreading wisp that wraithed above his head.

One of the phones rang. Pappenheim picked it up. One of his contacts was at the other end.

'The Graf von Röhnen,' the person immediately began.

'Ah!' Pappenheim said. 'Thought about it?'

'I have. I would still advise prudence. Even more so.'

'You've found something.'

'Perhaps.'

'Don't go coy on me.'

'There's just one very thin file. Two pages.'

Pappenheim drew on his cigarette. '*Two* pages?'

'Just the two.'

'That, in itself, makes my suspicion index hit the ceiling.'

'And mine . . . especially when you read the annotations.'

'That's it. Keep me waiting.'

'Such a wit you are, Pappi. The annotations say the main files are elsewhere.'

'Now why did I think that's what you'd be telling me? How do we get them?'

'Are you mad? Trying to locate them will set alarm bells ringing.'

'Alarm bells can be disabled. And while you're at it . . .'

'Something *else*?'

'Never rains, does it?'

A sigh came down the line. 'Who this time?'

'Ask one of your many contacts – discreetly – if they know of a Daood Hassan, peace activist from the Middle East.'

'A *peace* activist?'

'I know all the jokes,' Pappenheim said, 'so don't waste the irony on me.' He grinned at the phone. 'So? Can you do it?'

'I can but try. If you ever decide to leave the police, Pappi . . .'

'Are you trying to tempt me?'

'. . . you'd have a great career as a blackmailer.'

The person at the other end hung up.

Pappenheim put his phone down slowly. 'I like it when people pay me compliments.'

He continued his humming where he'd left off.

His own peace was short-lived. The door was flung open, and Kaltendorf stood there, going into the usual over-the-top act of coughing.

'My God, Pappenheim! *Do* something about this place. Open a window!' Kaltendorf waved pointlessly at the wisps of smoke. He left the door open. 'I saw Müller,' he went on. '*Leaving!*' It was an accusation.

Pappenheim remained seated. 'That child abduction case, sir . . .'

'*Kommissarin* Holtau is dealing with it. Don't throw any smokescreens at me, Pappenheim!'

29

'That, sir, is a fine piece of witticism . . .'

Kaltendorf glared at him. 'You may enjoy these sparring matches, Pappenheim, but I don't! Now tell me where Müller has gone.'

'To see Holtau, sir. She asked him for some advice. I believe she's at the child's parents'—'

'Get her. Now.'

'Yes, sir.' Pappenheim dialled Holtau's mobile.

Kaltendorf forced himself to go further into the smoke of Pappenheim's office and grabbed the phone.

As soon as Holtau answered, he barked, '*Kommissarin* Holtau, this is *Direktor* Kaltendorf. Is Müller with you?'

'He was here just a few minutes ago, sir,' Holtau lied smoothly. 'I think he may be on his way back to his office, but I can't swear to it.'

'Why was he with you?'

'I wanted him to talk to the father, sir.'

'And?'

'In the end, the father decided to talk to me, after all. Seems he has a problem with senior female police officers. Could be a macho thing.'

'Thank you, *Kommissarin*,' Kaltendorf said, face tight. He put the phone down firmly and stared at Pappenheim. 'You seem to have everyone in your pocket, Pappenheim. But that won't last forever. Count on it!'

'Yes, sir.'

Kaltendorf favoured Pappenheim with another stare then stomped out, exaggeratedly waving at the smoke, heels striking hard along the corridor. He still left the door open.

Pappenheim got out of his chair with a sigh, went to the door and shut it.

'Manners maketh the man,' he said. 'But definitely not this one.'

Kaltendorf stormed back to his office and entered just as his direct line began to ring.

He rushed to his desk and snatched up the phone. 'Kaltendorf.'

'We've got a problem.' It was the same person who had spoken to him earlier.

'What kind of problem?'

'One we certainly don't need at this time. Hassan is missing.'

Kaltendorf took his time before saying, 'How can he be missing? He's not due here until . . .'

'He did not turn up at his last rendezvous. He is supposed to be in Stockholm. His next stage is here. They have not seen him in Stockholm.'

'He missed his flight?'

'He caught the flight and arrived as expected.'

'I see.'

'No, you don't, Heinz. He was collected, but somewhere between his hotel and his rendezvous, he went missing.'

'Then it's a problem for the Swedes.'

'That it would be so easy.'

'I don't understand.'

'That's a problem, too, Heinz. I'll be in touch.' The caller again hung up, before Kaltendorf could say anything more.

Kaltendorf decided he would say nothing about Daood Hassan's disappearance either to Müller or to Pappenheim.

Schlosshotel Derrenberg was a medium-sized mansion that had seen rough DDR days. Derelict and overgrown through years of misuse, it had been stunningly renovated to its former glory. Aunt Isolde had inherited the former shell.

One of the lucky few to have found the family home still standing – just – after the fall of the Wall, she had performed a labour of love to transform it into what it now was: part family home and part luxury hotel. The hotel section was comprised of the main structure and the right wing. The left wing – reserved as the owner's residence – had its own secure entrance, with a garden and courtyard behind a high wall. Dotted around were ground-level spotlights that floodlit the building and illuminated the main garden at night.

A stream, with raised concrete banks to protect against flooding, flowed gently across the garden from the far, wooded part of the vast grounds and past the rear of the hotel to empty a kilometre or so later into the river Saale. A small wooden bridge spanned it.

Within the grounds was a separate building that was almost as luxuriously renovated. This was for the use of overnighting staff. Aunt Isolde maintained that if she treated her staff well they would remain loyal, and would be excellent. It was a philosophy that had paid off handsomely.

A well-surfaced country lane meandered through spectacular Thuringian scenery, leading towards the Derrenberg, and at exactly midday, Müller turned the Porsche off the road and on to the long, curving driveway that led to the mansion itself. He pulled up before the colonnaded entrance.

Christian the hussar, looking anxious, rushed out to meet him.

'Thank God you're here, sir!' Christian began as Müller got out of the car.

'How is she?'

'She . . . she's fine. In the residence. Kitchen. He's . . . he's there with her . . .' Christian looked extremely worried.

'Does he seem dangerous?'

Christian shook his head. 'He . . . he's been very kind to her . . .'

'And how has she reacted to him?'

'I think she is still in shock.'

'I'm not surprised. Do the hotel guests know anything about this?'

Christian again shook his head. 'No. We have a full house . . . but most of them are out, so . . . we managed to get her to the residence without anyone noticing.'

'And the staff?'

'They know, of course. But Herr Brennermann has everything under control.'

'Ah yes. He used to be deputy manager to Bulent Landauer. How do the staff take to him now?'

'It was difficult at first, Herr Landauer dying the way he did back then. No one can really replace him; but things are fine with Herr Brennermann.'

Müller nodded. 'Alright, Christian. I'll go to my aunt now. I'll use the gate to the courtyard.'

'Yes, sir.'

There were two gates: one secured by a keypad for pedestrian entrance, the other for vehicles, and opened by remote.

Müller went to the small entrance and tapped in the code. Locking bolts slid with a soft hiss and the gate swung open quietly. He walked through and the gate swung shut behind him.

He turned right and headed for the door next to the kitchen, whose large window looked out upon the courtyard. Though it had its own keypad, it was unlocked. Müller pushed it quietly open and entered on silent feet.

Pappenheim picked up his phone. 'Pappenheim.'

'I've got something on Daood Hassan,' the voice said.

'That was quick.'

'I've . . . er . . . got a contact outside . . .'

'Outside? What do you mean?'

'Outside Europe.'

'Ah.'

'Seems your man is clean.'

'He's not my man . . . and you mean *apparently* clean . . .'

'What a suspicious mind you have.'

'I'm a policeman.'

'I could say something, but I won't.'

'I'm pleased. So? What about Hassan?'

'Seems as if he was orphaned at twelve. The stuff I got

doesn't say how, except that mother went first – when he was six – then the father. Some philanthropist cared for him in absentia . . .'

'Any idea?'

'None given. Hassan apparently has no knowledge of his benefactor, to this day. He grew up with a reasonably wealthy family – people the benefactor had placed him with – and was well educated. Speaks at least four languages in addition to his own, fluently. Two of these languages are English and German. He has dedicated himself to peace in the Middle East.'

'We need angels wherever we can find them,' Pappenheim commented.

'Why do I get the feeling you are less than overwhelmed?'

'When the *Über*boss dumps something strange on us, I *always* sniff it for poison.'

'Some poisons don't smell.'

'As I know only too well. Anything else you can find, I'd be grateful.'

'There's "grateful" . . .'

'And then there's "grateful". How well you know me.'

'Sometimes I wonder whether I should laugh or cry.'

'Look on the bright side.'

'I prefer the dark.'

'You would.'

Pappenheim replaced the receiver, steepled his hands briefly, then as if suddenly realizing he did not have a lighted cigarette, quickly lit up. He inhaled deeply, leaned back in his chair and streamed smoke out of his nostrils.

'Well, Herr Daood Hassan, you've gone missing. Where to? And why? Were you kidnapped? Or is this of your own doing? If so, how did you escape your minders?'

Pappenheim took in another lungful of his Blondes, and slowly let the smoke out. 'Questions, questions, questions. I need answers. I . . .'

The same phone rang again. He stared at it, and let it ring.

'I'm very popular today.'

He picked it up. 'Pappenheim.'

This time it was the female voice. 'I've got that number you wanted.'

Pappenheim wrote it down as she told him. 'You're a genius.'

'Tell me again when you see them pulling my fingernails.'

'Nonsense. I have it on good authority they stopped doing that last week.'

'My backside's exposed, Pappi. I sailed very close to get this.'

'But you're out safely. I appreciate it,' he added, levity gone.

'You should. This time, *you* owe *me*.'

'I will reciprocate.'

'I'll hold you to that.'

The sudden emptiness told Pappenheim he would be talking to himself if he said anything more.

He replaced the phone and stared at the number he'd written down. 'You're in for a surprise,' he said to it.

Three

M üller stood in the doorway of the large kitchen and spoke in a soft voice. 'Aunt Isolde.'

Aunt Isolde and the man who had said he was her first husband sat opposite each other, at a solid wooden table that had the looks of a genuine antique. Two cups of barely drunk coffee stood between them.

The normally elegant Aunt Isolde looked somewhat less so. She seemed to be still in a state of shock. Given the circumstances, it was hardly surprising.

The man in white looked Arabic in complexion; but his eyes were a giveaway. A very pale blue. His hat was perched on the back of a nearby chair, baring a head with a slightly receding hairline, but with an otherwise full head of cropped, white hair.

Both Aunt Isolde and the man turned their heads to look at Müller; she with warm pleasure, he with watchful interest.

'Jens!' she said in greeting. Almost as tall as he, she eagerly stood up and hurried over to give him a warm hug, and a kiss on both cheeks. 'It wasn't necessary for you to come.'

'Yes it was.'

'Well I'm glad you are here. I won't deny it.'

Aunt Isolde turned to look back at the man who had now risen to his feet.

'Is it really . . .' Müller began.

'It is,' she confirmed. 'Shocking as it might seem, this is my first husband, Timmy.'

Even as she spoke, Müller noted she appeared undecided; as if uncertain whether she should be pleased that Timmy was still alive after all those years, or wish he had never returned.

'Timmy? But I thought . . .'

'You perhaps only remember his surname. His full name is Timothy Charles Wilton-Greville. Timmy was my name for him.'

The man she had called Timmy had approached and was studying Müller speculatively, head slightly tilted, very much like a bird of prey surveying its next meal.

'I remember,' Müller said, looking steadily back at the man in white. 'The Honourable Major Wilton-Greville.'

'Quite the man, you have become,' Aunt Isolde's Timmy said in his halting German. He held out a hand.

Müller looked at it, and after a moment's hesitation, briefly shook it. 'Major.' Then he added, 'We can speak English, if you'd like.'

'Would you?' the other said with eagerness as he switched. 'I can speak a few lingos, but haven't used the German in a while. 'The "major" is long gone,' he continued, 'as is the "honourable". Call me Timmy. If you find that too informal, Greville will do.'

'Very well,' Müller said. 'Greville.'

'It's just as well that you're here, Jens,' Aunt Isolde went on, in the same language. 'I believe Timmy wants to talk with you.'

Her accent was pure Sandhurst, still strong after her early years with Greville, whose own accent had influenced her.

Müller glanced at Greville, expression neutral. 'What about?'

'Care for a stroll in the main garden?' Greville countered.

Müller looked to Aunt Isolde.

'I'll be fine,' she assured him. 'Something to eat or drink, first?'

Müller shook his head. 'I'll wait. I had a bite on the autobahn.'

'Not one of those dreadful wurst things.'

He smiled at her. 'I still like them. Every so often.'

'Bad childhood habit,' she remarked with a tone of censure. 'You know better, Jens.'

'Of course.'

'Hopeless,' she said. She seemed to have brightened since his arrival, and looked fondly at him. 'I suppose you two had better go for your walk.'

Greville looked at her. 'Yes. I think we should.' He went back to get his hat. 'Shall we?' he said to Müller.

With a final glance at Aunt Isolde, Müller followed Greville out of the kitchen.

They were passing the main entrance of the hotel, on their way to the stream.

'My word!' Greville exclaimed when he saw the Porsche. 'That is a motor!' His speech rhythms sometimes appeared to be decades out of date. 'Fast, is she?'

'Very,' Müller said.

'My word!'

They stopped by the car. Then Greville began to walk slowly around it in open admiration, now and then pausing to peer closely.

He pointed to the wheels. 'Are those yellow things special callipers?'

Müller nodded. 'This means the brakes are ceramic.'

Greville gave him a quick look. 'Stop on a sixpence, eh? Don't do things by halves, do you? Good man.'

Müller said nothing as Greville continued his inspection, for all the world like a boy with a new toy. It was clear he had a taste for sports cars.

'My word!' he repeated to himself. He stopped once more, looked at the car from nose to tail, studying the seal-grey paintwork. 'Unusual colour. Subtly menacing. Says something about you, old boy.'

'Good? Or bad?'

'Bit of both. Bit of both. Seen a few of her sisters in the Gulf states, of course. But not one like this. Sit inside, may I?'

Müller squeezed the remote to unlock the car. 'Be my guest.' He wondered when Greville would start on the real reasons for their being there.

Greville got in behind the wheel, sat unmoving for long seconds, then he pointed to the darkened, small screen on the central console. 'What's that? Television?'

'Communication, navigation and audio system,' Müller replied.

'Good Lord!' Greville said. 'It's a jet fighter.' He smiled at his joke. 'Beautiful,' he continued, as he looked about him. 'Absolutely beautiful. Lovely rich smell of leather.' He climbed out, with more than a hint of reluctance. 'Give me a ride some time. Eh?'

'Anytime you would like . . . within reason.'

'Of course! Understood. Busy policeman.'

'Something like that,' Müller said, hiding his own smile.

'So, dear boy . . . on to the stream.'

They walked on in complete silence, came to the raised, artificial bank of the stream and stopped.

Greville peered down at the water. 'Bigger than one would expect. Almost a small river.'

'Someone else once said that to me.'

Greville shot him a sly glance. 'Young woman, I'll wager.'

Müller looked at him in mild surprise, but said nothing.

'Wondering how I could have hit the mark? Not difficult. There was a particular timbre to your voice. Had to be a young woman.' Greville smacked Müller's arm playfully. 'Who's the policeman here?'

He turned again to the stream and fell into a deep silence. Müller waited.

When Greville at last spoke, it was in a very soft voice. This gave added power to what he actually said.

'I'm dying. No, no,' he went on, interrupting what Müller

had been about to say. 'Anything you could say would be well off the mark. My . . . affliction is not a natural one; and it is a pernicious, evil way of dying. The irony is, I did it to myself.'

Greville stopped, eyes seemingly focused on the flowing water. In reality, he was a long way away.

'Nature,' he continued, 'has laws. Humankind bends, abuses and misuses them, in sometimes abominable ways. Thirty or so years ago – more or less hardly matters – I was young, and very keen to serve my country. I dare say, even knowing what I know now, I would be just as keen to do it all over again, albeit a little more carefully. Yes. Carefully.'

Müller looked on, and decided not to disturb Greville's unburdening.

'One of the reasons I vanished without apparent trace,' Greville went on after a short pause, 'was the job I was tasked to do. Understand this . . . the Middle East had an unseen, as well as a highly visible battlefield during the Cold War. There were many casualties the figures for which will never see the light of day. That unseen conflict was ferocious, and frequently murderous. People went out on seemingly innocuous activities, never to return. A sailing trip could end up with an empty boat. A visit to a beach, fatal. An empty road, more hazardous than a carload of drunks whizzing around Piccadilly on a Saturday night.

'I had a mission that required me to enter a laboratory in a supposedly benign country. Word had come that they were doing something particularly nasty in that lab. Whatever it was, however, the quantity was as yet minute. The science they employed then was in its infancy. Foreign scientists were involved. What they were making was very difficult to keep alive. Stocks were extremely low; so low, in fact, that only one vial existed.

'We had to get it and, at the same time, permanently sabotage the lab. Destroy their work. Getting in was relatively easy. They had no idea that anyone outside knew. We were therefore not expected. My job was to get the vial, while others carried out the sabotage. I knew exactly where to go. Easy.'

Greville paused once more.

Müller waited patiently.

'Easy,' Greville repeated, continuing to stare at the water and still far away. 'I got into the lab. Not even a guard. That's how sure of themselves they were. Whoever had supplied the information had done the job well. It was clearly someone who had worked there; quite possibly planted. I believe the person in question was "rescued" – if you see what I mean – and undoubtedly went on to live a long and wealthy life under an assumed name somewhere.' He gave a short, rueful laugh that had little humour and plenty of sadness. 'Rather like me, but without the riches.

'I got the vial – tiny thing – put it in a padded pocket. The vial was itself in a secure container . . . or so I thought. Speed was now of the essence. I began to leave the empty lab.'

Greville stopped again, shook his head slowly at the irony of it.

'It is one of those things in life that two people, totally oblivious of each other's existence, become fated to meet at the most inauspicious of moments. A conscientious guard, on miserable pay, doing the only job he could get, and wanting to do it well, chose that moment to walk into the lab. It was not even his beat. How he came to be there is still a mystery. Perhaps he was looking for someone. Perhaps he was just popping by to say hello. That day, the person he saw was yours truly. He shot first, and intended to ask questions later.

'He hit me . . . or rather, he hit the vial. I was thrown to the floor by the force of the impact. But his aim was not true. He hit the vial a glancing blow; but the vial and its container were not bullet-proof. I had my own gun already out, so, as I fell, I fired. I did not miss. Clean through the heart. I had not gone there intending to kill, even though I had a silenced weapon. I wanted a silent entry and a silent exit. No fireworks until we were well clear and the explosives went off.

'I saw his eyes as he fell,' Greville said to the water. 'So full of reproach. Only doing my job, they seemed to say, before they lost all life. His gun had made an awful racket, so I got out of there as fast as I could. Hell was breaking loose, but we were a good team. We made it safely away and dispersed. It was only after I got to my own safe house that I realized that the vial had not only broken, but its contents had vanished; some of it had evaporated, the remainder had seeped through my clothes and into my skin.

'I felt nothing. No after-effects. No symptoms whatsoever. I felt certain we had been fooled by our informant. Perhaps whoever it had been did not enjoy his or her riches, after all. There was nothing. It had all been a big con. At least, that was what we believed for years. I continued working in deep cover in the Middle East. I can speak many dialects. I once had a fight with a man who picked on me because my regional accent was from an area the local people despised.' Greville gave a deprecating smile. 'Can't know it all.'

'As the years passed, I gave the incident with the vial no further thought. The people who had sent me had long assumed, as I had, that we had been fooled. Then, one day, something happened. So innocuous I would have missed it had I not decided to check further.'

Greville suddenly cleared his throat and glanced at Müller sheepishly.

'Um, I did something which for me, given the circumstances at the time, was quite insane. However, I did it. I had sex with a young lass . . . er . . . um . . . unprotected. Considering she had been a complete stranger hours before, it was quite mad. But I had just returned from a highly dangerous and successful mission. I had faced death and had survived. In the madness of my euphoria, I ignored years of caution and went for it . . . so to speak.' Another sheepish glance.

42

'The next day, I went to an excellent doc I knew well and told him. After giving me the usual lecture on how I should have known better, he gave me a thorough examination, including urine, sperm and blood tests. He also scraped away inside my . . . er . . . tube. Days later, after the results were known, he asked to meet me. Not in his surgery. That alone set my antennae shivering.

'When we met, his look was very strange. Like a man who had seen something he wished he hadn't. He looked scared too. I began to *feel* scared, before I even knew what was up.'

At that moment, Müller's phone rang.

'Excuse me,' he said to Greville as he took the mobile out of his jacket pocket.

'Quite alright, old boy. Need a bit of a break anyway.'

Müller moved some distance away, while Greville continued his scrutiny of the water.

'Yes, Pappi.'

'Where are you?' Pappenheim enquired.

'At my aunt's. To be precise, in the garden, talking to her first husband.'

'You mean it really is?'

'It really is. Bizarre, but true. Wonders never cease.'

'Well, here's another wonder, which may well please you. Hassan's gone missing.'

'Was he already here?'

'This will make you even happier. No. The Swedes lost him. He was meant to be in Stockholm.'

'The Great White told you?'

'As if. Got that from one of my people.'

'Does he know, do you think?'

'If he does, he's not telling us. And if he doesn't, they're not telling him . . . whoever they are.'

'Interesting.'

'My thoughts exactly.'

'The undead husband has some interesting things to say too. Tell you all about it later.'

43

'Can't wait. So where are we with the Hassan thing?'

'Not our problem. That belongs to the Swedes, and Kaltendorf. And . . . I can take my holiday.'

'Knew I'd make you a happy man.'

'The day's still young.'

'Ouch,' Pappenheim said with a laugh as he ended the conversation.

Müller put his phone away and looked across to where Greville was still deep in his contemplation of the stream.

'Ouch has many meanings,' he said to himself. He went back to Greville. 'Sorry. A mobile phone can sometimes be a ball and chain.'

Greville gave him a fleeting smile. 'Busy policeman.'

'My cross. Please continue.'

Greville nodded absently and turned back to the water. 'The doc wanted to do further tests, to confirm or otherwise, what he thought he'd seen. I asked him what was wrong. "I want to be sure before I tell you anything," he said. His exact words. I'll remember them to my dying day. I was, of course, even more frightened. To appreciate how this was affecting me, remember I had been in all sorts of pretty dangerous situations and, while I was naturally concerned for my own survival, I was never actually *frightened*. But that day, the doc frightened me. I agreed to the further tests. What else could I do?

'This time he was even more thorough. The test results came back. They proved conclusively what the doc had feared. "You have been poisoned," he told me. Again, I use his exact words. They, too, will haunt me to the day I leave this earth. What kind of poison? I asked. And when? By the time he had finished explaining to me in detail, I finally understood. The vial.

'You see, we were all wrong. The people in the lab had succeeded. Only . . . no one realized at the time, nor by just how much. Quite probably, not even the scientists themselves. They had not yet managed to test it. But

44

this original, and only sample was quite virulent in its own way.

'What they had done in manipulating nature was to create a weapon; but a weapon so stealthy and so implacably vicious, that any nation possessing it would have in its hands the most effective genetic, long-term killer ever to enter our nightmares. Forget Aids. Whether you suspect it to be man-made, or a natural occurrence, is immaterial. Aids is a bludgeon. The thing in the vial was a masterpiece of evil: silent, long-term, supremely effective. A trojan horse of a weapon.'

Greville took another pause and gave a soft laugh, short and bitter.

'What had happened to me that day, old boy,' he went on, 'was that my reproduction kit turned into a poisoned chalice. That guard killed me, even as I killed him. In my case, the dying took rather longer. What those bastards in the lab had created was a monstrous silent instrument of sterility; a genetic killer of generations. The original donor – yours truly, for example – having successfully impregnated a woman, would ensure that any male child born therefrom grows up irreversibly sterile. Imagine this multiplied over hundreds of thousands. Millions. You could wipe out nations over time, without sacrificing a single soldier on the battlefield; and do it without the target nations ever suspecting it. Their populations would simply dwindle over time. Zero replacement rate.'

Greville paused to look at Müller. 'You seem a trifle ill . . .'

'Is this really true?'

'Every word, I'm afraid. Wish it weren't, believe you me. You're looking at the living nightmare. Fiendish, those bastards, what?'

'I have a stronger word.'

'Not as strong as those I have uttered over the years. Over time,' Greville said, 'the monster inside me began to destroy vital organs . . . so slowly as to be virtually undetectable. Sometimes it makes its presence felt with the odd twinge here and there. The doc warned he thought that might happen, though naturally he could not be certain. He was groping as blindly as I was. Nothing to alarm one, of course. One might think, ah, I've pulled a muscle, or some such. You look absolutely fit on the outside while, inside, the damned thing works away at you.'

'How . . . how does it finally happen?'

'Strangely enough . . . no pain. One night you go to sleep, and you don't wake up. Its *coup de grace* is so gentle it's obscene, given its true nature.'

'And how long . . . ?'

'Do I have? No idea, old son. No idea whatsoever. Just like the real thing, you see? Using nature.'

'Has that doctor told anyone?'

'Most trustworthy, that doc. He swore by his lab people too.'

'People can be bought.'

'Certainly. But not the doc.'

'And the lab people?'

'According to the doc, they had no idea what they were looking for. He was the one who spotted it. And he told no one.'

'And you? Did you tell your bosses?'

'No. They might themselves have cherished the idea of making such a weapon and devising clandestine methods of delivering the finished product. Almost certainly why they wanted that vial. Doubt they would have gone to all that trouble, only to destroy it without first replicating its constituent parts. Exhaustive tests on me at the time showed nothing. That's the beauty of the damned thing. It hides . . . for years. I never considered enlightening them, after the doc found out. Who knows? The vile thing may have the ability to transform itself into a wellspring, enabling them to use me as a source. It might not have worked out that way; but then, it might have. I was not prepared to be responsible for turning that iniquitous thing loose on the world.'

'A spy with a conscience?'

'There are many more of us than you might think. From all countries. You'd be surprised how, on some occasions, necessity made the strangest of bedfellows. Once teamed up with an East German who previously had been my mortal enemy. We allied ourselves with an American, to eliminate some privateers. People who did it for the money.'

'The brotherhood of moral spies?' a sceptic Müller asked.

'Strange as that might sound . . . yes. There's a sort of unwritten code. While not exactly *my enemy's enemy is my friend* . . . alliances of convenience, certainly. Naturally, as with anything to do with humans, there are many who do not follow this code. Some violently oppose this practice. The true ideologues. Rather like Hitler opposing the Christmas truce during the First World War. As a policeman, you will have come up against such people.'

'I certainly have. Quite a little story, Greville.'

'There is an even more ironic twist to it. Before I discovered what I was carrying inside of me, I made discreet enquiries about the guard I had killed. Found out he was a widower and had a young son. I arranged to have the boy taken care of. Never knew of me, naturally. Man now, of course. Any father would be proud of what he has become.'

'Why do I have the feeling there's a kink in that particular story?'

'Warned you with the mention of irony.' Greville had a world-weary look in his eyes, and a sad smile lived briefly on his lips. 'Betrayal. Someone ratted.'

'Who?'

'One of my own people. Certain of that. But not sure who.'

'Why? And why now?'

'Perhaps someone's found out – certainly not from the doc – that I've been holding out on them. That I had discovered the truth of what I'd really found, all those years ago. This is nicely cruel revenge, but in the person of the boy who became my detached son. He wants to kill me, for killing his father that day. Poetic. Ironic.'

'Does he know you had him cared for?'

'I very much doubt it. Even the people who set him on me don't know. They merely identified me as his father's killer.'

'You can't be totally certain.'

'Can one ever be? Life is so full of uncertainties. Most of the time we stumble blindly along.' Greville looked at the stream once more. 'Like my detached son, you are probably hunting out the killers of your own parents.'

It was almost a throwaway line. It stunned Müller, who snapped his head round in shock to stare at Greville.

Berlin, at the same moment in time.

Pappenheim, the inevitable cigarette dangling from his lips, looked at his watch.

'Still too early over there,' he muttered.

The cigarette danced to his words, sprinkling ash on his shirt and tie. He brushed the specks off the tie, but left them on the shirt. He picked up a phone and called the sergeants' office. Klemp answered.

'Ah, Udo,' Pappenheim began. 'Reimer or Berger with you?'

'Berger is here.'

'Oh good. Put her on will you, please?'

'She's just picking up her extension.'

Pappenheim could imagine Klemp miming to Berger to pick up her phone.

'Chief?'

'Ah. There you are. I have some good news.'

'And the bad?'

'Pessimist.'

'I have a good teacher.'

'I'll pretend I didn't hear that. Here's your good news. Your little babysitting jaunt may be off.'

'You won't hear me crying with disappointment, Chief. There must be the bad-news bit somewhere.'

'I said "may".'

'Thankful for small mercies then.'

'Life is tough.'

Berger put down her phone just as Reimer entered, T-shirted, with shoulder harness, in jeans and trainers, looking grim. A police-issue black leather jacket without insignia was slung over his left shoulder.

'Not your girlfriend again,' Berger said with the air of someone who had listened to tales of woe too many times.

'Another pissy row,' Reimer explained, going to his desk and almost throwing the jacket at it.

'What a nice surprise,' Klemp put in with a wink at Berger.

'You can laugh. It's not your ears she's bending. All because I told her we had some unexpected assignment.'

'So what?' Berger said. 'You're a policeman, for God's sake! She knows we work all hours, especially in this unit.'

'She had planned dinner with her parents. Our unexpected babysitting job clashes.'

'"Clashes",' Klemp mocked. 'You should be happy,' he went on. 'I never get a chance like that to cancel a dinner with my in-laws.'

'Why is the man always, *always* wrong?' Reimer asked in frustration.

'You're a man,' Berger said. 'That's wrong enough. Live with it.'

'Har har,' Reimer said.

'I can put a smile back on your face, Reimer,' Berger said.

He looked at her with suspicion. 'Oh sure.'

She nodded. 'Just heard from the chief. Babysitting's off.'

Reimer gave her a sideways look, suspicion still there. 'Is that a certain fact? You're not pulling my chain?'

'Reimer, I'll never pull anything of yours.'

Klemp burst out laughing.

Reimer rounded on him. 'Enjoying your laugh?'

'Stay calm, Reimer,' Berger told him. 'It's true.'

'Where's the catch?'

'What catch?'

'There's always a catch with the chief.'

'Ah, Reimer. Know him so well, do you?'

'There has to be a catch,' Reimer insisted.

'Well . . .'

'And?'

'He did say "may" be off . . .'

'I knew it!'

'Take it easy, Reimer.'

'Have you any idea –' he began to the room at large, returning to his favourite topic – 'how many times she's threatened to dump me?'

'She's still with you,' Klemp remarked heartlessly. 'So you must be doing something right, or –' he peered with deliberate intensity at Reimer's crotch – 'she likes something about you.'

'Klemp,' Berger said, 'you're disgusting.'

'So, what else is new?' Klemp was unrepentant.

Berger stood up. 'I give up. I'm off to the toilet, if anyone wants to know.'

'Need any help?' Klemp asked, grinning.

'Klemp,' Berger said. 'You're sick.'

'So, what else is new?' Klemp repeated.

Müller was still in shock as he stared at Greville, who looked back at him with a smile that was at once reflective and full of sympathy.

'You're wondering, of course,' Greville said, 'how I happen to know about it. Long story, old chap, which I shan't go into. Suffice to say I overheard something that perhaps I should not have; or, to be more precise, I was where I should not have been, at that given time.

'You will recall that I mentioned having the strangest of alliances in times of necessity; and the East German chappie I mentioned. One of the Stasi crowd, on a little overseas jaunt in the Middle East. There were a few of them out there, with their then Soviet comrades. The chap who became a temporary ally was under the command of a police major – young for the rank, but a cunning and totally amoral individual. I have seen some cold-blooded people in my time; but this . . . creature took the biscuit.'

The unexpectedness of the revelation about his parents still held Müller in thrall. Now he felt a strange shiver go through him at mention of the major. All his instincts told him he already knew the identity of the person Greville was talking about.

'This . . . major,' Müller heard himself say. 'What was his name?'

'Nothing to give you a clue, I'm afraid. No one used names that meant anything. Myself included. He went by the name of Schlange . . .'

'*Schlange* – snake. Very graphic.'

'And snake, indeed, he was. He revelled in the connotations of such a name. Of course, it was as fake as any of ours out there. We all had several aliases. It is a lying game, after all. I got interested in the conversation because I heard your father's real name mentioned.'

'My father's *real* name? Are you saying my father was a spy?'

Greville was now staring at Müller, as if seeing him for the first time. 'My dear boy . . . you knew nothing of this? Obviously not,' Greville continued softly. 'Your expression . . . is most eloquent. Very sorry to have given you a double shock like this. I had no idea you knew nothing of it. I assumed . . .'

Greville paused, studying Müller with genuine sympathy.

'Your father,' he continued, 'was a legend in his own time. If I had not heard his name that night, I would never have learned his true identity. Many of us had heard of the legendary Romeo Six . . .'

Müller felt a hot flush shoot through him. '*What?*' It was a shocked whisper.

Greville's scrutiny was now intense. 'You've heard of that name?'

Not knowing how to react to this news, Müller's response was terse. 'I have.'

'But I thought—'

'I had no idea my father was a spy. But I've heard of Romeo Six. A case I was investigating—'

'You investigate spies?'

'Not in the strictest sense. My particular unit—'

'Has the more – shall we say – sensitive and unusual cases, which no one else wants and which sometimes bring you up against my line of business.'

'You can put it like that. If Romeo Six really was my father, it opens up a can of worms. At least, for me. That police major you talked about . . .'

'Ah, him. Yes. After the fall of the Wall, he became a privateer. By then, he had become a full colonel. He returned to his old stamping ground, the Middle East. The things he did there . . .' Greville shook his head slowly. '. . . chill the blood. Apt cover name. Anyway. Heard he got his just deserts, at last. Not sure where, or when.'

'I knew him.'

Greville's look was of disbelief. 'Impossible, old boy. Not your territory at all. How—?'

'His name was Dahlberg. I am certain he is the police major, or colonel, you have spoken of. It's your mention of Romeo Six – my damned father – that makes me believe it.'

52

'Steady on, old chap. Don't damn your father. From the little I do know, he was an extremely brave man. Romeo Six was a *double*, you see. He had been fooling the other side for years. Then someone, somewhere, betrayed him. One of *his* side – just as happened to me.' Greville had his world-weary look. 'At times, there is no honour within our "brotherhood". What I heard Schlange and his colleagues discuss that night was the elimination of Romeo Six. Hell hath no fury; and I'm not talking about a woman scorned.'

Müller digested this further piece of news, emotions churning. 'You're saying my father spied for the West?'

'He most certainly did, from deep within the Stasi.'

'My God.'

'Quite so. Did it for years, by all accounts. Posed as a businessman, sympathetic to the DDR. Dangerous job, but very successful for a number of years. When they found out – with connivance from many on the opposite side, it seems – revenge was swift, and savage. I'm only guessing, but I believe that those who betrayed him had much to fear from him. After all, he would have had access to the identities of those in the West with plenty to hide.'

'So, the bastards had him, and my mother, killed.'

'From what I heard that night, it would seem so. Schlange – or Dahlberg, if the same man – must have been involved.'

'Dahlberg was a former police colonel from the East,' Müller said, voice tightly controlled, 'and he had gone private. He was cynical about the system he served, and he used it more than it used him. He died here, almost where you're now standing. He fell into the water.'

Greville looked down at the stream, then at Müller. 'You?'

Müller nodded. 'I had some help. If Schlange *was* Dahlberg, it puts some of the pieces of a puzzle together. He helped destroy the father, and he wanted the son as well. Did you know he was supposedly my distant cousin?'

Greville stared at him. 'Good Lord. No. I did not.'

'Whatever his political or financial motives, there was the

53

family needle in there too. He felt cheated of his birthright. He actually told me. Imagine, a comrade envious of a "decadent" title. It was his weakness; the chink in his armour.'

'I'll be damned. A family grudge. The worst of all hatreds.'

'It was much more than that; but yes, that was an ingredient.' Müller paused, staring beyond the stream to the wooded area of the garden. 'There are many others behind what happened to my parents,' he went on. 'They're hidden from me; for now.'

'And you will not stop until you have found them.'

'No. Schlange – or Dahlberg – was just one of the instruments. There were other such "instruments" that I know of. All dead now . . .'

'Working your way through the outer ring?' A tiny smile played about Greville's lips.

'It just turns out that way. I'd much rather arrest them.'

'Then they get expensive lawyers, and their powerful friends ensure you are hobbled, and they get off.'

Müller again nodded. 'Even so. I'm not that kind of policeman. I would prefer to take my chances with the legal process.'

'Don't be a boy scout all your life, old man. If you had been where I have, you would understand. And I know where I'm going. It's not like in the movies. The good guys are hard put to manage a win; because the bad have no constraints. Depressing, but also very true.'

'I have a very good colleague and friend whom I respect. He is always ready to rein me in, should I be tempted to step over the edge.'

'The noble Pappenheim, who would rather sully himself than have you sullied.'

'You seem to know a lot about me, Greville.'

'I made it my business to know,' Greville said, 'as soon as I found out about your parents. I took an interest from afar, so to speak. Unfortunately, my knowledge of the details concerning how they died is sparse, to say the least. It is important to certain individuals that they keep these details well secured. You will need to ferret very deeply and, of course, they will be very determined to stop you; at all costs. Whatever your father knew must be extremely damaging. But I may be able to supply a small piece of the puzzle.'

Müller gave him a quizzical look. 'Let's walk. There. Across the bridge.'

In Berlin, Pappenheim again checked his watch.

'Must be time now,' he muttered, and picked up a phone. He dialled the number he had been given.

The Pentagon, Washington.

The phone rang on a desk within an office where the sole occupant was a USAF lieutenant-colonel.

The lieutenant-colonel picked it up. 'Colonel Bloomfield.'

'He's in trouble,' Carey Bloomfield heard. 'Call me.'

'*Pappi?*' she whispered in astonishment. 'How did you get this number?'

'Call me,' he repeated, and hung up.

She put the phone down carefully, as if it had turned into something that would bite her if she mishandled it.

'"He's in trouble",' she repeated to herself. 'What the hell have you done now, Müller, to drive Pappi into tracing my secure number? And as for you, Pappi, how did you manage to get it?'

Four

T he silence that had followed Greville's revelation that he had something to contribute had continued as he and Müller walked to the small bridge and crossed the stream. Greville trailed along, hands in pockets.

'You can?' Müller at last said.

'I wrote down what I heard of that conversation, and left it with someone for safe keeping. I gave him strict instructions. Like the doc, I trust him implicitly.'

'Who is he?'

'My former batman. Salt of the earth, and a very good friend. He became my batman for about a year, when I was a newly minted lieutenant. Smart man, he went on to better things. Became a commando, and ended up a through-the-ranks lieutenant himself, which was the highest he could expect to reach by the time he was ready to leave the service.

'I was never one for class distinctions. Black sheep, as it were. My father tended to believe that the class system was sacrosanct. Everyone in his own place sort of thing. Some to serve, others to command. I scandalized him when I was a boy by choosing to make friends with the servants' children, rather than with those of my class, whatever that was. He was rather pleased – and much relieved, I might add – when I gained a commission.

'My former batman is William Malcolm Jacques – spelt the French way but pronounced Jakes as I have done. Welsh,

56

Scottish and French names, but as English as you're likely to find. Bill Jacques is a man to whom I would entrust my life. I know I can, because he once saved it. He now runs a school for gentlemen's gentlemen. Some of the customers who employ his students are far less gentlemanly than he is. Ironic, what?'

'Where does he live?'

'In England. Dorset. And in France. The south. Nice. The school has a branch there. I'll give you both addresses, and telephone numbers. I shall also tell you where my notes are hidden. You'll be the second person who knows.'

'Doesn't he?' Müller was surprised.

'No. Hid it myself when I last saw him. Some time ago. Got a favour to ask, old boy . . .'

Müller's phone interrupted what Greville had been about to say. He took out the mobile, stopped walking, and looked at Greville.

Greville made a brief hand movement. 'Do carry on.' He walked a short distance away to allow Müller some privacy.

'Yes, Pappi,' Müller said into the phone.

'The Swedes are getting agitated,' he heard Pappenheim say. 'Still no sign of our man.'

'What do your guts tell you?'

'It's what they're asking.'

'Try me.'

'For one, was he kidnapped? Or did he choose to go AWOL? If so, why?'

'What's going on in that suspicious, cynical brain of yours?'

'Compliments, compliments . . . If he has absconded,' Pappenheim continued, 'what's his agenda? I'd like to know what occupied Mr Hassan's time *before* he became a full-time peacenik. He's so clean, it hurts.'

'Perhaps he really is clean.'

A long silence greeted this.

57

'Got the message,' Müller said.

'See what I can dig up, shall I?'

'Which means you're already doing so.'

'How well you know me, oh Master. Speaking of which, when are you coming home?'

'Anyone asking?'

'Not yet. But bound to.'

'I'll let you know.'

Pappenheim's suck on his cigarette made a fluting sound. 'Like that, is it?'

'Like that.'

'Hokay,' Pappenheim said cheerfully. 'I'll enjoy watching the GW's veins pop, if he asks.'

'Something else . . . see if you can find out anything about the name Schlange . . .'

'*Snake?* How melodramatic, theatrical . . .' Pappenheim gave a sudden pause. 'Theatrical,' he repeated in a soft voice. 'You had a cousin, once . . . late, unlamented, given to such gestures. Any connection?'

'You're so quick, Pappi, it hurts.'

'Hey. That's *my* line.'

'I can borrow, now and then.'

'Feel free. So, why the interest?'

'Something I've just learned. More later. See if there's a connection.'

'Will do.'

'Thanks, Pappi.'

Müller put the phone away as their conversation ended, and strode on after Greville, who had walked a little way along the stream towards where it exited from the woods.

Greville had stopped and was again looking down at the water, its flow a gentle, soothing noise.

'It's very clean,' he said as Müller approached. 'Any fish to be had?'

Müller stopped and looked down at the stream. 'I think they caught a catfish here last year. In DDR times, the Saale,

58

into which this feeds, was itself a polluted hellhole; but things have improved enormously, so the fish have come back.'

'Any snakes? Not a joke. Just curious.'

'The odd viper perhaps goes for a crawl out in the woods. Truth is, I've never come across one.' Müller was still peering at the clear waters of the stream. 'You said you wanted a favour.'

'Ah. Yes. Um . . . the things I've told you . . . would you mind saying nothing to Isolde? Particularly about my little accident in the lab . . .'

'What you decide to tell, or not tell her, is entirely your affair. I am not here to pass judgement.'

'Thank you. Appreciate that.'

Müller looked at him. 'You do know she never stopped loving you, even when she married Helmut?'

'And I never stopped loving her. I once spent some time in a particularly nasty institution in the Middle East. My own fault. Careless. Got caught. People there in authority who enjoyed inflicting physical pain. I survived by thinking of Isolde.' Greville was again on one of his mental journeys into the past, and stared at the stream without really seeing it. 'One of those who administered the pain won't ever do it again. Took great pleasure in snapping his neck, once I'd got out. Shooting was too good. I wanted him to feel I was repaying him. Found him, of all places, in a whorehouse. The woman betrayed him for no payment. Seems he liked inflicting pain during love-making.'

'Schlange,' Müller said, jolting Greville back.

'What? Oh. Yes. What about him?'

'You said he was amoral . . .'

'An understatement if ever there were one.'

'Have you heard of someone called Bloomfield?'

Greville jerked his head round to stare at Müller. 'You do have surprising information. Never met the poor chap, but heard of him; or rather, what happened to him. American agent. Unfortunately, he met up with Schlange. That evil creature was in the process of peeling him alive, strip by strip, for information. Bloomfield was rescued. Too late for the poor devil, really. Schlange had virtually completed the job.'

'No doubt about it now,' Müller said, almost to himself. 'It was Dahlberg. I know about what happened to Bloomfield.'

Greville narrowed his eyes at Müller, as if contemplating something. 'How so?'

'A case spilled into your kind of territory.'

'World is indeed small,' Greville said, with one of his tiny smiles. 'Care to illuminate?'

Müller said nothing.

After a while, Greville said, 'You're seeing it again. The moment when you took him. I can understand that. I frequently revisit the moment when I snapped my torturer's neck.'

'It was raining,' Müller said. 'Heavily. The stream was swollen and flowing very fast. He had Aunt Isolde in an armlock—'

'*What?* The bastard!'

'He had just cold-bloodedly shot dead the manager, Bulent Landauer, who was the son of a close friend of my aunt; and he was using her as a shield to cover his escape. I was never going to let him make it.'

Müller drew in a deep breath, letting go of the vision.

'I think I understand that sound,' Greville said.

'I'm never going to let the people who killed my parents get away,' Müller told him. It was a vow.

'Didn't think you would.'

In Berlin, the duty sergeant at the front desk looked up from his security monitors to see a stern-faced man in a suit standing beyond the protective screen of armoured glass, staring at him. The man carried a large, padded white envelope.

'Can I help you?' the sergeant asked.

The tiny boom microphone of the skeletal headset he wore transmitted the question to tiny speakers on the other side of the glass. His words were heard clearly, and without electronic overtones.

The man kept looking at him. There was a wide counter at the base of the glass screen. The man dropped the envelope on it and turned away.

'Hey!' the sergeant called.

The man had gone a few steps. He stopped, turned slowly to direct his cold gaze back upon the sergeant. He said nothing.

'How do I know this isn't a bomb?' the sergeant asked.

'Then you've got a problem.' The voice, like the eyes, was cold.

The sergeant glanced warily at the parcel. 'I could make you take it back?'

'How?' It was both a question and a challenge.

The sergeant backed down. 'Who's it for?'

'Pappenheim.'

'*Oberkommissar* Pappenheim to you!'

The man walked deliberately up to the counter until he was leaning against it, as if he intended to push his way through.

'If rank is a problem for you, shithead,' he snarled, 'would you like to know mine?'

The sergeant stared at him, stunned by the unexpected verbal attack. 'You can't talk to me like that!' he finally retorted.

The man gave a smile that was close to a silent snarl, turned on his heels and walked out without a backwards glance.

'We know who's the shithead,' the sergeant said, glaring.

But the man had long made his exit.

The sergeant picked up a phone and called Berger.

'*In!*' Pappenheim called in response to the knock on his door.

Berger entered, carrying the white envelope.

'Beware of Greeks bearing gifts,' he intoned.

'I'm not the Greek here. Herman Spyros is.'

'I'll decide later whether that was a dry comment or not,' Pappenheim said. 'So, what's that you've got?'

'According to Jürgen Hirsch, who's on the duty desk, you've got a hard man in a suit to thank. Just your name on it.'

Pappenheim squinted through the smoke at her. 'A hard man in a suit. What did Hirsch actually say?'

As she handed the envelope to Pappenheim, Berger gave a detailed resumé of what Hirsch had related to her.

Pappenheim chuckled as he looked it over. 'Bet that soured his lunch.'

'You know the person who brought this, Chief?'

'No. But I know where he came from. OK. Thanks for bringing it, Lene.'

She remained where she was. 'What if it's a bomb?'

'I'm assuming you have already ensured it's been through the scanners,' Pappenheim said. 'If anyone can get a bomb through our extortionately expensive detectors, then the people who sent this certainly have the expertise.' He blew some smoke through his nostrils like a dragon with a misfire. 'However, much as they might probably be dreaming of doing away with me, they've not yet reached the stage of acting upon it. But . . . if I am wrong, better to have one set of body parts to scrape off the walls, instead of two.' He peered at her. 'Still here, Berger?'

'I was just wondering if this is to do with our baby-sitting . . .'

'If it is, I'm sure to tell you.'

'Of course you will, Chief,' she said, disbelief plain.

'You can trust me.'

'Hah!' she said, and went out.

Pappenheim smiled to himself as the door shut behind her; then he studied the envelope once more. It was quite thick, and heavy.

'If you're a bomb, I know where your sender lives. I'll come back to haunt.'

He jabbed the dying cigarette into the already full ashtray and began to open the envelope. There were three neatly bound documents of about twenty pages each, plus a hand-written note.

You never got these, the note said, *and I did not send them. They are copies, so there is no need to return them.*

The note was unsigned.

'Hmm,' Pappenheim said.

He put the note through a small, recently acquired shredder attached to his desk, and above his waste-paper basket. He watched as the thin, spaghetti-like strands curled about themselves as they floated down into it.

Satisfied, he turned his attention to the first of the documents. The subject matter was Daood Hassan.

He began to read.

Fifteen minutes later, he had still not lighted a replacement cigarette. He sucked in his cheeks as he came to the end of the document.

'Shit!' he exclaimed softly.

He lit a cigarette for the second document, which was about Neubauer. When he came to the end of that one, the cigarette was only half smoked. The remaining half lay in the ashtray, prematurely stubbed out.

He made no comment as he picked up the third. *Graf von Röhnen – Romeo Six*, was the handwritten title upon the first page.

Then he saw a yellow marker, barely protruding, near the end. He thumbed through to the page, four before the end. Another handwritten title: *Schlange Dahlberg*.

He read through the entire document without once lighting up. When he had finished, he put all three documents neatly together, then leaned back in his chair to study them from a distance. Still looking at them, he took a fresh ciga-rette out of the pack, lit it, drew deeply upon it, then blew the smoke at the neat stack he'd made of the documents.

'Not a bomb in the normal sense,' he said to the stack, 'but a bomb all the same. Just don't blow up in our faces. That's all I ask.'

He took his time with the cigarette, all the while staring at the pile of documents as if mesmerized. When he had reached the end of the Gauloise, he stubbed it out with great deliberation, then picked up a phone.

Müller and Greville were on their way back to the Derrenberg when the mobile rang.

'I'll carry on,' Greville said, and kept walking as Müller stopped to pull out the phone.

'Yes, Pappi.'

'I think you should get back here as soon as possible,' Pappenheim said.

The way Pappenheim had spoken made Müller say, 'Has *he* been at it?'

'He's been very quiet . . . for him. That's not the reason. Things you should see. I won't discuss them, even over this connection.'

Müller paused. If Pappenheim chose not to talk further on a secure connection protected by a scrambler, then there was little choice but to return to Berlin.

'Alright, Pappi. Back as soon as possible.'

'Fine. I think the rogues' gallery would be a good meeting place.'

Müller paused once more. The 'rogues' gallery' was their nickname for the documents room, the most secure area in the entire building. Only three people had free access: Müller, Pappenheim and Kaltendorf.

'I'll see you there,' Müller said. 'Give me roughly . . . two and a half hours from now.'

'OK.'

They ended the conversation and Müller looked across to

where Greville, taking his time about it, was crossing the bridge. Müller put the mobile away and walked quickly to catch up.

They reached the other bank together.

'Trouble?' Greville asked.

'Not sure. But I've got to return to Berlin.'

Greville nodded. 'Then I'll give you all the details before you leave.'

'What do you plan to do now?' Müller asked.

'To be quite frank, I'm at a bit of a loss.'

'Then stay here. I'm certain Aunt Isolde won't object. If your . . . detached son is after you, as you believe, then this place is well out of the way . . .'

'I have no intention of putting her in danger.'

'Talk to her. You'll find she's of sterner stuff than you might think. The years have not changed her that much.'

Greville's tiny smile lived briefly. 'Oh, I do know the stuff she's made of.'

'Then wait here until I return.'

'Is that Jens Müller offering me a haven? Or *Hauptkommissar* Müller giving me an order?'

'Both. Do you have luggage?'

'A small bag. Travel light. Lifetime habit. It's in reception. I'll stay in the hotel, if they can find me a room.'

They had reached the hotel entrance.

'As you wish,' Müller said. 'I'll say goodbye to Aunt Isolde.' He held out a hand. 'Be here when I get back.'

Greville shook it. 'Very well. I'll give you those details when you're done with Isolde. Just in case.'

'Pessimist?'

'Realist.' Greville's smile hung on for longer than before. He kept smiling as Müller went off to see Aunt Isolde.

Aunt Isolde had returned to the kitchen, where Müller found her.

'Aunt Isolde,' he began. 'Something's come up, and I've

got to return to Berlin immediately. But I'll be coming back as soon as I can. I've suggested to Greville that he remain here. He's decided on the hotel. Alright with you?'

She nodded. 'Of course. Perhaps,' she added wistfully, 'the hotel is best for now. I'm still coming to terms with his being alive.'

'Don't rush it. Let things take their course.'

She placed a gentle hand on his arm. 'Don't you worry. I'll be fine.'

'I'm sure you will be. Aunt Isolde,' he went on, 'this might seem a foolish question, but did my father leave anything with you?'

The hand on his arm was suddenly very still. 'What makes you ask?'

'Just a hunch. I don't really expect . . .'

'Yes,' she told him, in a very quiet voice. 'He did leave something for you.'

Before he could react, she went out of the kitchen.

Scarcely daring to believe his ears, Müller remained where he was and stared after her.

About five minutes later she returned, carrying a worn briefcase of soft brown leather.

She handed it to the astonished Müller. 'I've had this with me since you were twelve. There's a note in there from your father, addressed to me. You may read it. It will explain.'

He went over to the table and put the heavy briefcase down upon it. He stared at it for some time.

'Go on,' Aunt Isolde urged. 'Open it. It won't bite. It's not locked.'

Almost reverently, Müller snapped open the clasp. He then opened the briefcase, and looked in. It was full of thin files, something that looked like a jewellery box, and an opened envelope.

He took out the envelope, which was addressed to Aunt

Isolde. A single sheet of paper was in it. He drew that out, spread it open and began to read the short note.

If he does not ask, these contents do not matter. If he does, they might help him.

Müller slowly folded the note and returned it to the envelope, which he put back into the briefcase. He snapped the case shut.

'Do you know what's in there?' he asked her.

Aunt Isolde shook her head. 'This is meant for you. I would have had no business looking.'

He pushed the briefcase towards her. 'Put it back in its hiding place. I don't want to take it to Berlin with me at this moment, especially if it contains what I believe it does. I'll look at what's in there when I get back.'

She did not question his decision. 'Alright, Jens. And you?' she went on with some anxiety. 'Will *you* be alright?'

'Absolutely. No cause for you to worry.' He gave her a quick kiss on the cheek. 'Look after yourself. Call me at any time, if you need to.'

She nodded. 'I will.'

She stroked his arm, as she would a fond son.

In Berlin, Pappenheim was staring at the Daood Hassan document as he would a dangerous snake. The cigarette between his lips hung there, slowly consuming itself.

'A hired killer,' he said at the document. 'Why couldn't you have surprised me and been what you claim you are? So, Herr Daood Hassan . . . who's your target? And where? Sweden? Or here? That is the question.'

Pappenheim gathered the documents and returned them to the envelope. He then killed the cigarette, got to his feet and, taking the envelope with him, left the office.

A short distance along the corridor was the black, armoured steel door of the documents room, with its keypad-operated locking system.

Pappenheim stopped and entered the code. Solid internal bolts slid back, and the door swung open.

Pappenheim went in.

In an office that was not in Berlin, a man picked up his phone at the first ring.

'Disappearance successful,' he heard.

'Excellent. Do they know?'

'I very much doubt it.'

'I don't want your doubts! I want certainties!'

'I have already run a trawl,' came the affronted retort. 'We're clean.'

'I never take anything for granted. Run another check!'

The man slammed the phone down, abruptly ending the conversation.

'Morons everywhere,' he snarled.

The caller at the other end looked at his dead phone and made a sour face.

'Moron,' he said.

Pappenheim came out of the documents room.

He had placed the envelope in a cabinet holding other highly sensitive material that he and Müller had collected. Not even Kaltendorf knew of the existence of such material, much of it containing seriously compromising evidence against some of the very people with whom the senior policeman associated.

Pappenheim was almost at his office door when he heard the dreaded summons.

'Ah! Pappenheim!'

Pappenheim stifled a sigh and stopped. He turned round to see Kaltendorf striding hard-heeled towards him.

'Any sign of Müller as yet?' was the first question that came, like a hurled weapon, at Pappenheim.

'No, sir.'

'No, sir! No, sir!' Kaltendorf came to a belligerent halt

68

before Pappenheim. 'That's all I ever hear.' His eyes dared Pappenheim to disagree.

Pappenheim said nothing.

'When Müller finally returns, tell him I want to see him. In my office!'

'Yes, sir.'

With a final glare, Kaltendorf marched off.

Pappenheim waited until his superior had turned a corner, before entering his office.

'One day,' Pappenheim began in hope as he entered his haven, 'he might pound his way through to the floor below. Give us all some peace.'

At about the same time, Vincente Monleon was driving his souped-up, black Seat Ibiza FR south from Flensburg. The Agostini version of 'The Riddle' was playing loudly on the CD through six speakers. Monleon whistled happily in accompaniment.

A slim but athletic-looking man in his thirties, Monleon had close-cropped dark hair that strikingly resembled the patrician haircut of ancient Rome. The Valencia licence plates were adorned with the blue EU band and the E for España national ID letter. He was cruising well within the limit, and keeping legally to the inside lane of the Autobahn. Then Monleon saw that, some distance up ahead, two pairs of traffic police were doing spot checks. One pair waved off the car they had been dealing with.

'Nothing better to do?' he muttered to himself in Spanish.

Cars were slowing down. Some were waved on, then one was picked out by the pair that had just finished, and directed to the hard shoulder. By the time Monleon had reached the spot, he was the one who got waved to the hard shoulder by the other pair.

'Of course it would be me,' he muttered again.

He pulled up as directed, and stopped. He turned off the engine before being asked. One of the policemen came to his door. His partner stayed well away, watchful, hand on sidearm.

A little further on, the second pair of police – one a female officer – were seemingly too occupied with their own catch to take interest.

'Your papers, please, sir?' he was asked in German. 'And will you please get out of your vehicle?'

'Of course.'

Monleon made no hasty movements, and climbed out, taking both his personal and car documents with him. He handed them over.

The policeman stepped back a little and glanced at the number plate. 'Valencia,' he said. 'El Cid, and Don Quixote.' He smiled.

'You know Valencia?' Monleon spoke hesitant German.

'Sorry, no,' the policeman said as he studied the car documents. 'Only Ibiza. Like your car.' He smiled at his joke.

His partner, hand still on sidearm, gave a fleeting smirk.

As the policeman seemed to want to talk, Monleon decided to be friendly.

'Ibiza!' he said dismissively. 'Come to Valencia, city of culture, history, and the best paella in all Spain.'

The policeman did not look up as he said, 'I would like to, but my girlfriend seems to like Ibiza. And you appear to have brought the sun with you.'

'It's hotter here than in Spain. You have stolen it, I think.'

The policeman actually grinned as he finally looked up. 'That's exactly what my girlfriend said. Excuse me.'

The policeman ducked into his patrol car to run a check, while his partner maintained his alert stance.

The friendly one emerged from the car, expression neutral.

'So . . .' he continued, as if the conversation had not been interrupted. 'Is the paella really the best?'

Monleon played the game. 'The very best. It is made with meat *and* fish – and the shrimps, of course; but not like those others, with just bits of fish mixed with the usual shrimps.

70

Paella Valenciana. The original. Some are made with the eels from Lake Albufera. Best wine to have with it – to my taste – is Macabeo, and finish with Mendoza – that's brandy – and coffee. The very, very best.'

The policeman smiled again as he handed back the documents. 'I can almost taste it, the way you describe it. I'm not so sure I'd like the eels, but I'll try to persuade my girlfriend to visit next time we go to Spain. You have a long way to go, Mr Monleon. Drive carefully.'

'I will. Thank you. It is wonderful to be able to drive all over Europe. Like the States.'

'Well . . . not quite like the States, but I get your point.'

Both policemen watched carefully as Monleon got back behind the wheel.

'And don't forget,' Monleon said, as he clipped on his seat belt. 'Come to Valencia on your next holiday. Enjoy some great food.'

He started the car, gave them a wave and drove off.

The policemen watched, but did not wave back. Soon they were searching the traffic for their next victim.

Monleon turned 'The Riddle' back on.

'Police,' he said, reverting to Spanish. 'The same everywhere.'

He began to whistle again as the almost straight, 64-kilometre stretch of the A7 Autobahn between Tarp and Bordesholm unwound before him.

Five

'What? They've found him? Where?' Kaltendorf had received a phone call and was looking at once puzzled and relieved.

'In some back alley somewhere,' the caller replied. 'Seems he was mugged.'

'Mugged? In *Sweden*?'

'You don't think there are muggers in Sweden? Probably some asylum seeker,' the other added disparagingly.

'Probably,' Kaltendorf agreed.

'So now you're back on track. Make sure *your* people don't lose him as well, when he arrives on your patch.'

'I'll make certain of it. You can depend on me.'

'I do hope we can, Heinz. I do hope we can.'

The line went dead.

Pappenheim had received a phone call of his own.

'You're joking,' he now said.

'I don't make risky phone calls to joke.'

'Keep your shirt on,' Pappenheim soothed. 'So, what's the story?'

'He was mugged.'

Pappenheim burst out laughing. 'Is the mugger still alive?' he asked, laughter barely subsiding.

'Would you believe he was found dishevelled, bruised, and scared?'

Pappenheim stopped laughing. 'Dishevelled? Bruised? *Scared?*'

'Like repeating things, do you? But yes, I do share your scepticism.'

'Now why would someone like that go to the trouble of playing the victim of a mugger?'

'Strangely enough, I asked myself that very question. Wonderfully enough, it's not my problem.'

'Thanks.'

'I like that note of dryness I hear. Warms my heart. And Pappi . . .'

'Yes?'

'Don't call me again this century.'

'I didn't call you. You called me.'

'So I did.'

As had occurred with Kaltendorf, the line went dead.

'He's a comedian now,' Pappenheim said as he replaced the phone. 'And as for you, Herr Daood Hassan,' he added to the phone, 'what are you up to? And who's your target?'

He picked up another phone and called the sergeants' office. This time it was Berger who answered.

'Ah. Lene. Glad you're there. Bad news, I'm afraid.'

'What a relief, Chief. And here I was worrying.'

'You're too young to be so cynical. Leave that to old dogs like me.'

'If you say so, Chief. I take it the bad news means we're back on?'

'You are.'

'Reimer will love this.'

'Complaining again, is he?'

'Girlfriend trouble.'

'That's not news.'

'It's a dinner with her parents. Long planned.'

'He *wants* to go? The man's sick. Excellent policeman, but sometimes . . .'

73

'Exactly what we all think over here. Love makes you blind, they tell me . . .'

'Is that some kind of challenge I hear in your voice, Berger?'

'Me, Chief?' She was all innocence. Then she quickly added, 'I'll give him the glad news.'

'Thanks, Lene. And, by the way, when our man does finally get to Berlin, don't let him out of your sight.'

'What about the toilet?'

'That's what you've got Reimer for.'

'You do love making him happy, Chief.'

'That's what I'm here for . . . to make you all happy.'

'Can I laugh now?'

'You're being rude to your superior again. And Lene . . .'

'Chief?'

'Make sure your weapons are always ready for fast use. Both of you. If you're carrying your usual arsenals, so much the better.'

'Something you're not telling me, Chief?'

'Just being cautious. More later.'

In the sergeants' office, Klemp said to Berger as her conversation with Pappenheim ended, 'Did I hear you say you're back on?'

'We are.'

Klemp looked beyond her. 'Well, he's coming back from his run to the toilet. This should be interesting.'

'We're back on,' Berger said as soon as Reimer entered.

'Shit!' he swore. 'I just told her it was OK.'

'I thought you'd gone to the toilet.'

'I did. But I called her as well.'

Klemp shook his head slowly. 'Sad. Very sad.'

'What the hell do I do now?' Reimer implored.

Berger looked at him without sympathy. 'You're very hard to please, Reimer. Do you know that?'

'*Shit!*' Reimer said again.

Klemp looked at him and smiled, Schadenfreude off the scale. 'Isn't it nice when things work out just as you'd like?'

'Go sit on your . . .'

'Lady present, Reimer,' Berger said, baring her teeth at him in a fierce smile. 'Go yell at your girlfriend or something. I don't understand this, Reimer. I've seen you put a gun to the head of a slime who had one against your gut, and *he* backed down. What does your girlfriend carry? A poisoned dart?'

'I love her,' Reimer said in simple explanation.

'There's love, and then there's love. This sounds like domination to me.'

'Think what you like.' Reimer paused for a moment, then seemed to come to a decision. 'I'm going to tell her dinner's off.'

'There,' Berger said. 'Not so hard was it?'

Klemp gave a slow hand clap.

But Reimer looked unhappy as he went out again to make his call privately.

Klemp looked at Berger. 'Do you feel safe with him?'

'Reimer's OK.'

'We both know he's a top *bulle* and one of the best undercover people we have . . .'

'But?'

'That crazy woman of his could be blunting his edges. I'll be honest with you. The way he's been acting lately would worry me if I had to partner him on a sensitive job.'

'Sensitive is the wrong word, Klemp.'

'What do you mean?'

'What am I? Your language teacher?'

While Reimer was steeling himself to tell his girlfriend he would not be attending dinner, Pappenheim's phone rang again.

He picked it up. 'No peace for the wicked.'

'You said it.'

'You again? Short century.'

'Do you want this, or not?'

'I want.'

'It appears that your man needed a pee on his way to the meeting . . .'

'Convenient.'

'Wait for the rest.'

'I'm suitably chastened.' Pappenheim blew smoke at his nicotine-decorated ceiling and waited.

'They stopped at a small café-cum-restaurant and asked if they could use the toilet, which just happened to be at the back . . .'

'With a door to the outside?'

'With a door to the wide open spaces.'

'Gets better and better.'

'His minders remained a discreet distance away, while he exercised his waterworks.'

'Ah, discreet minders. Where would we be without them?'

'I don't envy those particular two.'

'If they worked for me . . .' Pappenheim began in a hard voice. 'But do go on. I'm interrupting again.'

'Thank you.'

Pappenheim ignored the sarcasm as the caller went on, 'They realized something was wrong when the pee turned into a marathon. By then, of course, it was far too late.'

'So, what's their excuse?'

'Not "their". His. He claims two people came in from the back, grabbed him and chucked him into a car. He was driven round Stockholm, then dumped. All his cash stolen – he had plenty on him – and, naturally, his credit cards. They even took his mobile phone. Oh yes, they roughed him up a bit before leaving him in that alley. That's why he's so scared.'

'There's that word again. Are we talking about the same person? I would have thought his so-called abductors would have had more to fear from *him*.'

'The word is, he really *is* scared.'

'Who could possibly be frightening enough to actually scare this man?'

'You'll be seeing him soon. You judge.'

'I still find it difficult to believe. Unless someone's been feeding you very badly, and deliberately, if you see what I mean.'

'The thought had crossed my mind.'

'Better and better,' Pappenheim repeated. 'How come you're so up-to-date on this . . . er . . . incident?'

'We monitor these things.'

'"Monitor". What a multitude of sins that word covers.'

'Time to go.'

The line went dead in its sudden, familiar way.

'You and Kaltendorf should get together,' Pappenheim said as he replaced the phone. 'You both have a way with exits.'

He took the cigarette out of his mouth and looked at the glowing end. 'Think about it,' he said to the cigarette. 'Abduction, theft, bodily harm, terror. But left alive.' He put the cigarette back into his mouth with the urgency of a drowning man grabbing at a lifebelt. 'Left alive to tell the tale. Why?'

Klemp was engrossed in a newspaper he had taken from one of the drawers of his desk.

Berger glanced up from a report she was in the process of writing and saw a picture. 'You're looking at the wrong page, Klemp. The bikini is on this side.'

'Better bikini here. Full-page.' Klemp did not even look up.

Berger shook her head in resignation, and continued with her report.

'It says here,' Klemp began, still not looking up, 'that this hot weather will continue for a week or more.'

'Is that why you're so glued to that page? They've got the usual pictures of women in their underwear lying in a park, or standing in a fountain, just to show how hot it is?'

'Why shouldn't I look at something that pleases me?' Klemp countered.

'That's a good point.'

'I know what that is. It's sarcasm.'

'Now I know you really went to school.'

Klemp folded his paper with a sigh. 'You're being very bitchy today, Lene.'

'That's a good word. Bitchy.'

Klemp cocked his head to one side. 'It must be that time of—'

'Say it, and I'll shoot you.'

'My lips are sealed.' Movement distracted Klemp. 'And here comes loverboy, looking very sick.'

Berger looked up again as Reimer returned. He did appear to be ill.

'Uh-oh,' Berger said. 'Bad, was it?'

'Worse.'

'Ah well. Don't worry too much, Reimer. Must be that time of the month.' She glanced at Klemp, straight-faced.

Müller was on his way back to Berlin.

As with the journey down, he decided to drive without music, preferring instead to listen to the sounds of the car. Churning through his mind was the story Greville had told: the reasons for Greville's long disappearance; the terrible genetic poison, the revelation of yet another dark side to Dahlberg; the detached son's mission of revenge; and, at last, the true identity of Romeo Six.

'My own father,' Müller said to the sounds of the Porsche.

Then, to crown it all, the discovery of the documents left for him by his father, all those years ago. So many pieces, all one by one being teased into place. But there were many, many more still to come.

He had not wanted to look at the documents. Not just yet.

Unsure of what he would find, or how he would react, he had preferred to give himself some thinking time. Greville had said his father had not been a traitor but, instead, had been doing extremely dangerous work for his country. If true, it was work that had eventually got him killed.

'And my mother with him.'

Müller tightened his lips until he felt they would split. A great anger was building within him. Whatever it took, and whoever he had to go through, he would find out the truth.

'I want to see your faces,' he said into the car, voice low, and very cold. 'I want you to see me, knowing I have found you, under whatever stone or rock you've been hiding; in whatever hole you have crawled into. Whoever you are, no matter how powerful, how high you may be, I will have my reckoning.'

Then what would he do?

'I'll see when the time comes,' he said, answering aloud the question he had mentally asked himself.

The road ahead was a streaming ribbon as the Porsche, its fat wheels gripping at the surface, hurled itself at high speed along the fast lane of the Autobahn.

About half an hour later Müller acted on impulse and took the next exit. Once off the Autobahn, the road fed him on to a narrow *Landstrasse* that led to a small village. He went through, and the road continued into open countryside. A kilometre or so later, he saw a track that entered a wooded area. The track turned out to be a former military road of DDR vintage. Parallel lines of evenly spaced, embedded blocks swept down a slope and into a hollow. The blocks had been laid in such a manner that heavy vehicles would have been able to travel upon the 'road', even in wet weather, without danger of bogging down.

As he drove down, the big ultra-low-profile tyres rumbled loudly, the vibrations transmitting via the sports suspension throughout the car. Even so, it took the punishment in its stride.

He stopped the car at the bottom and got out. A small pool of clear water, situated in the middle of the hollow, looked incongruously ornamental, though it clearly was not. As he walked towards it, Müller saw that it was fed by a trickling brook, but the water level remained constant. He assumed there was an underground run-off somewhere.

He looked about him. The place had every appearance of an area that had not been visited in years. It was also very silent, as if his arrival had sent every woodland creature scurrying into hiding. Tall trees enclosed it, save for the track, which created its own gateway. It would have been very difficult to spot from the air, Müller thought.

'They probably once had a surface-to-air missile battery sited here,' he said to himself.

He looked about him once more. Then, suddenly, he raised his clenched fists above his shoulders and let out a resounding yell. It was a yell. It was a roar. It was a scream; and it went on, and on, and on, echoing into the woods. The years of pain from the age of twelve, the sense of loss, the anger, the rage, the feeling of betrayal, all went into that sound, which at times sounded scarcely human. It was a primeval bellow that was at once a howl of mourning and an implacable challenge.

When it was at last over, Müller lowered his hands, unclenched his fists and stood there taking deep, measured breaths until he had calmed himself.

Then he returned to the car, got in, and drove back the way he had come.

Pappenheim finally got the call he'd been anxiously waiting for.

He grabbed the phone as soon as it rang, hoping. The voice at the other end confirmed that the waiting was over.

'Thank you for returning the call, Colonel. And congratulations on the promotion.'

'Thank you,' Carey Bloomfield said. 'I'm not a full colonel. Just lieutenant-colonel.'

'"Just"?'

'And I could lose that in a heartbeat for making this call. Is it worth it?'

'Very much so.'

'I'm not in my office and this phone may be wide open. How big is his trouble?'

'Big enough.'

Carey Bloomfield was smart enough not to ask questions. 'I see.'

'Your presence would be helpful.'

'Are you crazy? I can't just . . . Doesn't he listen to you anymore?'

'In this situation, no.'

'Not good.'

'My precise thoughts.'

'Do you still smoke?'

'What a question.' As if to prove it, Pappenheim blew a smoke ring at a wall.

There was a moment's silence. 'I think we've talked long enough on this phone.'

'So do I,' he agreed.

They hung up together.

'I hope you'll find a way to make it, Colonel Bloomfield,' Pappenheim said to the still-floating smoke ring. 'He does need you.'

He picked up another phone and called the goth.

'Miss Meyer,' he began when she had answered, 'did anyone listen in?'

'Yes, sir.'

'Got a trace?'

'I have.'

'Well done.'

'That was easy,' Hedi Meyer said. It was not a boast.

'Computer kids!' Pappenheim said. 'Another world entirely.'

There was a smile in her voice when she said, 'Do I hit them now?'

'Give it a few moments, then do your worst.'

'My pleasure.'

'Computer kids!' he repeated when he'd hung up.

In a small room full of electronic equipment, a man with headphones pressed a button. The entire conversation of Pappenheim and Carey Bloomfield was played through.

He stopped the recording and turned to his companion. 'They were smart. Not enough to get anything worth much. But what do you make of it? He seems to be having some sort of crisis.'

The other man, older, was silent for some moments. 'He is not a man given to having crises. At least, not enough to worry Pappenheim and certainly not important enough to drive Pappenheim into making contact with the good colonel.'

'So? Do we pass this on?'

The older one gave it some thought. 'Look at it this way – if it's important and we do nothing, it's our necks. If it isn't, we can't be faulted for being conscientious. Let them decide.'

'Passing the buck?'

'Where my neck is concerned, anytime of the day, week, month, or year.'

'I think I've got the message.' The operator pressed another button, then yelled, whipped the headphones off and clapped his hands to his ears. '*Jesus!*' His eyes were screwed up in pain. 'Bastards!'

The other man watched dispassionately as his companion suffered.

'Bastards!' the operator repeated, gasping. He still held his hands to his ears. 'They knew!'

'Did we lose that recording?'

'I'm in pain here!'

'Did we lose it?'

'Check . . . check for yourself! My bloody ears hurt!'

The older man pressed a red button on an adjacent console and studied a monitor. A flat line greeted him.

'Damn it! Erased!'

'The bastards suckered us. They knew we were there.'

'They didn't know *we* were listening. They assumed some-one would be. What does that tell us?'

'You're asking *me*? My fucking ears hurt!'

The older man looked at his companion neutrally. 'Stop being such a baby.'

He tapped furiously at a computer keyboard for some minutes, trying to find a way of retrieving the recorded conversation; but the flat line remained resolutely unaltered.

'Ah, shit!' he swore in frustration. '*Nothing*. All fucking gone!'

The man with the painful ears gingerly took his hands away from them. 'What now?'

The older one continued to tap at the keyboard. 'Removing any evidence of the interception. Better never to have made it than to have done so and lost it.' He looked at his companion. 'Do you have a problem with that?'

'None at all.'

'Good.' A few more taps. 'Finished. We never started the intercept.'

At that moment, a door opened behind them. There was just enough time for them to turn to stare in surprise, before two silenced shots hit each of them.

'Who watches the watchers?' the killer remarked to the dead bodies. 'I hate incompetence. But I despise cowardly deceit,' he added, putting his gun away.

He glanced behind him to address someone beyond the door. 'Take care of these two, then clear this place of everything. I don't want even the tiniest screw left here. That would greatly displease me, and those who pay us and give the orders. When it comes to risking necks, it's theirs and yours over mine.'

He stood back. Four men entered and immediately set to work.

'If they can intercept our intercept,' he continued, 'they

can find this location. So be quick about it, then make this place look as if no one's been here for a while.'

He walked out, leaving them to it.

Pappenheim got a call from Hedi Meyer.

'And?' he enquired.

'Done,' she said, blissfully unaware of the fatal consequences of her actions. 'They won't be doing that again in a hurry.'

'Do you have a source?'

'Tracing even as we speak, sir. Coming up. Here we are . . . an address in . . . Marzahn-Hellersdorf.'

Marzahn was in the former East Berlin.

'Give it to me.'

She gave him the details.

'Thank you, Miss Meyer. You're a genius.'

'I know,' she said.

'Marzahn . . . Marzahn,' Pappenheim said thoughtfully as they ended the call. 'None of the people I know are out there. So who's so interested in my phone calls?'

He called Berger. 'A nice little run in the sun for you and Reimer.'

'I always wanted a run in the sun.'

'Don't be flippant. Here's the address.' Pappenheim passed on the details he'd got from the goth. 'Check out an office there for eavesdropping equipment.'

'Just where I wanted to go today . . . Marzahn.' She made no effort to hide her distinct lack of enthusiasm. 'When should we go?'

'I'm still hearing your voice.'

'We're gone.'

Berger stopped the car and stared.

Reimer peered upwards at a gigantic crane. 'It's a building site!'

'The whole of Berlin is a building site,' Berger retorted.

The address to which they had been sent was an office block still in the throes of construction.

'Now what?' he demanded.

'We look for the man in the hard hat.'

'They're all wearing hard hats.'

'There's a pecking order. The ones we're looking at all have the same colour. Look for the one that's different. The top dog.'

She got out of the car. Reimer followed, frowning as he did so. Both of them wore jackets which effectively hid their weapons; Reimer his leather jacket, Berger a denim jacket.

'You're not seriously suggesting,' Reimer began complaining, 'that we check *every* office here? Even though the thing's not finished, there must be a few offices that are done. And –' he stared up at the partly finished building – 'it's a big place.'

'We do it,' Berger said. 'There,' she went on. 'The one with the tie, looking at us with hard eyes. He's the foreman. Bet he has that look when he gets home and yells where's my dinner at his wife.'

'You see all that in a look? What have you been taking, Berger?'

'You're the undercover man. You tell me.'

'I don't divine good husbands from bad.'

'Follow me, and learn.'

Berger began walking towards the man in question, who was already on his way towards them. Reimer sauntered along.

The foreman stopped, blocking their route. 'Can I help you?'

Berger showed him her ID.

He peered at it, unimpressed. '*Obermeisterin* Berger. You're not local.' He was looking at Reimer.

'Very observant,' she said.

The man was still looking at Reimer.

Berger persisted. 'Has anyone been using the offices?'

'Does she give the orders?' the foreman asked Reimer.

Berger shot Reimer a triumphant glance.

Reimer looked back at the foreman with eyes of stone.

'Don't upset him,' Berger advised the rude foreman. 'He's in a foul mood today. And mine is worse.'

The foreman turned his reluctant attention upon her.

'That's better,' she said to him. 'I'll ask again. Is anyone using the offices?'

'Can't you see for yourself?' His tone was contemptuous. 'This is a construction site. No one is here who hasn't the right to be,' he added pointedly.

'We'd like to have a look, sir,' Berger said with extreme politeness.

Reimer, familiar with the tone, swivelled his eyes to look at her with interest.

The foreman was still unimpressed. 'I don't care what you'd like. I won't have you getting in the way of my work. There's nothing here for you. If you want to make an issue of it, get someone more grown-up to come here.'

Berger was sweetness itself. 'Someone more grown-up, sir? Fine.'

The man cocked his head at her and frowned, not quite sure what to make of her attitude.

She took out her mobile and pressed a single digit. Pappenheim answered immediately.

'Chief? Someone wants to talk to you.' Leaving the connection open so that Pappenheim could hear, she looked at the foreman. 'That's my boss, *Oberkommissar* Pappenheim. Grown-up enough for you? His temper is worse than Reimer's and mine put together.' She held the phone towards the foreman. 'Tell him all about grown-ups.'

Like bullies everywhere when their bluff has been called, the foreman decided to give in, if with bad grace.

'Put that thing away,' he said. 'Have your look, if you've nothing better to do. Just keep out of my way. Bloody *Beamte*.' He turned his back on them and began to leave.

'Thank you for your cooperation, sir,' Berger said in a loud voice. She put the phone to her ear and continued to Pappenheim, 'Problem solved, Chief. Incidentally, you've sent us to a building site. An unfinished office block.'

'Intriguing.'

'We'll see what we can find, if anything.'

'Alright. But take no chances, building site or not.'

'We'll watch it.'

'Temper worse than both of yours, have I?'

'I had to say something.'

'I'll remember that, Berger.'

'Yes, sir. Well, Reimer,' she continued as she ended the call and put the mobile away, 'let's see what's in this pile of concrete and glass.'

'You were right about him,' Reimer said in wonder, as they made for the already completed entrance.

'It's all in the look,' she said.

'Windows of the soul, huh?'

'You've been reading again, Reimer. Pass it on to Klemp. Wean him from the bikini tabloids.'

'Too late for him.' Reimer actually grinned.

'That's better, Reimer. Life isn't so bad, after all. Now let's see if we can find something to wipe that smug look off the foreman's face and make you really happy.'

It took them about half an hour to work their way to the top floor of the partially completed, seven-storey building.

They had searched the first six floors: offices with doors or windows still to be installed; half-completed lavatories; executive suites; company coffee shops in mid-decoration; everything they could possibly check, they had checked; with no result. Throughout, they had kept as much as possible from getting in anyone's way. From time to time they noticed the foreman giving them hard-eyed stares; but he did not intervene. The multiple sounds of the construction work were deafening, being muted only when they entered a finished office.

All the lifts had already been installed, but only one was fully operational. This now deposited them at the top floor. The all-pervasive noise was suddenly less so.

'This,' Reimer began as he stepped out, 'will be an office to die for. And thank God it's a lot quieter. It's almost like silence.'

The entire floor was a huge oval, with doors leading off a vast central area. The roof was a transparent cupola, flooding the place with natural light. Some of the doors were open, showing wide panes of glass through which the city skyline could be seen.

'Great, great view,' Reimer enthused, 'if you're lucky enough to work here.'

'We're not doing so badly, Reimer,' Berger said, as she looked about her.

'Yes. But we're not on the top floor.'

'If you're very, very good, you'll become a *Direktor* one day, and you'll get your own glass palace. Put in a good word for you, shall I?'

'Har har. Funny.'

'Notice anything?' Berger asked suddenly.

'No. What?' Reimer paused. 'It's quieter.'

'You've already said that.' She peered through one of the open doors. 'All the other floors had people. This seems empty. I—'

'No it's not.'

She followed Reimer's gaze. Two workmen had come out of a far office. Both wore hard hats and work clothes. One was tall, with a smooth, almost baby-like face. He was in the lead. His companion was slightly shorter, and stockier.

He stopped before them. His colleague stayed further back.

'You should not be up here,' he began, looking at each in turn.

'We spoke to the foreman,' Berger told him. She took out her ID.

The man barely looked at it. 'I see. Well. Help yourself.'

'Thank you. We'll try not to disturb you.'

'No problem.' The man turned and, followed by his companion, returned to the office he had come from.

'If only everyone behaved like that,' Berger said, 'life would be so much easier.'

Reimer had been staring at the man's back. 'Perhaps,' he now said in a low voice, and began to walk further away from the office the men had gone into.

Berger gave him a sharp glance, but followed.

When they were far enough to satisfy him, Reimer said in the same low voice, 'Now it's my question. Notice anything?'

She looked about her. 'No.'

'Their shoes.'

'What about them?'

'Even the foreman with the tie was wearing solid, cleated ankle boots. These guys are wearing city shoes.'

'So? They're in an office . . . not on the building site outside . . .'

'OK. This part of the building is more complete, but the people we saw on the other floors were all wearing heavy work shoes, and they were all over the place . . .' Reimer stopped and looked at Berger, who seemed thoughtful. 'What is it?'

'The man who just talked to us. First, it was . . . "you shouldn't be up here" . . . then it was all OK. He didn't even really look at my ID . . .'

'He expected us.'

'Which means he either talked with the foreman . . .'

'In which case he shouldn't have given us the macho greeting . . .'

'Or he was expecting us, but not because he had spoken with the foreman . . .'

'Who already told us no one was *using* the building . . .'

'Anomalies,' Berger said.

Reimer stared at her. 'What?' The word came out in a sharp whisper.

'What our boss, the Graf, would say. Spot the anomalies.'

'You're beginning to talk like him now?'

'I'm not even going to answer that. If you're right about those two at the other end . . .'

'If I am right, what do you want to do?'

'This.' Then she raised her voice to normal speaking level. 'Let's see what's in this one. Then we work our way through all the others.'

She entered the nearest office, making no effort to be particularly quiet. Like all the others they had seen on the lower floors, this was also devoid of furniture. Reimer followed her in and together they searched it minutely.

And drew a blank.

They worked their way through a further five offices; all similarly without a single item of furniture, all with the same result.

The sixth was different. It was Reimer who spotted it.

'The anomaly,' he whispered to her, then continued in the normal conversational level, 'I can think of better things I could do on a hot day like this.' He pointed to a slight discolouration on the new carpet.

'Same here,' she grumbled, playing the game. 'I'm getting fed up.' She lowered herself to the carpet, and gingerly touched the discolouration. *Damp*, she mouthed.

She quickly got out a pair of cotton gloves, put them on, then took a tiny, opaque plastic bag out of a pocket. Reimer passed her a penknife, which she used to scrape fibres into the bag. She returned the penknife, then sealed the bag and put it away.

As she straightened up, she saw that Reimer was now staring at the bottom of the window. He pointed again.

She almost missed it: the tiniest piece of black masking tape, stuck in a low corner of the window.

Reimer, with his own gloves on, pried it off and put it into another bag. He put that into a jacket pocket.

They studied the carpet closely, looking for any indentations that would betray the former presence of furniture. But there was nothing.

'Nothing here, either,' Reimer said in his normal voice. 'I'm beginning to think we've come to the wrong place.'

'It's starting to look like it,' Berger agreed. 'Next one, then.'

With his gloves still on, Reimer touched the window pane with an exploratory hand, then motioned to Berger to do the same.

She felt a slight stickiness, and briefly rubbed the tips of her fingers together.

'Then can we go?' Reimer pleaded, removing his gloves to put them away.

Berger did likewise. 'We do them all,' she told him sternly.

Reimer was looking at her with a question in his eyes. She indicated they would talk when they were back in the car. He nodded.

They left the office and made a show of inspecting all the others. They also discovered what seemed to be a storeroom with a large double door. It was locked.

Berger and Reimer looked at each other, then went to the office they had left to the very last.

She knocked on the door. The taller man opened it.

'Sorry to disturb,' she began. 'This is the last one. Do you mind?'

'Not at all,' he said. 'Do come in.' He stood back to allow them to enter. Building plans were spread out on the carpet. 'As you can see, there is no furniture as yet, so the floor is our desk.'

The stocky one was looking at them neutrally through pebbly eyes.

Berger nodded. 'We won't bother you any further. Thank

you for your cooperation. Oh . . . we found a locked door. Do you have the keys?'

He shook his head. 'Sorry. I think the foreman might.'

'I see. Well, thank you again, Herr . . .'

'Rorsch.'

'Thank you, Herr Rorsch. We'll see ourselves out.'

Berger nodded at the stocky man whose eyes seemingly bore no spark of life, and led Reimer out of the office.

She did not speak again until they were back down at the main entrance. The foreman was waiting.

'Well?' he challenged. 'Found anything?'

'No,' she replied.

'I told you there was no one here who didn't have a right to be.'

'So you did. Thank you for your cooperation. We'll be leaving now.'

As they left, the foreman said, 'Bloody *Beamte*!'

'I could seriously dislike that man,' Berger said as they got back into the car. She did not start it.

'What are you up to?' Reimer began. 'You said nothing about that storeroom, or the men we saw.'

'With good reason. The foreman is either a big liar, or a fake, or he's been fooled. Look over there.' She indicated with a head movement.

Reimer looked. 'I don't see . . . ah! Dark van. No lettering on the side. Not a work van. Can't see the number plate.'

'It wasn't there before. It seems to be waiting. We should be able to see the plate later.'

Reimer looked from the van to the building and back. 'Waiting for the men?'

'Let's find out.' She started the car and moved off.

'I thought you said—'

'We're not leaving. Just relocating. Call the chief. Tell him about the van, and tell him we need heavy artillery to break down a door; and fast.'

While Reimer did so, she went away from the area just far

92

enough to give the impression they had gone, then turned into a side street to backtrack. By the time she had come to a halt once more, Reimer had relayed the message to Pappenheim, and they were now parked where they could not be observed by either anyone in the van, or the foreman. But they had a clear view of their target area, and the number plate on the van.

The back doors of the van were also now open.

'Shit!' Reimer swore. 'Our colleagues won't make it here in time.'

'Don't panic. It's not going to be easy to get all that stuff out of the storeroom, down seven floors and into that van quickly.'

'Sure the storeroom is not empty?'

'I'd bet your romance with your girlfriend on it.'

'Leave her out of this.'

'If you say so. Now tell me, what does that number plate say to you?'

Reimer stared at it. 'It's official!'

'The chief will love this.'

'But how . . . ?'

'You're asking *me*? Do I know all the official organizations in this country? I'm just an *Obermeisterin*. That plate may even be fake. Look,' Berger went on. 'Here come the comedians from the top floor . . . and not empty-handed, either.'

As they watched, the two men, each carrying a piece of electronic equipment, came out of the building and headed for the van.

'Now, where do you think that stuff came from, Reimer?'

'So much for the key being with the foreman,' he said.

'You spotted the shoes.'

'Yes,' he said, pleased, watching as the men loaded the van, then went back into the building. 'If they go on at this rate, our people might just get here in time, after all.'

'Perhaps,' Berger said. 'Perhaps not. Look.'

Two more men, also carrying equipment, had come out of the building, just as the first two had gone in.

'*Shit!*' Reimer said again. '*Four* of them! Well, that changes things. Do we take them on if our people don't make it?'

'Do we have a choice?'

'I was afraid you'd say that.'

Six

G reville was again by the stream in the garden, hands in pockets, deep in thought. He still wore his hat, and its wide brim was snapped down, casting a faint shadow about his face. His eyes looked into the farthest of distances.

Soft footsteps brought him back from his reverie. He turned his body at the hip and saw Aunt Isolde approaching. He gave a gentle smile as he waited for her to join him, then turned back the way he'd been facing, as soon as she was at his side.

'Thank you for putting me up, Isolde,' he said, looking at her. 'I shall pay, of course. I've got a fair bit of money, and—'

'Nonsense, Timmy. I won't take a penny from you. And I won't have an argument about it.'

'Very well.'

They spoke English to each other.

'I do hope you don't mind staying at the hotel,' she continued. 'For the moment, I think it's best.'

'Quite understandable.'

'You're not . . . offended?'

'My dear Isolde, absolutely not. More than I expected, all things considered.'

There was a silence between them after that.

Then she said, 'What happened to you out there, Timmy?'

'Life,' he said after a while.

'You know what I mean, Timmy.'

'Don't follow, old girl . . .'

'This is the "Red Baroness" of '68, Timmy . . . not some giggling schoolgirl.'

He gave a short chuckle. 'The "Red Baroness". The society rags gave you that sobriquet, and others followed. What would they say now, eh?'

'That was years ago. Since then, I have managed to keep my life well away from them.'

'Quite right too.'

'You haven't answered my question, Timmy. What really happened out there?'

'Don't quite grasp what you mean.'

'You spoke for some time with Jens. Then he comes in and asks me about his father.'

Greville pursed his lips briefly, looked down at the water, then out into the woods.

'Quite an impressive young man,' he said to her. He peered down at the water. 'Told me someone caught a catfish in there, once.'

'Don't change the subject, Timmy.'

'You brought him up well,' Greville said. 'You have every right to feel proud.'

'I would like to think,' she said, 'if you and I had had a son, he would have been like Jens.'

That sent Greville into another silence. It took him a full minute to break it.

'You asked me what happened out there,' he began. 'I answered . . . life. That is indeed what happened. Sometimes, the things we wish for never come. Sometimes they do . . . but not in the way we imagined, or had hoped for. A terrible tragedy brought Jens to you. And another kept me away.'

Greville scuffed for a moment at the raised bank with a shoe.

'I'm going to give him my Healey . . .'

She was astonished. 'You've still got it?'

'Oh yes. In perfect condition. Haven't been using it, of

course; but someone's been keeping it safe, caring for it. Barely any miles on the clock. Seeing your policeman son's remarkable machine gave me the idea. He'll know how to appreciate it.'

'You make that sound like a will.'

'Do I? Didn't mean to.'

Aunt Isolde looked searchingly at her first husband. 'I don't expect you to tell me about the things you have done, Timmy. But if anything is the matter . . .'

'Nothing's the matter, old girl. Perfectly fine.'

She smiled at him in a sad little way, as if she did not quite believe him.

In Marzahn, Berger and Reimer continued to watch with anxious impatience as the men continued to load the dark van.

She called Pappenheim. 'Chief? The van's being loaded. Electronic equipment. Four men, including the two from the top floor. And Chief, we may have a complication.'

'I hate complications,' Pappenheim said. 'What kind?'

'The van has official plates.'

Seconds of silence greeted this, before Pappenheim said, 'Do nothing before the back-up arrives.'

'And if the van starts to leave?'

'Stop it. Back-up won't be far. They're making good time. No sirens. And, Lene . . .'

'Chief?'

'Don't get yourselves killed.'

Pappenheim ended the conversation.

Reimer looked at Berger. 'What did he say?'

'Don't get ourselves killed.'

'Oh great.'

'And the back-up's nearly here. No sirens.'

'I damned well hope so.'

Suddenly, Berger got excited. 'Well, well. Just look at that. The foreman.'

Reimer stared as the man who had blocked their way when

they had first arrived came out of the building, carrying some equipment to the van.

'As fake as Klemp's hair.'

Reimer gave her a stunned look. '*Klemp? Klemp has a wig?*'

She nodded. 'Yep. It's a good one. I'll give him that. Expensive.' She kept her eyes on the activities by the van.

Reimer was having a hard time trying to decide whether she was telling the truth, or just winding him up.

'Come on, Lene! You're putting me on.'

'I've told you before, Reimer . . . I'll never pull anything of yours, and I'll never put you on, no matter what.'

'You know what I mean,' Reimer said, unabashed.

'It's the truth. Long before our unit was created, Klemp's old unit sent him on an exchange to America. Los Angeles. Everybody there seems to have a Hollywood connection, wants to have a Hollywood connection, or just hopes someone with a Hollywood connection will spot them . . . according to a female colleague who worked with him.

'In LA, believe it or not, his American partner actually had a sister with a Hollywood connection . . . a friend who worked as a wig-maker. If you look at Klemp's hair, you can see she's good.'

Reimer was staring at Berger as if he thought she'd gone mad. 'Klemp's hair comes from a *Hollywood* wig-maker? Oh come on!'

'Ask him, if you feel brave enough. I'm not supposed to know. Better not tell him you heard this from me . . . unless you really want to know hell. Your girlfriend will seem like a mouse by comparison.' Berger still had her eyes on what was going on by the van. 'If our people don't turn up soon, we're really going to have to do the job by ourselves.'

She drew her weapon, keeping it low in the car, and checked it.

Reimer gave a sigh of resignation and did the same. Then

he looked up, while Berger was still concerned with her weapon.

'The cavalry's arrived,' he said.

Weapon ready, she snapped her head up to look.

Two unmarked, dark-blue Mercedes transporters with darkened windows swooped from separate directions to effectively block the van. The men from the top floor, plus the fake foreman, were surprised with their arms laden. They stopped in disbelief, and gaped helplessly as police in full riot gear spilled out of the vehicles and surrounded them. Others charged through the building entrance.

Berger and Reimer were about to join the fun when Pappenheim made contact.

'Just got the update,' he said to Berger. 'Go and take your bow, then leave our colleagues to it and come back to my office to give me the details. Well done, Lene. Reimer too.'

'Thank you, Chief.'

She smiled as Pappenheim ended contact, and turned to Reimer. 'He says well done. We're to go over there and say hello to our friends from the top floor, and the pisshead foreman, then go back to the office. So let's go, shall we?'

'What if they're really official?'

'Not our problem.'

The raid leader, a *Kommissarin* with helmet visor raised, was by the van as they walked up.

'Lene!' she greeted. 'Do you know what you've caught?'

'Hello, Ilona. I don't want to know.'

Ilona Fohlmeister grinned. 'Don't blame you.'

Berger walked up to the foreman, who glared back at her as she tapped at the monitor he carried.

'No one who isn't supposed to be there,' she said to him. 'Those words will haunt you.'

'You're playing with the grown-ups,' he snarled.

Her eyes bored into him. 'Is that a threat?'

'We never threaten. We act.'

'Now I'm really frightened.'

Berger turned to the men from the top floor, who stood there, still with items of equipment in their arms, looking like boys caught out in some act of mischief.

'How are the building plans?' she asked the tall one.

'Smugness is a bad habit,' he said.

She smiled at him. 'It must hurt . . . being caught like a rat in a trap.'

The stoney-eyed one fixed her with his lifeless stare, but said nothing.

She glanced back at the foreman. 'And by a bloody *Beamter* too. A *woman*, at that. Horrible, isn't it?' She turned to Ilona Fohlmeister. 'These pissers are all yours, Ilona.' She spoke loudly enough for the eavesdroppers to hear.

The fake foreman wouldn't leave it. 'You!' he snapped at Reimer. 'Enjoy being told what to do by a woman, do you?'

Reimer walked slowly up to him, smiled, then suddenly brought the open palm of his left hand in an upward sweeping motion. It connected with the monitor in the foreman's arms, taking the man completely by surprise. The monitor had simply been supported, but not gripped. It toppled and crashed to the ground, smashing explosively into countless expensive pieces.

'Oops,' Reimer said. 'Sorry. Cost a lot, did it?'

'You did that on purpose!' the foreman raged.

Reimer looked at his colleagues. 'Did I?'

'No!' they chorused.

'I thought so. Are we leaving, Lene?'

'We are,' she said. To Ilona Fohlmeister, she added, 'Thanks for the back-up.'

'Anytime.'

Müller was driving at high speed back to Berlin.

He had deliberately switched off his mobile, as well as the in-car, hands-off phone. He had no desire to talk with anyone, including Pappenheim, during the course of the journey. No music came through on the car's extensive sound system. He listened instead to its challenging roar, feeling at one with it.

The Porsche howled towards Berlin, a seal-grey streak hurtling along the Autobahn on its fat wheels.

All hell was breaking loose.

Pappenheim picked up his phone at the first ring. 'Pappenheim.'

'Do you enjoy poking at ant nests?'

'You're persistent . . . especially for someone who told me not to call you again this century.'

The caller ignored Pappenheim's dry remark. 'I've just heard.'

'Good news travels fast.'

'That's supposed to be bad news . . .'

'I know what I'm saying.'

'Have you any idea who these people are?'

Pappenheim blew smoke at the base unit of the phone. 'The way you've said that tells me *you* know. But I don't, and don't particularly care. I've taken down some people who were eavesdropping on my conversations . . . Hello? Hello?'

Pappenheim took the receiver away from his ear and stared at it. 'Did you hang up on me again? Or were you cut off?'

Kaltendorf was also on the phone.

'What the devil are your people doing?' the voice snapped in his ear. 'Who ordered that officials be arrested by officers . . . *in full riot gear*?'

Not wanting to admit that he knew nothing about it, Kaltendorf tightened his lips, then said, 'It was an error of judgement . . .'

'Not yours, I do hope, Heinz. Find out who did this. I'll have his head, if you don't. And yours, for good measure!'

The phone was suddenly dead as the caller hung up on Kaltendorf, whose face became suffused with a dark-pink shade that grew increasingly darker.

'*Pappenheim!*' he said tightly. 'If Müller is still out, it must be Pappenheim.'

He slammed the phone down, then stood up, expression clouded by something very close to rage.

Pappenheim was in the process of lighting a fresh cigarette when the door was flung open and Kaltendorf stood framed in the doorway.

Pappenheim did not interrupt his lighting of the cigarette.

'*Stand up when I enter this cesspit you call an office!*' Kaltendorf yelled.

Pappenheim drew calmly on the cigarette and slowly got to his feet. The entire building must have heard, he thought. He said nothing and gazed at Kaltendorf through the smoke he blew out of his nostrils.

Kaltendorf was so taken by his own fury, he forgot to go into his coughing act.

'What the hell did you think you were doing?' he shouted.

Pappenheim remained controlled. 'What did I do, sir?'

'You had people who were going about their official duties arrested by officers from this unit, as you well know! In *full* riot equipment!'

'No, sir. I did not. I had people who were intercepting communications from this unit arrested. As far as I know, this is a serious offence. As would be expected of me, I took immediate action to stop it. Thanks to excellent work by our colleagues, this was efficiently done. The culprits *and* their equipment – important evidence – are on their way here under escort.'

Kaltendorf's mouth worked, but nothing came out for some time. Pappenheim took another pull on his cigarette and squinted at his superior.

'Intercepts?' Kaltendorf finally got out. '*Intercepts?* This unit's communications were being intercepted?'

'Intercepted. Yes, sir. I don't think we were expected to find out.'

Kaltendorf stood there for some irresolute moments, then abruptly turned away to stomp along the corridor.

Pappenheim waited until the angry footsteps had faded before going to close the door.

'Something your pals were keeping from you?' he murmured as he pushed the door home, cigarette clamped between his teeth.

He had barely sat down again when a knock sounded.

'In!' he commanded.

Berger and Reimer entered.

'Well. You two are certainly more welcome than my last visitor,' he greeted.

'We heard.'

'The whole building heard,' Reimer put in.

'An exaggeration,' an unperturbed Pappenheim said. 'But close enough. Good work, you two,' he went on. He stopped, watching as Reimer looked about him. 'What grabs your interest, Reimer?'

Reimer stopped himself. 'Er . . .'

'It's an office, Reimer. My office. You've been here before.'

'Er . . . yes, Chief.'

Pappenheim's baby-blue eyes seemed to impale Reimer for long seconds. 'A smart man would not voice any thoughts he has at this moment.'

'I'm very smart, Chief.'

'I know it. Or you would not be working for me.'

'No, Chief. I wouldn't.'

'Now that's out of the way, you two can tell me exactly what happened. Berger, you first.'

They gave him a comprehensive report of the incident. When they had finished, he nodded in satisfaction.

'Very good work, both of you,' he said. 'I want you to write this all down, exactly as you've told me. We may need your reports if this thing turns sour.'

'Any idea who they could be, Chief?' Berger asked. 'Assuming they really are official.'

'No idea whatsoever. If they are official, someone's got a lot of explaining to do. If they're not, impersonation will be just one of their problems. Then we'll see just how grown-up they are.'

Berger smiled at this.

'Alright,' Pappenheim said. 'Off you go. I want those reports by yesterday. Oh . . . and Reimer . . .'

'Chief?' Reimer looked worried, as if expecting the worst.

'I particularly like the part where you accidentally destroyed that pricey piece of equipment.'

Unsure of how to take this, Reimer gave a weak smile.

'I would have kicked his balls. But then, that's me.'

Reimer grinned.

'Now, out of here, you two.'

The phone rang again, bare minutes after they had gone.

'Be with you in half an hour,' Pappenheim heard Müller say when he had answered.

'There you are,' Pappenheim said. 'I've tried to reach you at least seven times . . . well, perhaps five . . .'

'I've had everything shut down. I wanted some thinking time.'

'I can well understand.'

'Any further excitement?'

'Funny you should ask. What a day this is turning out to be.'

'Can it wait till I'm back?'

'All things considered, it's probably the wiser course.'

'I smell all kinds of messages in that little statement.'

'You don't know the half of it.'

'So, the world hasn't come to an end as yet.'

'Give it time.'

'Then the gallery in thirty minutes from now.'

'I'll be waiting.'

'You say such nice things, Pappi.'

'It's because my heart is pure.'

'I'll laugh about that later.'

As they ended the conversation, Pappenheim put the receiver down slowly, clasped his hands behind his head and looked up at the ceiling. His third cigarette within just over thirty minutes was planted between his lips. It sent writhing smoke signals upwards.

'He made a joke,' Pappenheim mused. 'Sort of. He must be OK.'

It was not Vincente Monleon's day.

Deciding he wanted to eat but not motorway food, he left the Autobahn just before Münster, intending to find a countryside restaurant with good eating. A short distance from the Autobahn, he found himself on a deserted *Landstrasse*. The road sign indicated 3 kilometres to the next town or village.

Cruising along, he glanced in his rear-view mirror and saw a police car approaching with lights flashing. He slowed down and made room, expecting it to pass. It did, but only to slow down again, one of the officers waving a lollipop sign at him. He slowed down further, then came to a halt. He did not turn off the engine this time. The patrol car pulled up in front of him, blocking his path.

'The only car on this road,' he said to himself in Spanish, 'and it had to be me.'

The two officers, both women, got out of their car. As with the earlier checkpoint, one came towards him, the other hanging back with hand on sidearm.

'They don't look as if they would like Valencia paella,' he muttered.

Monleon looked up as she came nearer, and smiled.

'Hello, ladies,' he said to her in his accented German.

It was not the right thing to say. She scowled at him and looked suspicious.

'Your driving licence, please, sir. And please turn off the engine and get out of the car.'

'Of course.' Monleon complied, ensuring he did nothing to cause alarm. He handed over his licence.

The officer took it and went back to her car to check, while her partner stared unsmilingly at Monleon.

She returned, handed the licence back.

Relieved, Monleon took it and began to get back into his car.

'You are heading for Spain?'

Monleon paused. 'Yes.'

'A long way.'

'Yes. I am hoping to be near the French border at Mülheim before it gets dark. So, if I may, I would like to—'

'Please open the boot,' she demanded.

'Of course.'

Patiently, Monleon went to the back of the Seat and opened the boot.

She peered in at his neatly packed suitcases. One was an aluminium travel case.

'What's in that one?'

'Just my cameras. I like taking pictures on my trips, just like most people.'

'Show me.'

'Of course.'

What happened next took the policewoman completely by surprise. She had moved too close to Monleon, and he moved very swiftly; far too swiftly for an inoffensive tourist. Before she knew what was happening to her, he had grabbed her in a powerful armlock across the throat, and her weapon was in his hand. He jabbed it against her spine.

'If you make the wrong move,' he barked at her partner. 'She's dead!'

The partner froze.

Monleon quickly raised the pistol and fired once. It was a fatal shot. The partner fell heavily, dead hand still gripping the pistol which she had tried to draw, even as she fell.

The policewoman in Monleon's grip now swivelled fearful eyes towards him.

'Don't . . .' she began.

She never finished. Still within the hook of his arm, Monleon moved her sideways, calmly put the pistol against her chest and fired, letting her go at the same time. Her body thudded to the ground.

'You should have left well alone,' he said to the body.

From the moment he had been stopped, no other car had passed. He now moved quickly, hoping no other traffic would appear in the meantime.

He wiped the pistol clean on the fallen police officer's shirt, after partially pulling it out of her trousers. He left the pistol next to her. He checked himself for specks of blood. There were none. He shut the boot of his car, then, with a swift but unhurried movement, got back behind the wheel and drove off.

As he passed the police car, he heard the radio squawking, and wondered if the shots had been heard.

He took the first turning that would lead him back to the Autobahn.

'And all because I wanted to eat,' he said in Spanish.

There was still no other car on that road.

Once back on the Autobahn, Monleon now drove much faster than before, though still scrupulously observing any speed-limited sections.

In this manner, he would put a great distance between himself and the dead policewomen by the time they were found; and his route would take him not towards Mülheim, but towards Berlin.

The car he drove would be different, and his documents would no longer say he was Vincente Monleon.

Back on the *Landstrasse*, the bright sun burned down from

a cloudless sky to heat the bodies of the policewomen; and the first, tentative flies began to arrive.

Pappenheim got a call from the forensics department.

'Those scrapings that Berger brought in,' the person began.

'Go on, Peter.'

'Mostly damp carpet,' Peter Marl said.

'But?'

'Traces of blood.'

'Ah.'

'Someone tried to clean the carpet, and had practically succeeded. Whoever it was couldn't have imagined that Berger would come and scrape away at it. There are always residues, sometimes even when a cleaning machine is used. Could be anything, of course . . . someone smashes a finger with a hammer, steps on a nail . . .'

'Big nail to go through the sole of a working boot . . .'

'OK. Not a nail. Cut with a carpet knife perhaps. These things are very sharp.'

'I know. Done it myself, laying carpets in my distant youth. Just suppose none of the above . . .' Pappenheim let the suggestion hang.

'Someone hurt more dramatically, you mean. Possibly.'

'It's a scenario. Got enough to determine blood group?'

'Just about. The wonders of science. Gone are the days when you needed a bucketful. That's a joke.'

'Imagine. Don't know where this might lead, Peter, but let me have as full a report as you can, as soon as you can.'

'Will do. And the piece of tape Reimer found . . .'

'Don't tell me there was blood on it.'

'I won't. There wasn't. It's just a piece of tape.'

'I can take a joke, Peter.' Pappenheim bared his teeth at the phone. 'See? I'm smiling.'

Marl gave a short laugh. 'Same old Pappi.'

'I wouldn't be different.'

'I know. I have a suggestion about the tape,' Marl added.

'You know me and suggestions . . . as long as they're not the rude kind.'

'I'll spare your blushes. There are traces of a dark material on the adhesive side. I'm guessing, mind you . . . but I would say the tape is part of a roll they used to mask a window, or windows. They used it to attach the material I just mentioned.'

'Didn't want anyone to spot what they were getting up to.'

'Could be. There are some powerful binoculars around, they tell me.'

'Yes. Even the police have got them.'

Both laughed.

'Thanks for the quick work, Peter.'

'Don't mention it.'

'This is turning out to be quite a day,' Pappenheim said as he replaced the phone. 'And it's still very young.' He glanced at his watch. 'Time for the rogues' gallery.'

He left the office, hoping he would not run into Kaltendorf on the way. He made it safely to the solid door of the documents room. Just above the numbers on the keypad, a tiny green light was showing. Someone was already inside.

Pappenheim tapped in the code and the heavy door swung open. The bright lighting and the low hum of the air-conditioning greeted him as he entered, pushing the door shut behind him.

The large room had no windows and every wall save one, from floor to ceiling, was lined with wide, steel cabinets. Each of these had its own keypad. At the single wall without a cabinet was a big desk with a computer on it. Already very powerful, it had been tweaked by Hedi Meyer, who had locked herself into a continuing upgrade cycle. She had already made it the most powerful computer in the entire building, beating even those in her own department. On either side of the keyboard were two items of totally unexpected equipment: a joystick and throttle that seemed to have come out of an F-16 jet fighter, courtesy of the goth herself.

Kaltendorf had once barged in and had seen her using them. A major fit later, he had demanded that they be removed; but Müller had managed to convince him that they were necessary investigative tools. The war of the joystick and throttle was far from over.

The computer, with its large plasma screen monitor, was connected to a cinema-quality, multi-speaker sound system. A high-backed leather chair was pushed close to the desk.

Müller was leaning against the centrepiece of the room, a wide and solidly built central table with a white top that also served as a photographic lightbox.

'Right on time,' Pappenheim said.

'No other way to be.'

'Unless it's for a meeting with the Great White,' Pappenheim said as he approached the table. He studied Müller closely. 'You OK?'

'I'm fine. Lots of interesting things to tell?'

'Oh yes.'

'On my way up, I caught a rumour that we've arrested some people who may be loosely termed colleagues. Anything I should know?'

'Make yourself comfortable,' Pappenheim replied. 'As I said, I have a few tales to tell.' He pointed to the cabinet into which he had put the envelope the stern-faced man had brought. 'There's an envelope in there with dynamite. Which would you like first? The envelope? Or the events leading up to the arrest?'

'Laughter before tears. Let's hear about the arrest.'

Pappenheim seemed almost relieved to start on that first. He gave Müller a detailed breakdown of what had occurred, but omitted to add that it was the trace of his call to Carey Bloomfield that had sparked it all off.

'Blood on the carpet,' Müller said with a straight face when

Pappenheim had finished. 'Are they real officials?' he went on. 'Or fakes . . . ?'

'Or private operators under contract? That can hide plenty of sins.'

'Kaltendorf will probably have them released, no questions asked,' Müller said, 'if they are in any way tied officially.'

'We could let them go,' Pappenheim suggested, 'but keep all that nice equipment. The goth would weep for joy if she could get her hands on that stuff. Very expensive, very up to date. I saved the best for last. Guns.'

'Guns?'

'A veritable armoury. Five automatic pistols – one with a silencer; three light sub-machine guns. The SMGs are one Heckler and Koch MP5/10, and *two* Calico M960s. One a top German gun – normally official issue – the others, two fierce American 50-round barrage-makers. Brand new, all three. Interesting, no?'

Müller stared at him. 'Were they going to war? And the blood traces in the carpet fibres? Can they explain that? And I want to know about that silenced gun. Who's questioned them so far?'

'The raid leader, *Kommissarin* Fohlmeister . . .'

'Ilona's good.'

'That she is. But she didn't get far. Kaltendorf stepped in.'

'Of course he would,' Müller commented drily. 'I think we should pay our friends a visit when we're finished here.'

'My very thought. Before you start on the envelope, some gossip from one of my contacts.'

Pappenheim told Müller about the saga of the lost and found Hassan.

'What do you think?' Müller asked when Pappenheim had finished.

'I think it stinks. You'll agree, when you've read what's in that envelope.'

'Alright. We've had the laughter. Now the tears.'

Pappenheim gave Müller a wary look as he went to the cabinet, tapped at the keypad and opened it. The entire front moved outwards, revealing the serried banks of plain brown envelopes, each with a group of identification letters and numbers at the top left-hand corner. He took out the envelope, which he handed to Müller. He went back to the cabinet and leaned against it, as if keeping out of gun range.

He watched carefully as Müller emptied the envelope of its contents and began to read the first of the documents.

Müller said nothing as he read his way through the first. He picked up the second and his face paled.

Pappenheim knew this was the document about Romeo Six.

The planes of Müller's face tightened and became so still they might have been inanimate. He read with an eerie immobility, body seemingly carved from stone. He read the entire remainder of the documents in that manner, moving only to put one down when he'd finished with it. When he had read them all, he straightened to his feet, the last document in his hand.

'Well,' he began in a voice that was almost inaudible, 'I've got my tears.'

Then, without warning, Müller slammed the document hard against the table, letting it go as he did so. The force of the impact actually made the sheaf of paper bounce slightly. It then skidded across the white surface and almost off the table. Briefly, he passed the hand that had held the document against his forehead.

'Even the black-box recordings from the crash were faked!' he said with a savagery that seemed to come from deep within him. 'All those *years*, that lie . . . that my mother crashed the plane because my father betrayed her. Not satisfied with killing them, those bastards smeared them as well.'

Müller walked to the door, then back to the table, while Pappenheim looked on with concern.

112

'I'll get them, Pappi,' he said, voice now unnaturally calm. 'I'll get them if it's the last thing I do.'

'And you've got some names now.'

Müller's eyes were baleful. 'I've got names.' He enunciated each word one by one.

'And I'll help you.'

Standing at the table, breathing deeply but not looking at Pappenheim, Müller nodded slowly.

'Thanks, Pappi,' he said at last. 'I have my own tale to tell. There is a bizarre synchronicity to all this. What came with this envelope is confirmed by another source I would never have imagined in my wildest dreams. My aunt's resurrected husband had a long talk with me. You will blench when you hear what he had to say. And, on top of that, I discover that my father has also left something for me: a briefcase full of sensitive information. He must have known something was going to happen to him. I suppose he did not believe they would go after my mother as well. I've not yet read what is in them. I've left the briefcase down there for now. I'll be going back, and staying overnight.'

Müller then leaned once more against the table and told an increasingly wide-eyed Pappenheim about Greville.

When Müller had finished, Pappenheim muttered in disgust, 'What a great world we've got.'

'It's not the world, Pappi.'

'I'll amend that. Great planet, shame about some of the people.'

'More than a shame. Much more, much nastier than shame.' Müller paused, mind churning. 'We've got a professional killer masquerading as a peace activist; a man dying from a decades-long, deliberately created biological poison; a conspiracy to kill my parents; a bunch of heavily armed eavesdroppers claiming to be official; and a boss who knows at least some of the people behind this, even if his guilt is as yet unproven. This same boss might well be about to let our prisoners go. I am in the perfect mood to pay them a visit.'

113

'Not without me,' Pappenheim said.

He collected the documents, put them back into the envelope, returned the envelope to the cabinet, and locked it.

'Ready?' he said to Müller.

'More than ready.'

Seven

They walked purposefully along the corridor, heading for the second floor, where the prisoners were being held in an unused office.

They decided not to take the lift, choosing instead to go via the stairs. Their shoes slammed in unison, and by the time they were approaching the office where the men were being held, they had put themselves into the hard frame of mind they wanted.

'Find out who owns the building,' Müller said, 'who is behind the construction – that means *every* firm involved – who's put up the money, who has done the hiring, and so on. Someone had enough connections to put an entire snoop team in there with no questions asked. If they *are* official, we must find out which of our many national organizations is responsible, and who gave the order . . .'

'And if not official?'

'They'll be very sorry. This was a comprehensively equipped team. Someone, somewhere has access to the kind of stuff that even we can't get our hands on . . .'

'The honest way,' Pappenheim remarked with a straight face.

Müller glanced at him. 'You're up to something. Do I want to know?'

'I think not.'

'I never heard that.'

'I know you didn't.'

*   *   *

Two of Ilona Fohlmeister's crew – one male, one female officer – were on guard outside. Both knew Müller and Pappenheim well.

'Is that to keep us out?' Müller asked. 'Or them in?'

'We can't even see you, sir,' one said with a grin.

'Thanks,' Müller said, and shoved the door open. 'Comfortable, everyone?' he asked the five prisoners in a hard voice.

They had been lounging about, drinking coffee out of mugs. All looked back at Müller and Pappenheim with disdain. There was no other reaction.

'That's it,' Müller said to Pappenheim. 'They're deaf.'

Pappenheim took a packet of his Gauloises out of a pocket, knocked out a cigarette, returned the pack to the pocket, lit the cigarette, inhaled, blew smoke at the ceiling, then sighed with pleasure.

'That must be it,' he said. 'Deaf as posts.'

The man with the baby face decided to speak, and did so with contempt. 'The Müller and Pappenheim double act. You've really bitten off more than you can chew this time.'

Müller smiled coldly at him. 'Shooting people in supposedly unoccupied offices can also be difficult to chew on.'

No one in the room had remotely expected the remark. The man gave a startled blink. He could not have helped himself. Even Pappenheim stared in astonishment at Müller.

'Yes,' Müller said to the man, pressing home his advantage. 'We found the blood.'

The baby-faced man was trying hard to work out whether Müller was bluffing, and not succeeding. His attempts were further complicated by the fact that his companions were visibly beginning to look uneasy.

'Whoever you claim to be working for,' Müller went on, 'is going to have a hard time pulling you out of this one.'

Baby-face regained some of his composure. 'And who's going to make this "hard time"?' His lips curled as he gave Müller's earring a pointed stare. 'You, Herr Graf von

Röhnen? The rich boy with the earring, playing at being a policeman?'

'And me,' Pappenheim said to him. 'I'm not rich, and I don't play . . . unless it's rough. And I wouldn't underestimate him. He can play very rough. Especially today.'

Pappenheim went up close to the baby-faced man and blew smoke at him. The man coughed.

'Filthy habit,' he snapped. 'You two have your fun. Pride comes before the fall. You have no idea what you're dealing with.'

'How many times have I heard that before?' Müller asked Pappenheim.

'Let me see . . . oh . . . many, many times,' Pappenheim answered, staring at the baby-faced man.

'You can't do anything without Kaltendorf.'

'He's not going to save you,' Müller said. 'What name did you give my colleague? I'm talking about *Kommissarin* Fohlmeister.'

'Call me Schmidt.' The man transformed his supercilious expression into a smile and looked at his companions.

They smiled back.

'Very original,' Pappenheim said in wonder. 'And here I was thinking it was Rorsch. They really do know something we don't,' he added to Müller.

The man who said he was Schmidt misunderstood, and favoured Pappenheim with an amused look. 'That's the first smart thing you've said.'

'I can say many smart things. Where would you like me to start? How about lying when questioned by an investigating officer? Committing murder . . . with a *silenced* weapon? That speaks of serious premeditation. Murder is murder . . . but you know what I mean. You could have stabbed him – or them . . .'

Pappenheim paused at that instant and raked all five with a swift glance. At least two of the men gave each other surreptitious glances.

'You could have strangled them, poisoned them, thrown snakes at them . . .'

'Are you quite finished?'

'No. You could have done all that but instead you deliberately screwed on a silencer and . . .' Pappenheim stopped, looked at Müller. 'Want to continue?'

'Only to say this. Herr Schmidt, Rorsch, or whoever you are, get used to it. Until I find out what you and your friends have really been up to, you're going nowhere.'

'Kaltendorf will—'

'Kaltendorf will what?' Kaltendorf came through, interrupting whatever Schmidt had been about to say. He looked at Müller. 'I have already told *Kommissarin* Fohlmeister that I am taking this over.'

'Yes, sir,' Müller said, deceptively acquiescent. 'I was just wondering whether you know these people are murderers, as well as illegal eavesdroppers.'

Kaltendorf's eyes danced with uncertainty. '*Murderers?*' He looked at Schmidt, the man with many names. '*Murderers?*'

Kaltendorf was so shocked, he seemed completely oblivious of Pappenheim's smoking.

Schmidt was definitely rattled, but he kept his head. 'The *Hauptkommissar* is making wild accusations . . .'

'We found blood, sir,' Müller interrupted. 'And a pistol with a silencer . . . which has recently been fired. As you're here, sir,' Müller continued, 'I'll leave it to you.'

He walked out, followed by Pappenheim.

The two guards remained poker-faced as they came out. Pappenheim winked at them as he hastily killed his cigarette by pinching it out in the no-smoking zone of the corridor, waiting for the glowing end to die and then putting the lot into a pocket.

'Let's put in some distance before he wakes up,' Müller said as they hurried away.

'You don't have to say that twice. But what was all that

about in there? You could have blown me over when you came up with that shooting scenario.'

'I threw it in blindly, and hit home. Once that had happened, it was just a matter of applying pressure.'

'I hope that gun has been fired.'

Müller gave a tired smile. 'So do I.'

'What if one of those powerful people Schmidt – or Rorsch – kept hinting about with as much subtlety as a sledgehammer pressures the Great White into handing over the guns without a check?'

'What's to stop us from having it checked now, just in case?'

'Thought you'd never ask.' Pappenheim took out his mobile and called Fohlmeister. 'Ilona,' he began when she'd answered. 'Those guns . . . where are they?'

'Still in the van. The *Direktor* gave orders not to move them.'

'Suppose you had checked the silenced gun, *before* he gave the order, but didn't put it in your report, pending release of the others?'

'You mean, I did so on the way back, just out of curiosity? The prisoners were in other vehicles, so they would not have seen whether I did or not.'

'Something like that makes sense to me.'

'Ah, that curiosity of mine.'

'Thanks, Ilona.' Pappenheim ended the call. 'Now we wait.'

'We wait,' Müller said. 'Meanwhile there's a dead person, or more than one, to be accounted for.'

'Do you think the GW will buckle and let them go?'

'If that man were a bridge, I would not walk over him. Does that answer you?'

'Graphically.' After some moments, Pappenheim said, 'Should I ask the question?'

'Ask away.'

'Do you believe Hassan is Greville's son, and that Greville is the target?'

'Greville *may* be a target, given what he has said. Whether Hassan is the "detached" son or not . . . I'm keeping an open mind at this stage. It all seems too neat. Of course, stranger things have happened. Older man meets young woman of his dreams, falls in love . . . only to discover she's the daughter he never knew he had. Why not a son about to kill a father he doesn't know? But even so.'

Müller paused. They walked up a flight of stairs before he spoke again.

'The primary target is not Greville. Greville may be a decoy kill.'

'I love headaches,' Pappenheim said. 'So healthy.'

'Greville is safe for now,' Müller went on. 'These people have done their homework, but they may not know about Saalfeld . . .'

'Then again, as you would say . . .'

'They might. So, I still won't take chances, especially with my aunt. She nearly got killed by Dahlberg. Once is enough. I'll look after Greville down there tonight, bring him to Berlin tomorrow and leave him at my place for the day. As you know, it's not an easy place to get into. He'll be quite safe. Then, during the night, we'll head off for the Eifel. I've got some friends with a country house out there. I can't see Hassan's people knowing about that. But even so . . .'

'You still won't take chances.'

'No.'

'Why not have some of the Rhineland-Pfalz colleagues keep an eye—'

'A police presence would be a beacon. I'll handle it.'

They were approaching Pappenheim's office, when Pappenheim's mobile rang.

It was Ilona Fohlmeister. 'It's been fired,' she said immediately.

'As expected. Thanks, Ilona. Whatever you do, don't let that gun disappear.'

'And if the *Direktor* asks?'

'Refer him to Jens. He's got a broad back.'

'Thanks!' Müller said.

'And if that doesn't get him spitting blood,' Pappenheim went on to Fohlmeister, 'refer him to me. That will really have him walking the ceiling.'

'Better you than me. But I'll hold on to the gun.'

'Thanks, Ilona,' he repeated. 'I mean that.'

'OK.'

'Do you know why he hates you so much?' Pappenheim said as he put the mobile away.

'You've told me many times, in so many different ways. You find new ones each time you tell me.'

'Perhaps. But there is one that burns him more than all the others. He sees something of himself in you, when he was an ace of a policeman.'

'Wash your mouth when you say that.'

'I'm very serious, Jens. That's what makes him dangerous to you. Forget you saved his daughter once. That only adds to it. That time, you saw him weak . . .'

'So did you.'

'Ah, but I don't matter. He doesn't envy me . . .'

'He envies *me*?'

'Oh ho-ho-ho. Does he!' They had reached the office, and Pappenheim opened the door. 'Aah . . . smell that nectar!'

Müller caught a whiff of the trapped nicotine. 'I'll take your word for it.'

Pappenheim went back to his theme. 'If you were the kind to party and mingle with the *Adel* crowd, you could do that in your sleep. You are part of them. He has to work at it, never certain whether he's being accepted or not. Me? I'm something he sees crawling on the toe of his shoe. He doesn't envy me at all . . .'

A phone in the office began to ring. There was an insistence about it that made Müller follow Pappenheim inside. Müller shut the door as Pappenheim made for the phone and grabbed it.

'Pappenheim . . .'

'Where have you been?' the voice demanded. 'I've been trying to reach you.'

'What am I? Your wife?' Pappenheim grinned at Müller, then, abruptly, his face grew hard. '*What?* Are you sure? OK, OK. Not doubting you. But this is . . .'

'I can't say at this stage whether it's connected to anything we've discussed,' the contact said. 'But it's a strange one. So perhaps you should keep it in mind. I'll get back to you as soon as I know more. And Pappi, tell Müller to watch his back. Something is going on.'

'I will. Thanks.'

Pappenheim put the phone down slowly, expression grim.

He turned to Müller. 'One of my contacts. The one who sent us the stuff you read in the rogues' gallery. There's been an incident on a *Landstrasse*, not far from Münster. Two colleagues down. Female officers. Clean shots. One at short range, the other very close . . . against the body. Her weapon was used for both killings.'

'My God,' Müller said.

'Whoever the bastard was, he was no amateur. He came up against two armed officers and took them out with one of their own weapons. The one taken at short range was actually trying to pull her weapon as she fell. But she didn't last long. The one with the contact shot had bruising on her throat. Armlock. It looks as if they stopped him for a routine check and he must have been able to grab one, used her as a human shield, popped the free one first, then let his captive have the second shot.'

Pappenheim lit up and drew the smoke powerfully into his lungs, then let it out slowly.

'The reason he could not possibly have been a panicky driver losing it,' Pappenheim went on, 'is that the slime was calm enough to wipe the weapon of any prints whatsoever. He used her shirt.'

'He *stripped* her?'

'Nothing so crude. This is a cool customer. He pulled out just enough to enable him to wipe the gun. And residues, if found, will be hers. Smart bastard.'

'What about the armlock? No residues there?'

Pappenheim shook his head. 'Must have been wearing long sleeves. Nothing on her neck. The only moisture is hers.' Pappenheim looked at Müller through a fresh cloud of smoke. 'My contact sends a warning. I'll give it to you word for word. "And Pappi, tell Müller to watch his back. Something is going on." Make of that what you will; but I'd take it seriously. This person is not an alarmist. Didn't Greville say as much to you? Would you call *him* alarmist?'

'Not in the least. Given what he's been through, and what he's carrying inside of him, his calmness can sometimes be quite unnerving.'

'Two warnings. Time to raise the drawbridge, Herr Graf.' For once, Pappenheim was using the title seriously.

'What would you have me do? Go into hiding?' Müller paused, then stared at Pappenheim. 'Oh come on, Pappi. You are not suggesting that *I* am Hassan's primary?'

'As you just said, stranger things have happened.'

'Indeed. And while we're imagining anyone would spend a large sum of money to hire a professional killer to get a policeman . . .'

'Not *a* policeman . . . but a very special policeman who happens to be the son of a murdered double-agent, and who may just possibly have access to some very incriminating material; whose uncle by marriage has for the time being survived a nasty biological weapon, who possibly also has some time-bomb evidence; *and –*' Pappenheim paused for effect – 'a policeman who has been making life hell for a group of shadowy people . . . Need I go on?'

'Quite enough, Pappi, thank you! I'm a policeman doing my job . . .'

'Sorry to interrupt, but if I were talking about anyone else, you'd be the first to say, give him cover. Why not take your own advice? Your professional instincts must be ringing those alarm bells like a few thousand maniacs.'

'And if you're wrong and the primary is someone else entirely? These people are very clever. They can run several hares, to confuse us. Case in point. Hassan disappears. Hassan reappears. Someone, or some people, as yet unknown, perhaps killed in Marzahn. Two colleagues killed near Münster. The deaths of those two colleagues may have absolutely nothing to do with this . . .'

'But we can't ignore it.'

'We won't. There's a picture forming in there somewhere. I don't accept that I'm the primary . . . but . . .'

'You won't take chances.'

'I never take chances, as you well know.'

'All I wanted to hear.'

'Now stop worrying, grandma.'

'Grin when you say that.'

'I—'

The phone rang again.

'What a day,' Pappenheim said, snatching at it.

'More developments,' the voice began immediately.

'I'm all ears.'

'I did a trawl. Something came up. May be nothing, may be a part of the picture.'

'Someone just used a similar phrase.'

'Must be the esteemed Graf.'

'The man's a star,' Pappenheim said, pretending not to notice Müller's frown. 'So? What's turned up?'

'Routine Autobahn check near Flensburg. Black Seat Ibiza, Spanish driver, not driving in a hurry. Vincente Monleon from Valencia. Valencia plates, anyway.'

'Valencia!' Pappenheim said, in a failed attempt to sing. 'El Cid,' he went on normally, 'and the best paella money can buy.'

There was a sudden silence.

'Hello?' Pappenheim called. 'Hello! My singing that bad?'

'How did you know?' the voice asked.

'Valencia? What do you think? I've spent all my life sitting in a police office?'

'That's not far from the truth.'

'Well, for your information, my wife and I used to go to Valencia for—' Pappenheim stopped, not wanting to remember. 'What about Valencia?' he asked gruffly.

'That's what the driver said. Best paella. It seems he had a pleasant chat with the officers who did the check. One of them has regular holidays in Spain. He saw the plates and made a comment about El Cid. That's when this Monleon went on about the joys of the Valenciana. That's why they remembered him. He also told them he wanted to make it to Mülheim before dark.'

'I can see the hook coming,' Pappenheim said.

'Yes. The two officers on the *Landstrasse* stopped a black Seat Ibiza with Valencia plates. They were running a check. That was all they had time for. I suppose they must have been bored. Their earlier transmissions showed there was little traffic, they were just sitting there watching out for speeders who never turned up, and were thinking of moving on to another patch with more prospects. Then along comes the Seat.'

Pappenheim shut his eyes briefly. 'Christ.'

'So do things turn.'

'Well, thanks for the info. Not nice to hear, but it definitely helps to fill in the picture.'

'Pappi.'

'Yes?'

'Never nice to hear news of colleagues going down, no matter where from. You make certain the Graf takes my advice. There's something with his name on it.'

'I'll nail him to a wall if I have to. Thanks again. Did you get most of that?' Pappenheim added to Müller as he hung up.

'I could hear much of what he said, so I can guess the rest. A boring day turned into their last.'

'Why the hell did they have to stop him?' Pappenheim asked rhetorically. 'And what did they do to get themselves shot?'

'Asked him to open the boot?' Müller suggested.

'And he had something in there he didn't want them to see.'

'If I were a betting man, I would call that a certainty.'

'But that would mean . . .' Pappenheim stopped. 'We know it can't be Hassan. He's in Stockholm.'

'This may have nothing at all to do with Hassan. On the other hand . . .'

'I know what is coming.'

'. . . why not two killers, if the target is important? Without your contact, without Greville's information, there is no way anyone outside those who planned this would know what is going on. We are all focused on Hassan up there in Stockholm, not due here for another forty-eight hours at least; possibly more since his "roughing up".'

'While we're watching Hassan, the other killer is running.'

Müller nodded. '*If* that's what is really happening. And we would have been none the wiser, if Monleon had not had some bad luck – worse for the two female officers – with the spot checks. These things do happen. Wrong place at the wrong time for both parties. Like Greville. Everything was set. No one meant to be in the lab. Along comes the guard. One dead, leaving a young son; the other receives a vicious, decades-long death sentence. If he is tied to Hassan, Monleon may not be his real name at all. There are two other options.'

'Options. I like those.' Pappenheim moved behind his desk and sat down. He waved at the laden chair. 'Take a perch.'

Müller looked at the chair. 'I'll pace.'

'As you wish. Just don't make me dizzy.'

'The other options.' Müller began a slow pace from door to window and back. 'First, Monleon – or whatever his

126

name is – is simply an ordinary criminal, perhaps doing some smuggling: drugs, dirty money, dirty weapons. If so, he should be sweating, having killed two police officers. Unfortunately, the nature of the killings, and the way he behaved up near Flensburg, doesn't fit that scenario. There are killers, and then there are killers.

'Second option. He *is* a professional killer. The officers got in his way . . .'

'But why leave the Autobahn? He was clear. He had a straight run to wherever he was headed.'

Müller paused in front of the desk. 'Not such a mystery. Perhaps he was looking for somewhere to eat.'

Pappenheim was doubtful. 'There are some good restaurants on the Autobahn; some bad too, of course. But worth the trouble of going off?'

Müller began pacing again. 'He had time. He wasn't rushing, although he said he wanted to get to Mülheim before dark. He had plenty of time to make it. Lots of daylight so close to summer. In case you think it unlikely that he would leave the Autobahn, remember I tend to do that. I will travel quite a few kilometres to find a nice little café in pleasant surroundings, if I can spare the time.'

'I know. There's that one by the Rhine near St Goar. Your favourite cake place. Alright. I'll buy that, as Miss Bloomfield would say.'

Müller stopped again. This time he gave Pappenheim a questioning look. 'Miss Bloomfield? What has she to do with this? Are you sending out a coded signal, Pappi?'

'No,' Pappenheim said, innocence itself. 'It's just one of the things she says.'

'And you just thought you would . . . borrow it.'

Pappenheim shrugged.

Müller looked as if he didn't believe it for a moment, but paced on. 'So, he goes off the Autobahn, looking for somewhere. The man who likes Valencia paella wants to eat something other than Autobahn food. Perfectly natural. He's in Germany. He wants some real country cooking. Whenever I go to France, I hunt out likely watering holes. It is something I quite enjoy doing.

'He finds himself on a nice, empty stretch of *Landstrasse*. Life is good. Then it all goes wrong. Two apparently bored officers decide to stop him. How could they possibly have expected a tourist to be dangerous? According to what we just heard, they followed the procedure; but the one with the contact shot must have allowed herself to get too close . . . with dreadful results. Two parties meeting at the wrong time, in the wrong place. If he had arrived earlier, or later, it might never have happened. If he had continued on the Autobahn for a few more kilometres, it would certainly never have happened.'

'Hard as it is to say,' Pappenheim put in, 'had that not happened, we would never have found out about him.'

Müller again stopped before the desk. 'Until too late. Which leads us to the professional-killer scenario. As a hired pro, he will have had relay stations set up along whatever route he has mapped out. I very much doubt he's going anywhere near Mülheim. His mention of it was deliberate, in case he was remembered for any particular reason; except perhaps this one. Those officers were inconveniences that had to be eliminated. They meant little more to him than that, and he would certainly not have betrayed his presence otherwise. People like that work best when they blend with the scenery.

'This means we can forget about the Seat Ibiza. He will have got to his emergency station and will now be someone else, in a different car. He is once more anonymous. If you are correct and he really is after me, the only way is to flush him out. In short, make myself visible.'

'High risk.'

'Certainly. But I'm not supposed to know any of this. Hiding would show that I do, and make them even more cautious. And what's the best way to remain visible? Annoy the hell out of them, starting with our friends downstairs.'

'And if the target is not – as you believe – you, then what?'

'We still annoy them. We still have the edge, because they don't know what we know.' Müller's eyes held a fire Pappenheim had never seen before. 'I want them, Pappi. And I will bring them down, one by one!'

Shutters came down over Pappenheim's own eyes, as if he did not want Müller to see the anxiety in them.

'Blood on the tongue,' he said.

Müller looked at Pappenheim, as if unsure that he was all there. 'What?'

'Something someone said to me a long time ago, when I was a green novice. Blood on the tongue. When you want it so much, you taste the blood of your prey.'

Müller said nothing to that, but continued to look at Pappenheim as if the *Oberkommissar* had suddenly grown a third eye.

'When do you plan to go back to Saalfeld?' Pappenheim now asked quickly.

'After I've spoken with Kaltendorf.'

Pappenheim was surprised. 'You're actually going to his office?'

'Better than having him come to mine.'

'He'll never believe it. He'll die of shock.'

'There's a first time for everything.'

Pappenheim jabbed the cigarette he'd been smoking into the full ashtray. As if suddenly remembering, he dug into the pocket in which he had placed the old stub and dropped that too into the ashtray. He then reached into a drawer to pull out a paper handkerchief, with which he scrupulously wiped his fingers.

'I've got something to tell you, Jens,' he said.

Müller, alerted by the tone of his voice, looked intrigued. 'Bad?'

129

'I hope you won't think so.'

Pappenheim decided to go straight in. No point wasting any more time. It had taken him long enough, months of soul-searching and suppressed guilt, to get to this point.

'When you went to France after the Romeo case,' Pappenheim began, 'someone – and to this day I have no idea who – left a note in a white envelope, under your door. I took it.'

Pappenheim paused, waiting to see what Müller would say.

Again, Müller said nothing.

'It was a long, slim envelope; no stamp, and no return address. Just your name in block capitals. *MÜLLER*. That was all. At first, I thought it could be a letter bomb, so I took it to my office.' Pappenheim held Müller's gaze. 'I opened it.'

Müller still said nothing.

'Inside was a single sheet of paper. *You may think you have won, Müller. But you haven't. Your father was Romeo Six.* That's the exact quote. I'll never forget it. There was no signature.'

'Where is it now?'

'I tore it to pieces. Since it had not turned out to be a bomb, I assumed someone hostile was trying to get to you. With what we now know, I was right.'

'Have there been others?'

'One more. I kept a very sharp lookout.'

'You've been acting as a filter for my mail?'

'Yes.'

Müller once more said nothing, this time for long moments; then his expression relaxed. 'Join the club.'

'What do you mean?' a relieved Pappenheim asked.

'Aunt Isolde. I know something that part of me feels she should know. The other feels she should be protected from it.'

'You mean Greville.'

'I do mean Greville. If she knew the truth, it would be

terrible for her. I have decided it would be best to allow her to at least try to recapture something of what they had. If he decides to tell her, it's his affair, and not my place to do so. Sometimes, deciding what is best for someone you respect, care for, or otherwise hold in regard, is not easy.' Müller paused. 'Thanks, Pappi. I appreciate it.'

Müller went out, and closed the door quietly.

'Yes. Well.' Pappenheim cleared his throat. 'I need a cigarette.'

Müller decided that, as he was in the frame of mind for it, it was a good time to see Kaltendorf.

As he made his way along the corridor, he reflected upon what Pappenheim had done. Far from feeling angry, he was touched by the gesture. And who would have believed that, all these years later, the truth of what had happened to his parents would at last be coming out, piece by piece, into the light of day?

But, as first Grogan – the mysterious Russian–American, or American–Russian, or neither of those – had begun teasing out his highly sensitive information, then Pappenheim's contacts, and now Greville, had made their own contributions, a dark, hidden world was being opened up to him. Within that world were the players who had murdered his parents, and many others besides, in order to protect themselves and their interests.

And they would not stop.

'Unless stopped first,' he said aloud.

But was he mad to go up against such people? Unseen, powerful enemies with resources at their command that so far outmatched his, which were puny by comparison.

'They are stealing my country,' he said to himself.

And they had killed his parents.

And he had names. Not many, but it was a start.

He arrived at Kaltendorf's door and knocked.

'Come in!'

Kaltendorf's office was more than twice the size of Müller's, and had twice the window space. Yet, for all that, it seemed utilitarian by comparison. First impression was that it was decorated with police badges, national and international. Befitting his status as he saw it, Kaltendorf's pristine desk was huge.

He looked up from something he was writing as Müller entered.

'Ah, Müller! This is a surprise. When were you last in here?'

'Well, sir . . .'

'You don't remember. Neither do I.'

It was a challenge, but Müller chose not to accept it. 'I thought we'd talk about the prisoners, sir.'

Kaltendorf steepled his fingers and looked at Müller over the top of them. 'Ah yes. You mean our colleagues.'

'Technically, sir, they are prisoners.'

'"Technically". Interesting choice of word, Müller.'

'One of these people, sir, killed or injured someone, with a weapon that has recently been fired . . .'

Kaltendorf's eyes stared with a strange intensity at Müller. 'How do you know that? Have you been inspecting the weapons, against my orders?'

'No, sir. *Kommissarin* Fohlmeister, who led the raid, checked one of the weapons on the way back here. It had recently been fired.'

'Why didn't she say so?'

'I believe she is waiting for the release of all the weapons so that they too can be checked. Sir,' Müller went on, 'if I am correct about this . . .'

Kaltendorf tightened his lips, and Müller knew that this round at least was about to be lost. Nevertheless, he pressed on.

'Sir, these people were caught trying to escape with eaves-dropping equipment with which they had been intercepting *our* communications. We are a police unit. That in itself—'

132

'I know exactly what you're going to say, Müller. But I am afraid it is of no use. The men are gone, and their weapons and equipment with them.'

Müller stood there gaping. '*What?*' he finally got out. '*Gone?* But we were just with them, sir! They—'

'*Hauptkommissar* Müller! When you are *Direktor* – if that day ever comes – you can make the decisions around here. But until then, *I make them. Is that clear?*'

'Very clear, sir! And while you're at it, try and get your balls back!'

Furious, Müller stormed out.

'*Müller!*' Kaltendorf shouted. '*Come back here! I am not finished. Müller! Damn you, Müller!*'

Müller kept on walking. Heads popped out of offices to look. Eyes stared in disbelief. One or two people tried to talk to Müller, but one look at his expression was enough to make them think better of it.

Kaltendorf's outraged yells seemed to echo round the building. They were the sounds of an animal at bay.

When Müller had reached Pappenheim's office, he knocked and entered.

Pappenheim took one look at Müller's face and said, 'You're not going to tell me he's let them go.'

'He's let them go.'

'*Damn it!* Berger, Reimer and the assault team. All for *nothing!*'

'I just told him to find his balls.'

Pappenheim stared. 'You *did*? Not good. He won't forget that one easily. This is very close to the wind. You're playing roulette with your career.'

'And he's playing political roulette with us for his own damned reasons, his aspirations, and his cronies. How can he allow those people to go? One of them is a murderer. I'm sure of it.'

'Probably all are,' Pappenheim put in. 'They've got that killing look. Those guns were not pieces of sculpture.'

Müller jammed his hands in his pockets and went over to the window. 'God, Pappi. I can't see out of this.'

'Same window since you were here last . . . a few minutes ago.'

'Even so . . .'

The phone rang. Pappenheim got it at the second ring.

'Ilona!' he greeted. 'What? You're joking. But I thought . . . Well done!' Pappenheim was grinning. 'Some people are on the side of the angels. Fohlmeister has just delayed her advancement to *Oberkommissarin.* She's confiscated the van, and everything in it.'

'*What?* She disobeyed the Great White?'

'Not . . . exactly. She had the van under lock and key, and just happened not to be around when the GW told the slimes they could leave. They went to find their van but, very sad to say, there was no one around to open up. She had also left particular instructions for her subordinates: any release of the van and its contents had to be accompanied by the proper release documents, with full identification, so that no one could later say anything was missing.'

'Clever.'

'Not bad at all. As our mystery men are so desperate to keep their identities mysterious, this raises some problems for them. The GW can't fault her for doing things by the book, so she's in the clear.'

'But – as you've just said – bad for her future prospects regarding promotion. Things, however, do change.'

'They certainly do. The GW can get promoted out of here . . . A car came to pick up our joyous guests,' Pappenheim added, 'and they left, muttering darkly that this was our doing.'

'*Our* doing?'

'You, and me. I don't think we've heard the last of it.'

'What it is to be popular,' Müller said. 'But at least we can now examine everything properly. It is possible that they may never reclaim their equipment, for the very reasons you just mentioned.'

'The goth will be happy if that turns out to be the case. It was her excellent work that caught them, which was why they were trying to leave in such a hurry. Without her electronic wizardry, they would still be listening to everything that came in, and went out of here. And, as for the guns, I always wanted to see how a Calico handles.'

'What would you want with a fifty-round sub-machine gun, Pappi?'

'Pretend I'm in one of those black and white gangster movies?'

Eight

The black BMW 645ci Coupé was rushing along the A2 Autobahn towards Berlin.

The man driving it was once known as Vincente Monleon, lover of Valencian paellas. He was now Emilio Garadini, from Tuscany, purveyor of fine Italian wines. He wore designer sunglasses and a finely groomed, slightly droopy moustache. Unexpectedly, it went well with the Roman cut of his hair. His cream linen trousers and white polo shirt spoke of a wealth that fitted the car he was driving. He drove with the driver's window all the way down. D'Agostino's version of 'The Riddle' filled the car and was wafted away on the slipstream.

As with his persona as Vincente Monleon, he had long relegated the killing of the policewomen to the far recesses of his mind.

Müller was in his office, getting ready to return to Saalfeld. Then he paused, and called the friends who owned the house in the Eifel.

'Jutta . . .' he began when the call was answered.

'My God, Jens! What a pleasant surprise. Are you coming over to see us? Your godson is a year old now.'

'Is he?' Müller felt guilty. 'When?'

She laughed. 'Don't panic. It was only two days ago.'

'Two days! Jutta, I am so sorry . . .'

'Police work. I know. Just come and see us soon.'

'I promise.'

'I'll hold you to that. So, if it's not about a visit, how can I help?'

'Now I feel terrible.'

'Don't be ridiculous, Jens! We have much to thank you for. We're like family. So? What is it?'

'The house in the Eifel . . .'

'Of course you can. Taking her there? Who is she? Anyone we know?'

'Not the reason at all, but you do give me an idea.'

'Aha! So there is a she . . .'

'Stop prying, Jutta.'

'I'm a woman. I pry. But of course you can have the place,' Jutta von Gersch went on. 'Frau Holz has the keys as always. I'll let her know.'

'Thanks, Jutta. I appreciate it. Wish little Jens a happy birthday from me. I'll make it up to him.'

'I know you will. Look after yourself, Jens.'

'I will. You too.'

When they had ended the conversation, Müller briefly rubbed his face with his hands.

'God. I'd completely forgotten about the birthday. And they live in Berlin! Some godfather you are, Müller.'

He called Pappenheim. 'Pappi, I'm about to leave. Better sooner than later. I don't want another heart-to-heart with Kaltendorf today. Tell Ilona to be as bureaucratic as she wants with that van.'

'Don't worry. I'll make certain she'll tie it up for a year if she has to.'

'Good. I've remembered something you mentioned about Hassan after he returned from his magical tour of Stockholm. You said your contact maintained he was terrified . . .'

'Yes. I made a joke about that, but my contact insisted he was.'

'What if it really were true? What if the person we think is Hassan *isn't*? What if the terrified Hassan is in reality a decoy? And what if his "mugging" is in fact a reminder that he, the decoy, should behave himself? Peace activist mugged. Great headlines. Attention diverted. Decoy reminded of what could *really* happen to him if he puts a foot wrong. Meanwhile, the real killer's already on his way, while we're all concentrating on Sweden . . .'

'Our man in the black Ibiza, travelling south . . .'

'And almost certainly heading in a new direction. It's a theory . . .'

'That makes sense, if that's how it's being worked. We already know, thanks to that piece of nastiness near Münster, that we do have a pro killer on the loose.'

'Now heading anywhere.'

'If you *are* the primary, his destination is Berlin.'

'And if I am not?'

'Then we don't know the primary; but we do know he's after Greville as well.'

'Which is why it's back to Saalfeld for me. Keep my eye on Greville.'

'Of course, if you are the primary, he'll have both of you at the same location. Making his job easy.'

'I think he'll find it harder than he expects.'

'And where will you be . . . if you-know-who asks?'

'If he does,' Müller said, 'you don't know.'

'The sum of my knowledge is so minute these days.'

Müller smiled at the phone. 'Keep me posted.'

'Will do. And watch your back. My contact was serious.'

'I'm a serious man. And, talking of serious, can you believe I forgot my godson's birthday? He was one year old, two days ago.'

'Of course I can,' Pappenheim said.

A short while after Müller had gone, Pappenheim received another call from his contact.

'We should stop meeting like this,' Pappenheim said.

'You'd miss me,' the voice at the other end told him.

'And you'd miss having me to talk to,' Pappenheim countered.

'Alright. You win this round. Something more about Hassan.'

'Anything.'

'It seems he had gone for his walk along the waterfront. His hotel's in that area. According to him, he wanted to see that floating hotel they've got up there; the one they made from the yacht that used to belong to the millionairess . . .'

'Hutton,' Pappenheim said.

'That's the one. Seems he'd always wanted to see it, and thought, as he was so close, he'd take the opportunity . . .'

'When along came those bad men to kidnap him, rob him, beat him up, then dump him in a back alley.'

'He's sticking to that.'

'Something's sticky, that's for sure.'

'Just giving the facts.'

'Talking of which,' Pappenheim began.

A sigh was plainly heard. 'Here it comes.'

'Those people we . . . er . . . caught,' Pappenheim went on, unmoved. 'My boss would like to know who's responsible for the building, its construction, the hiring and firing, who bankrolled it . . .'

'Why not the shareholders as well, while you're at it?'

'Even better.'

'That was sarcasm.'

Pappenheim grinned at the phone. 'I know.'

'Sometimes . . .' the other said in resignation, and hung up.

'What it is to be loved,' Pappenheim said to the dead phone. He put it down, then picked it up again to call Hedi Meyer. 'Ah. Miss Meyer. How are we doing?'

'Clean.'

'Don't rest on your laurels. These people may yet find a way to set up another team. We monitor round the clock.'

'Don't worry, sir. I've set up an automatic intercept intercept, if you see what I mean . . .'

'Don't blind me with science, young woman. As long as it works.'

'It works.'

'All I need to know. Get us some more fish.'

'If they're out there, they're as good as hooked.'

'Miss Meyer, you know how to make an old wreck happy.'

'And how's the young wreck, sir?' Hedi Meyer enquired boldly.

'First, don't let him hear you call him a wreck. That's the one thing he isn't. Secondly, he's fine. I think.'

'Hmm,' she said.

'And Miss Meyer . . .'

'Sir?'

'A word to the wise . . . don't throw your heart at him.'

'I wasn't!' she said quickly. 'Can I hang up now?'

'You may.'

'Of course you were,' Pappenheim said as the line went dead. He smiled at the phone as he put it down. 'Oh, the joys of spring. Well . . . late spring.'

The black BMW had just passed Braunschweig when the hands-off phone warbled. 'The Riddle' was playing on a loop. The volume was turned down automatically.

'Yes?' Garadini said.

'Everything going smoothly?' came through on the speakers.

'Yes. Is there a reason for this call?'

'There are slight complications.'

'I don't like complications, no matter how slight.' Garadini's German was perfect.

'Stop at the next point. There'll be a message for you there.'

The conversation ended, and 'The Riddle' swelled back to its previous volume.

Garadini began to whistle in accompaniment.

*　　*　　*

140

The Porsche was speeding south along the A116 Autobahn towards the junction that would lead to the A9.

Müller had escaped without running into Kaltendorf. He had no idea how Kaltendorf would respond to what had occurred in his office. Müller was almost past caring. He could not understand, even allowing for Kaltendorf's own political networking habits, why the man had allowed the five eavesdroppers to leave without so much as a word of protest.

Who had such a hold upon Kaltendorf that a senior policeman of his high rank had turned into such a puppy? What was the carrot dangling at the end of the stick that kept Kaltendorf so acquiescent? Was it the same people who had used Neubauer, and in the end had finished him off when they'd had no further use for him? Was Kaltendorf blindly heading in the same direction?

Müller found he could not feel sympathy. Kaltendorf was his own worst enemy; a formerly tough and highly professional policeman turned into . . . what exactly?

People were pulling Kaltendorf's strings and, as a result, he was becoming a serious liability, as far as policing was concerned. The trouble was, Müller felt certain, this was precisely what those in the shadows wanted. How many others of the nation's institutions had such shadowy movers behind the scenes?

As the car hurtled south, Müller glanced at the rushing scenery. A distant house was on the periphery of his vision. The people within would be blissfully going about their normal business.

'What do you know?' he asked of them.

In Berlin, the door to Pappenheim's office swung open, and Kaltendorf stood there. Remembering the last encounter, Pappenheim got to his feet. But Kaltendorf was strangely subdued.

'Where's Müller?' he asked.

'Out, sir.'

Kaltendorf nodded but, unusually, did not ask where Müller had gone to. 'Tell him . . . Tell him I am prepared to overlook his outburst, on this occasion. I have not forgotten that he once saved my daughter's life. Tell him also, do not rush to judgement. There are sometimes . . . considerations that have to be made.'

Kaltendorf stopped abruptly, turned and walked away. He actually shut the door behind him.

Pappenheim, mouth agape, sat down heavily. He stared at the closed door.

'Did I just see and hear that?' he asked aloud.

Still staring at the door, he reached out and fumbled around until his hand touched his opened pack of cigarettes. He slid one out and put it to his lips. He lit it, and drew deeply.

'I think I just had a waking dream,' he said, blowing out a double stream through his nostrils. 'Yes. That must have been it.'

The five men released by Kaltendorf were sitting at a conference table in an office on the top floor of a building whose foundations had been laid during the thirties. At the head of the table was a man whose name was on one of the documents that Pappenheim's contact had supplied.

He stared coldly at the baby-faced man who had said his name was Rorsch. 'This is a mess!'

'We had no choice,' Rorsch began in his defence. 'They moved very fast. We did not expect them to intercept our own intercepts . . . Our information was that they had no such capability. Our equipment is the most up to date . . .'

'Clearly not sufficiently so! They now know you exist! Your invisibility was your strength. Now you are a beacon! You may as well stand on any rooftop and shout it! To make matters worse, all your equipment *and* your weapons are still in their custody!'

'That woman who led the raid has demanded proper documentation, which we obviously cannot give. This smells like one of Müller's—'

'Müller, Müller, *Müller*! The son is worse than the father! Von Röhnen senior was about to do considerable damage before a solution was found. The same will have to be done with the son.'

'I thought that was already in hand,' Rorsch said.

The man glared at him. 'You have your own sphere of responsibility. Stay within it! You would be wise to ensure that what happened to your two operators remains a mystery. They have your gun.'

'Kaltendorf will ensure—'

The man snorted with contempt. 'Kaltendorf! One day, he will outlive his usefulness.' He looked at them all with hard eyes. 'I suggest you all migrate for a while. Plenty of foreign work for your undoubted skills. You will be relocated. Become invisible again. You will be told when it is the right time to return. But before you do, you've got a chance to redeem yourselves.' He got to his feet. 'And remember this . . . no one is indispensable.'

They got the message.

He moved from their table, turned his back upon them and stared out of a window.

'*Müller!*' he snarled. It was a heartfelt curse. 'We are plagued by that family!'

The BMW was approaching Magdeburg when the phone again warbled. 'The Riddle' was still in its loop, and Garadini sighed in annoyance as the volume automatically lowered.

'Yes?' Garadini said.

'Your lucky day, after all. The package has left Berlin and is going south on the A9. Have you passed Magdeburg?'

'Coming up to it soon.'

'Perfect. Take the A14 exit to Halle. Join with the A9 after Halle. You should be in position for an intercept. If you do not make it at that point, do not worry . . .'

'I never worry.'

'Glad to hear it. If you miss this intercept, there is a relay of spotters. You will be guided. You have all the descriptions you need.'

'I have.'

'Good hunting.'

'The Riddle' again swelled to its original volume, and Garadini continued his whistling.

Müller could not remember precisely when he began to wonder about the helicopter.

He had spotted one near the Halle/Leipzig junction. That in itself had not been odd. Helicopters clattered over the Autobahns everywhere: traffic police, television news channels, private ones. At any given time, they could be seen dragonflying their way from point A to point B, sometimes loitering, sometimes not.

There was nothing in particular to cause any apprehension about the helicopter he now saw. It was not even the same helicopter. Yet he felt uneasy for some reason.

'Twitchy, Müller?' he chided himself, and settled down into his fast drive.

The BMW was now on the A9, but was still quite some distance from the Porsche. At the rate Müller was driving, it would never catch up. If anything, the Porsche was increasing its distance.

This time it was Garadini who made the call. 'What is he driving? A rocket ship?'

'You have the best car we can supply. Use it!'

'And get stopped again?'

'You leave that concern to us. We expect a result.'

'You will have your result. Just lead me to my primary.'

'That will be done.'

The man who had spoken to the five eavesdroppers was now alone at the big conference table. Directly before him was a cord-free phone. He sat there, thoughtfully rubbing at the signet ring on the little finger of his left hand.

Had Müller and Pappenheim been there to see it, both would have recognized the seal. It was exactly the same as one they had seen in a clandestine film sent to them by the mysterious Grogan/Vladimir, months before. In that film was a man with a ring on his little finger.

Hedi Meyer's computer wizardry had enabled her to enlarge the ring until the seal itself had filled the screen. She had then adjusted the definition so well that the image had become as sharp as if it had been photographed close up. Then it had been printed. The print was now safely stored with the other sensitive material, in one of the cabinets in the rogues' gallery.

The seal was a doctored variation of one of the ancient seals of the Knights Templar. The familiar two knights on the one horse was there; but over this was superimposed a jagged **X**.

The man had another ring, on the little finger of his right hand. This was also a variation, but of the first seal of Berlin: the 1253 Brandenburg eagle before the city walls. Its original inscription had been replaced by a single word in Latin, beneath the eagle: *Semper.* Forever.

The man gave the phone a hard stare, before picking it up and turning it over. He began dialling. The phone made soft electronic noises as he hit each button. The number was not in Berlin, nor was it within Germany.

'The intercept was compromised,' he began, as soon as he heard the other person's voice.

'How?'

'The interceptors were themselves intercepted.'

'I was led to believe the targets did not have the capability.'

145

'That judgement was wrong.'

'Whose responsibility?'

'It is being attended to.'

There was a pause.

'Any indications that Müller knows the truth?' the person outside Germany asked.

'None so far. After all these years, it seems most unlikely. He would have acted by now.'

'Yet he continues to get in our way.'

'He is a policeman; a conscientious one. Perhaps too conscientious for his own good.'

'We know how to deal with the conscientious. We have done so before. This is no different.'

'Also being attended to.'

'The father could have caused us considerable damage, traitor that he was. Make certain the son does not.'

'That, is a priority.'

'My position cannot be compromised.'

'And that, is understood.'

'Anything else?'

'Our man is running to target.'

'Excellent. The hare has outlived its usefulness.'

'That will be seen to.'

After they had ended their terse conversation, the man in Berlin made another call to a second number. As with the first, it was not a German number. The conversation was short, and to the point. When he put the phone down the man got up and walked to the window. He looked out over the city.

'Forever,' he said quietly.

Stockholm waterfront, Sweden, some minutes later.

The peace activist who had been kidnapped, robbed and beaten up looked afraid as he walked along the edge of the water. He had two bodyguards with him, but he still seemed afraid. That is, his eyes showed their fear, but to all other outward appearances, he was calm and at ease with himself as he chatted to the men tasked with guarding him.

Tall, solid individuals, they cast alert glances about them, covering every possible direction of attack. Each wore an earphone with a throat mike. Their heads were never still, tracking this way and that, searching out possible assassins. It was not a particularly busy time; not many people about, so the bodyguards had plenty of time to react, should anything hostile appear.

The activist saw, up ahead, the reason he had decided to go for the walk in the first place. A big, white yacht, moored permanently, it seemed.

'You really do want to see that boat, don't you?' one of the bodyguards said in English. His accent was vague mid-Atlantic; but his native tongue was not English.

'Yes. I have heard a lot about it. I would like to have a meal there.'

'Even after what happened the last time?'

'I never got to it.'

'You're the boss,' the bodyguard said with resignation. 'And this time, don't go off walking on your own.'

'Don't worry. I have learned my lesson.'

The bodyguards looked at each other, shrugged, and escorted their charge to the luxury yacht that had become a moored hotel.

They were perhaps still a couple of hundred metres or so away when the bodyguard who had been speaking put a hand to his ear. His body became still as he listened.

'Alright,' he said to the other two, hand continuingly held to his ear. 'The restaurant will have to wait. We have a warning. Back to the car!' He took his charge by one arm, the other was held by the second bodyguard. 'Come on, sir. Let's get you out of here. It's no longer safe.'

Fearful eyes, no longer hiding what they truly felt, darted questioning glances at his two protectors.

'What . . . what have you heard?'

'It seems as if some asshole militant is trying to get to you,' the bodyguard replied. 'So, it's back to the hotel. Now, please, sir. Hurry!'

They bundled him into the dark-blue Volvo they had just left, and the car shot off at speed, urgent to return to the relative safety of the hotel, a short distance away.

When they got back, they went straight up to his suite. One bodyguard remained on watch outside. The one with whom he had been speaking entered the suite with him.

'Sorry about that,' the bodyguard said in apology. 'Didn't want to take any chances.'

'That's OK. I understand.' The activist gave a shaky smile. 'I appreciate what you're doing.'

'Just our job, sir.'

'That's true, but I still appreciate it.'

'And this, sir, is also my job.'

The man the world had seen on television stared, eyes round with shock. A silenced gun was pointing at him.

'What . . . what are you *doing*?' Meant to be a shout, the words had risen to a petrified squeak.

'This, sir.'

The gun coughed twice. Its victim gave a tired little wheeze as the breath was knocked out of him forever by two neatly placed shots to the chest.

He was dead by the time he hit the rich carpet of his suite. His erstwhile bodyguard stepped uncaringly over the body and went out.

The bodyguard shut the door quietly. It clicked home. Only a swipe card could open it again.

His partner looked at him. 'Done?'

'Done. It can only be opened from inside, and the person who can do it is dead. It will take them a while to realize anything's wrong and use their security swipe card to find him. Gives us plenty of time to disappear. Come on.'

They walked away in a brisk but controlled hurry.

Unfortunately for them, they were wrong.

The unexpected return to the hotel had trapped someone in the suite: a member of the hotel staff placing items in the bathroom. She had been about to leave when she had heard people enter. Preparing her apologies, she had heard the frightened cry of the victim and had opened the door a crack to peer through.

She had seen the gun. Wisely remaining hidden, she had waited and had seen all that had happened. Terrified, she had continued to wait until she had heard the door of the suite click shut; then she had waited some more, just in case the bodyguard decided to return, for whatever reason.

At last satisfied that the bodyguard had gone for good, she forced herself to leave the bathroom. Keeping her eyes averted from the body, she went to the door to listen.

He would be gone, she told herself. He would not hang around after killing the man he was supposed to protect.

She went to a phone and called reception.

When Müller took the Saalfeld exit, there was a speck-like helicopter in the distance.

As he drove towards the *Schlosshotel*, he came to a decision. It could be nothing, he thought; but better wrong than sorry. Change of plan. He would take Greville to the Eifel immediately.

When he arrived at the Derrenberg, he parked by the entrance and hurried in. Christian, standing by the reception desk, looked at him in surprise.

'Herr Graf! Can I help?'

'Herr Greville. Where is he?'

'With your aunt, sir . . .'

'Thank you, Christian.'

Müller hurried out, leaving the confused hussar staring after him. He went to the owner's gate, quickly punched in the entry code and went through almost before the gate had opened properly.

He found them in quiet conversation at the kitchen table.

'Sorry to interrupt,' he began as they looked up at him in astonishment. 'But I've got to take you out of here, Greville. Now.'

'My dear boy, but—'

'I am sorry, Greville, but this is urgent.'

'Got it, dear boy. Say no more.' Greville got to his feet and picked up his hat from the back of the chair next to him.

Aunt Isolde, having risen to her feet as well, looked anxiously at Greville and Müller in turn.

'Jens? What is going on?'

'Later, Aunt Isolde. I am sorry, but we have got to leave right away.'

'Shall I get my bag from the hotel?' Greville asked in his calm voice.

Müller nodded. 'Yes.'

'Very well. Meet you outside, then, shall I?'

Again, Müller nodded.

Greville gave Aunt Isolde a fond kiss near her mouth. 'Not goodbye, my dear. See you again soon.'

He went out, leaving Aunt Isolde with Müller.

There was a moisture in her eyes as she looked at him. 'Bring him back, Jens, will you?'

'I will, Aunt Isolde. I'm taking my father's documents with me, so would you mind getting the briefcase for me, please?'

'Of course not. I won't be long.'

Aunt Isolde went out to get it.

She was soon back with the now-familiar, worn brown leather case, and handed it to him.

'So heavy,' he remarked as he took it. 'Must be full of interesting things.'

She looked at him anxiously. 'From what your father said at the time, you may find answers in there which could upset you. Whatever it is, think very carefully before you do anything. Will you promise me you will?'

'I will, Aunt Isolde. That *is* a promise.'

That appeared to satisfy her. She nodded, seemingly more to herself, as if confirming something.

'I must go,' Müller told her gently, and kissed her on the cheek. 'Don't worry.'

He hurried out.

'But I do,' she said softly, after he'd gone. 'You're all we've got left of the male line.'

Bag in hand, Greville was staring at the car when Müller got to the entrance, carrying the brown leather briefcase.

'My word! Getting my ride at last.' There was a smile of boyish pleasure upon his face.

'You certainly are,' Müller said. 'A long one. We're going west. To the Eifel. Safer there. I'll take your bag. Get in while I put it away.'

Greville looked at the briefcase, then back to Müller. 'That's your father's.'

'Yes.'

Greville nodded, but said nothing as he got into the passenger seat. He seemed to forget about the briefcase, and stared as Müller reached down by the driver's seat to press the switch that would open the luggage compartment.

'Of course!' he said, remembering. 'Forgot these cars have it back to front. The boot's in the nose.'

Müller gave a tight smile as he put bag and briefcase into the luggage well and shut the bonnet with a soft click. 'As ever was.'

He got in behind the wheel and shut the door.

'Belt on?'

'Belt on,' Greville confirmed. He peered out. 'Is she watching?'

'No.'

'Thought not. Better.'

Müller started the engine and 450 units of turbocharged brake horsepower snarled into life behind their heads.

'Oh my God!' Greville exclaimed softly.

He said nothing more as Müller turned the car round and headed away from the hotel; but he had a big, child-like grin upon his face. He did not speak again until they were back on the Autobahn and Müller let the car have its head.

As the acceleration pinned him back in his seat, Greville again uttered the same three words.

'Oh my God. What a superb machine!' he added.

'Not frightened?'

'Good Lord, no! Enjoying, old boy. Enjoying it. Whooo! Hah-hah!' Greville looked as if he had just been given the best present of his life.

'And now, old boy,' he went on after a couple of minutes enjoying the speed, 'tell me. What has happened? And please don't try to make things easy. Give me the facts, no matter how hard.'

'We believe your son is here.'

'Ah. My detached son. Yes. Well. Had to happen eventually. Is that why we are ground-flying?'

'Yes. We won't be using the Autobahns all the way. I'm going to take the most direct route westwards, from Hof to Koblenz. Though the going may be a little slower in parts, we'll make better time on the route I'll take.'

Greville looked at Müller with one of his hovering little smiles. 'Are we avoiding someone? Is he already here? By "here", I mean, in this area.'

'I am not certain. It's a feeling.'

'Ah. Always trust feelings. I did. Many times; and many times they saved my life. Something primeval. The old survival instinct. Many people have either lost it, or ignore it when it comes knocking. Not you, eh?'

'Not me.'

The phone rang, and Greville watched the antics of the communications display with great interest.

'That's the UK double ring,' he said.

152

'Yes. I had it changed to tease someone.'

'Ah. The mystery gel.' Greville looked at the name on the display. 'Pappi? *The* Pappi?'

Müller nodded. 'Yes, Pappi,' he said aloud as the connection was made.

'Where are you?' came Pappenheim's voice on the speakers.

'Leaving with a companion.'

'What made you decide?'

'Gut feeling.'

'Just as well. News from Sweden. The peace activist is dead.'

'*What?*' Müller glanced at the console in astonishment.

Greville was staring at the display as if he could actually see Pappenheim.

'No doubt about it,' Pappenheim said. 'Two neat holes through the chest. It will be all over the news tonight.'

'How?'

'The bodyguard did it.'

'You're joking!'

'Nope. They entered the hotel room together, having a friendly conversation, when suddenly the bodyguard pulls a weapon and, pop. Silenced gun. Unfortunately for him, the chambermaid or some other hotel staff member was still in the place. She hid in the bathroom and waited until the bodyguard had gone. He joins up with his mate, and they disappear. It would all have worked out, but for the hotel woman. She reported it to reception and the police went on the hunt. Caught them at the airport. They resisted with gunfire. Both now dead, so no one can question them.'

'Very neat.'

'Impressively so. Our peace man was never intended to arrive here. So, it looks as if your theory was right.'

'More so now.'

'I know there's more.'

153

'I've been seeing things. Helicopters. More frequently than normal. Different ones.'

'A relay chase?'

'Possibly.'

'And acting as beaters for the hunter. Anything you want me to do?'

'No. Then he'll know he's been spotted. That might send him to ground, which means we'd have to start all over again. I want him to come after us.'

'Risk–y,' Pappenheim said.

'Has to be taken.'

'Just don't get yourselves killed.'

'We won't,' Greville said.

'Pleased to meet you, Mr Greville,' Pappenheim said in English. 'I have heard a lot about you.'

'And I know a lot about *you*.'

'All things considered, I am not surprised. You have my respect, sir.'

'I thank you.' Greville glanced at Müller. 'Did you mind?'

'Not at all. Anything else, Pappi?'

'At the moment, no. Oh yes. Kaltendorf came to apologize.'

'He *what*?'

'Tell you about it later, when this is all over.'

'Alright.'

'So, we are now prey,' Greville said when the phone conversation ended.

'It would seem like it.'

'Do you have a spare weapon? I am still very good.'

'Yes, I have. But I'm hoping it won't be necessary.'

'Understood.'

'But if it is, I will give it to you.'

'Fair enough.'

'And if my driving frightens you at anytime . . .'

'It won't. I have observed you in the short time since we started. You are one with the car. I am totally relaxed, old boy. Enjoying the speed.'

Müller smiled at this, and settled down into the fast drive. There were several hours of daylight still left.

He could see no helicopters.

Garadini made the call.

'Where is he?'

'He was spotted heading back.'

'You lost him!'

'We'll soon find him. We have a wide net. Take the next exit and double back.'

Garadini bit back a retort.

It was another ten kilometres before the next exit. That did not please him. He turned off 'The Riddle'.

Despite staying off the Autobahn, Müller made excellent time.

'Decided to give you a present,' Greville said as they were approaching Fulda.

'There is no need . . .'

'Let me enjoy giving it to you, old boy. What do you say?'

'Alright.'

'It's my pride and joy. No need for it anymore. Haven't used it in years, of course. Classic. Austin Healey BN1. Original. The one with the long cranked-over gear lever. Know it?'

'Yes. I do. It certainly is a classic.'

'Worth a mint these days, I suppose. Hardly any mileage since I first got it. Other . . . concerns got in the way, as it were. Bill Jacques looks after it. My letter to him will explain everything when you see him. He sometimes gives it a run. I believe he keeps it in France. Mediterranean climate and all that.'

'You don't have to do this . . .'

'I know I don't. I want you to have it. You'll give it a good home, and give it the use it deserves. Old Bill Jacques treats it like porcelain. Afraid to break it. Not his, you see. Besides, he's not really a sports car man. You are. Can't think of a better home for it. So. Agreed?'

'Agreed,' Müller said, shaking his head slowly in wonder.

'That's the spirit.'

'You'll like where we're going . . .'

'To the Eifel.'

'Yes. But something you'll like, just happens to be a mere two kilometres as the crow flies – give or take a few hundred metres – from the house we're going to.'

'And that is?'

'The Nürburgring.'

'Good Lord. Really? The famous Nordschleife. Always wanted to see that. Other things to do. Life, eh?'

'Life indeed.'

Then their luck ran out.

'We've spotted him!' Garadini heard. 'Near Fulda. Going west. How far are you?'

'Too damned far!'

'Alright. Take it easy. We have an idea where he may be going, even though it's not certain at this stage. Use the motorways as much as you can, try to cut him off near Koblenz. When we're certain, we'll give you new directions.'

'And if he is not heading there?'

'Just do it.'

Garadini fumed as the conversation ended. He had now been driving non-stop for years, it felt.

Frustrated, he put 'The Riddle' back on and began to whistle.

Once past Frankfurt, they were back on the Autobahn network and crossed over to the A61 towards Koblenz. They had stopped only to fill up, and for Greville to visit the toilet.

The Porsche was sweeping along a great curve on the Autobahn.

'The Laacher See is somewhere over to the right, isn't it?' Greville said.

'Yes.' Müller was a little surprised by the question. He glanced at Greville as they sped along. 'You can't see it from here.'

'Long time since I came past these parts,' Greville said, as if in a dream. 'The volcanic Eifel. Craters, lakes, superb landscape, four hundred and eighty or so dormant volcanoes, I believe. I used to imagine what would happen if they all suddenly woke up.'

'I think,' Müller began half-seriously, 'the scene would look like something out of Dante.'

Greville nodded. 'Horrific, and madly beautiful in a dawn-of-creation way. I was talking to an old Arab friend, years ago. He had an interesting perspective on life. One day, he said, the planet will wake up when it's thoroughly fed up with our behaviour, and wipe us all out. Then it will start all over again with a clean slate. He spoke of it as he would a sentient being.'

'How did you answer that?'

'I said the planet need not bother. We'll do the job ourselves.' Greville paused for long moments. 'I had no idea how I would one day come to rue my own prophecy; something I said at the time, with more than a little dry humour.' He paused once more. 'It's started with me.'

Along the A61, they had been baulked by traffic jams caused by roadworks, though Müller had found slots where he could drive at high speed. Listening to what Greville had just said about his own fate, Müller continued to be impressed by the man's calmness.

Up ahead, the traffic had thinned considerably, and he was able to put on a good burst of speed until the Nürburgring exit on the *Bundestrasse* 412.

'Not far now,' he said to Greville. 'The house is on the outskirts of Döttingen. Great countryside.'

It was about thirty kilometres later, nearing their destination, when they rounded a bend and saw the black BMW moving slowly ahead of them.

Greville noted it. 'Lost, do you think?'

Before Müller could answer, the driver seemed to wake up and the car shot off at speed.

'Look for a helicopter!' Müller said urgently.

Greville saw it instantly. 'There! To the right!'

'I'm not going to waste time trying to work out how they've managed to find us,' Müller said as he chased after the BMW. 'The helicopters will have helped; but even so, they must have had a good idea of our intended route in the first place. If it is our hunter, he must have misjudged and thought we were ahead. Now he's trying to get away far enough to lay an ambush. I'm not going to give him the chance.'

The Porsche began to gain on the BMW.

Garadini was fuming.

'*You told me they were ahead!*' he yelled. '*You took me too far!*'

He was not talking to anyone but himself. As soon as he had seen the nose of the Porsche in his mirror, he had realized what had happened. The helicopter relay had called to him, but it had been too late. In fury, he had cut the link.

He was now on his own, able to employ his own tactics as he saw fit. He wanted to extend the distance from the Porsche, so that he had space to act.

As he drove, Garadini began looking for likely places to turn off. He was on an unfamiliar road with sometimes blind corners, and despite its technology, he was not sufficiently at home with the car to handle such a road at the kind of speed he needed.

It was then that he saw a turning to the right. It had a flimsy barrier across it, blocking an opening in a high fence, with a wide road beyond. It looked as if some roadwork was in progress, but no one was there. The road surface itself looked good.

Garadini swung the car and crashed through the barrier, which gave way easily, with hardly a jolt to the BMW. Where were the workers? He turned left and found himself on a road that was remarkably free of traffic.

Was it blocked off somewhere? he wondered.

But the situation pleased him. There was plenty of greenery and woodland for an ambush. If the road really was blocked, so much the better. He would not have to worry about traffic.

Perhaps the long drive had fractionally dulled his instincts, but the man who now called himself Garadini had made a huge blunder.

'I don't believe it!' Müller exclaimed as the Porsche raced after the BMW. 'He's just crashed on to the Nordschleife!'

'What?'

'He's mistaken the racetrack for a road! Now he's really out of his depth; but we've got to catch up with him. There are many places where he can stop to set up an ambush. He's spoilt for choice.'

Müller turned into the entrance to what normally doubled as a car park on Grand Prix race days. The downed barrier gave no problem, and he turned left to follow.

'You wanted to see the Nordschleife, Greville. Now you've got your wish.'

'Not the way I expected, old boy.' But Greville had a grin pasted upon his face.

'There are four sizeable villages within the perimeter of the Nordschleife itself,' Müller said, 'and the main one, Nürburg, is virtually adjacent to one end of the Grand Prix track. Roads run parallel to the Nordschleife in places, and some cross over, and under it, for access to the villages.'

The road Garadini had mistakenly gone on to was the twenty-plus kilometre track itself, and he had entered at the sixteenth kilometre.

Müller powered into the right-hand curve of the Brünnchen, accelerating as he went. The car squatted and launched itself, then settled as he got ready for the following, tighter left-hander into the switchback of the Pflantzgarten.

'What's her top speed?' Greville asked over the furious roar of the engine.

'A little over three hundred and twelve kilometres an hour . . .'

'My word. That's over a hundred and ninety miles per hour! Are we likely to do that?'

'There's a longish straight – about two and a bit kilometres – coming up soon, just after the bend at the nineteenth kilometre – Döttinger-Höhe – but I doubt she'll reach that with two up, despite her slight tuning. We should soon be seeing our hunter in his BMW, if he hasn't yet spun, or rolled himself off. The Nordschleife is notorious for catching the unwary, or the novice going beyond his capabilities.

'Usually,' Müller went on, 'the track is open at special times to private drivers, when there are no other activities. But everything usually ends by seven-thirty. We may see a few of the track staff, marshals and so on; but that depends.'

'On what?'

'How big today's event was . . . assuming there was one. There should also be track-side cameras, so, if we miss our man, we'll still have him on film. I hope.'

Watching as the car rode a tilted bend, Greville said, 'The "Green Hell". Place of history. Always wanted to be here one day.'

Müller glanced at him. 'Yes. It is. If one wishes to be pedantic, the "Hell" is actually the straight itself; but the entire North Loop can punish severely. It's a rollercoaster of a ride. I have the hope that our man in the BMW will make a second error of judgement and save us a lot of trouble. His first was coming on to the track.'

A sweeping right-hander curved towards the eighteenth kilometre, which led into a hairpin bend.

'We're coming into the hairpin,' Müller said. 'The Schwalbenschwanz. There's a right-hand bend after that, then we're into the straight.'

Müller's rapid change of gears was so smooth, Greville looked at him with respect. The car clawed its way round, lateral G forcing them to the right, then it fed itself into the right-hand Galgenkopf, to power up into the straight.

'Döttinger-Höhe,' Müller announced.

'And there he is!' Greville shouted.

The long straight had opened up before them and there in the distance was the BMW.

'Yes. I've got him.'

Greville took a quick glance at the speedometer. The 220kph mark had long been passed and the needle was sweeping further, in an apparently non-stop increase.

They were catching up so rapidly, it was obvious that the BMW had undergone a drastic cut in speed.

Müller eased off, dabbed at the brakes. The ceramic discs were grabbed fiercely by their calipers. The car decelerated as if pulled from behind by a giant claw. The inertia reels got excited and their seat belts went into grab mode, and held them fast against the leather.

'Either he's managed to frighten himself,' Müller remarked, attention fixed upon the car ahead, 'he's up to something, or he's wondering about the road he thinks he's on.'

He changed down, so as to have the power instantly available when he needed it. The car growled its impatience, as if eager to be unleashed.

Suddenly, the BMW was off again, fast receding into the distance.

Müller floored the accelerator and worked his way smoothly through the gears. The Porsche howled forward in an increasing surge. They rocketed past the zero kilometre mark and shot towards the first.

There was the slightest of kinks to the right. Greville glanced dreamily across his right shoulder to the ruined castle of Nürburg perched upon its nearly 700-metre hill.

'Looks as if he wants to do the entire circuit,' Müller said as they came up to the tight little right-hander that would feed into another sweeping bend, which curved past the top end of the Grand Prix circuit.

The BMW was again slowing down.

'What the devil . . . ?' Müller eased off. 'I think he wants us close enough for a shot.' He glanced at the digital timer on the console screen. 'Half an hour of full daylight left . . . at the very least. We should try to get him before it starts to fade.'

Then the black car was suddenly off again.

'He tries for distance,' Müller said, 'to give him time to set up his ambush. When that doesn't work, he then tries to entice us closer. As he did with the policewomen.'

Müller sent the car surging ahead again. Again they began to close the distance rapidly.

'What policewomen?'

'He killed two, earlier today. With one of their own weapons.'

Greville's face creased with a haunted sadness when he heard this. 'If he really is my detached son, I must ask myself whether I did the right thing. Should I perhaps have left him to the mercies of fate? What might he have turned out to be then?'

'You cannot blame yourself. The people who set him on you would still have done so. He is what he is, because he wants to be. He does not have the excuse of a deprived background. I'm going to push him,' Müller continued. 'Give him no room to manoeuvre.'

After the Hocheichen, the rising and plunging sweep of the Quiddelbacher-Höhe opened out before them as Müller chased after the BMW. Again, closure was rapid. This time, the BMW did not slow down; but the driver appeared to have reached his limit of control.

They swept out of Quiddelbacher and into the open bend at the fourth kilometre, and raced the wide sweep towards the tight Aremberg right-hander.

On occasion, the black car would run perilously wide, nearly going off the track, fishtailing slightly to remain on course, and it was in that manner that they went through. On one occasion, they were close enough to see the driver glance at them through his mirror.

'Adenauer-Forst coming up,' Müller said to Greville. 'Mark these places, in case you ever decide to do the track yourself.'

'I'm marking them. Marking something else too,' Greville went on, peering at the greenery and the thick screen of trees which, despite the unusual heat, looked richly lush. 'I can see what you mean about his being spoilt for choice. In this forest, he can pick and choose. Numerous hides for a good sniper with a good rifle. We're out in the open, funnelling our way through what in some circumstances could be an endless ambush position.'

'Are you speaking from experience in some other place?'

'The sniper's? Or the sniped?'

'Both.'

'Both,' Greville said.

'That's lucid enough.'

This nose-to-tail formation continued through towards the ninth kilometre, Müller keeping power in reserve, the BMW driver fighting to stay on the track. Müller kept a safe distance, while remaining close enough to apply a continuous psychological pressure.

The Porsche roared its challenge, hugging the track as it fed itself smoothly through the bends. The track swooped down.

'Wehrseifen,' Müller called, as he changed down to take the tight left-hand bend. 'After this, and just at the next bend, there's an entry point near the village of Breidscheid. He might decide he can go off the track that way. We'll see if he tries to. There should be a gated barrier, and it could be shut. So, perhaps he won't be able to.'

The track continued downwards, and the BMW swept round the bend without pause.

'If he did think of it,' Greville said, 'this could be the reason he did nothing. He would never have made it.'

Just beyond the apex of the left-hand bend, a dashed white line spanned the route of entry which filtered on to the track. It would have been difficult to turn into it, given the speed and the direction of travel. A parked blue car was also blocking it nose on, in front of some high fencing.

The eleventh kilometre; the twelfth. Soon it would be the thirteenth, and into the tight, tight, and tilted hairpin of the Karussell. The man in the BMW had to do something soon.

He did; and that coincided with the return of the helicopter.

Just before the apex of the bend that led into the Karussell itself, a rising, straight section of track filtered to the left, its entry marked by a white line. This short straight joined the two arms of the Karussell to the main loop, between the thirteenth and fifteenth kilometres.

The BMW, entering the bend at speed, suddenly swerved left, almost going out of control as it tried to push the boundaries of the laws of physics. It yawed wildly, swung its tail out, but just managed to scrape through. Luckily, the gated barrier in the fencing was open.

'My God,' Greville said. 'Will you look at that.'

Müller had already hit the brakes and had slowed right down. He pulled over to the left side of the track and on to the grass verge, stopping close to the low track-side barrier.

'We get out here,' he said to Greville, unclipping his belt. 'Can you manage?'

Greville had already freed himself. 'Of course, old boy.'

Müller reached behind Greville's seat to the right-hand occasional seat at the back and lifted it. A special recess was beneath and in it was a big Beretta 92R with spare magazines. He took out the gun and a spare magazine, and handed them to Greville.

'This is the "just in case".'

Greville took the weapon with the ease of one familiar with

their use. 'I see you do like your classics. 92R. Good solid artillery.'

Müller got out and, when Greville had done so, locked the car and pulled out his own gun.

Instinctively, both men crouched down.

Greville raised an eyebrow: '*Two* 92Rs. More of those in there?'

Müller was studying the track – bordered by woods – that the BMW had taken. Over to the right was an open patch of ground with more woods beyond it. Just where the low barrier ended, a footpath ran from the woods on the right side of the track entrance, into the open patch, then curved left to go up the slope. Some fencing went from left to right, starting by the track entrance, near the beginning of the path.

'No,' Müller replied.

He looked up briefly. Twilight was still some time away, but already the promise of a spectacular sunset was there.

'Got more of them, though?' Greville said.

'I used to have three.'

'And now?'

'Four.'

'You *do* like the things. Not standard issue, I'll wager.'

'No.'

'Man after my own heart.'

'Do you hear anything?'

'I don't hear an engine,' Greville answered.

'Exactly. We'll have to flush him out. Sure you can handle it?'

'My dear boy. This evil thing I've got in me isn't debilitating in the normal sense of the word. I am other-wise perfectly healthy and –' he checked the Beretta with consummate expertise – 'I can cope with this piece of artillery quite effectively.' He paused. 'Although, to be quite honest, the thought of killing the son – murderer though he be – as I did the father, does not settle one's stomach.'

'I will understand it if you feel—'

165

'No. No, old boy. Who knows? Perhaps I am arriving at a point in time that is the logical conclusion of what began years ago.' Greville's hovering smile fluttered. 'Who knows indeed.' He looked at the track. 'Go up, shall we?'

'Your white suit . . .'

'Not a problem. If I don't want him to see me . . . he won't.'

'Alright. You take the left side of the track. I'll cut across to that open patch, and move up the right.'

Greville nodded. 'Right you are.' He seemed thoughtful. 'Are you . . .'

'I'm fine. Fine. I was just thinking. Finally got to the Nordschleife. Always wanted to bring the Healey. Never had the time.' Greville glanced at the gun in his hand. 'Now here I am. Strange thing, life.'

Without another word, he stepped over the barrier and began to make his way up through the woods on the left side of the track. He moved with the speed of someone half his age.

Müller darted along the white line that marked the track entrance. He half expected to be shot at; but nothing happened.

Something up the track caught his eye. Staying in cover, he peered upwards. The BMW, broadside on, was an effective roadblock.

Cautiously, he went through and turned right, behind a screen of tall bushes and on to the path. But he did not go far into the open patch of ground. Instead, leaving the path, he made his way upwards, all the while staying within the cover of the screen of bushes on his side of the track.

166

Nine

Greville had made his way upwards until he had reached where the BMW was parked. From cover, he could see it quite clearly. There was no sign of the driver.

Greville then did something that would have astonished and alarmed Müller: he put both gun and magazine beneath a clump of shrubbery. When he withdrew his hands, neither the weapon nor the magazine could be seen. Greville then stood up, brushed down his suit, and strolled out on to the track.

He went up to the BMW and waited, leaning against the bonnet.

Before long, he heard a soft footfall. He did not turn to look.

Then something hard was pressed into the indentation just behind his lower ear.

'Killer of my father!' a voice hissed softly at him in English. 'It is time for my revenge.'

Greville did not move; nor did he say anything.

'Have you nothing to say to me?'

'What would you like me to say?' Greville was calmness itself.

'Do you think I am joking?'

'Certainly not. I never believe someone is joking when he puts a gun against my head.'

'At least you are not a coward.' This was grudgingly said.

'Thank you. Did you come all the way here to kill me? Seems a great deal of effort to me.'

'No. You are my personal kill. The other is professional.'

'The other?'

'The one with the car. The one who is out there now, looking for me. It will be of no use. I will kill him as I have been contracted to do. Pity I cannot take his car. It is a fine, beautiful car, but would be a liability.'

'That is a very pragmatic way of looking at it. Why have you been contracted to kill him?'

'I do not know, and I do not care. It is a job.'

'Have you no feelings for your potential victims?'

'What would that make me? A very poor professional; in every sense. And I am very successful. Did you care when you killed my father?' Keeping his gun firmly on Greville, the man began to search him for a weapon. 'You have no gun.' He sounded very surprised. 'Why?'

'That is a good question, which you should consider carefully.'

'I have not the time to stand here talking with you, so that your friend has the opportunity to surprise me. I will now shoot you as you shot my father. In the back.'

'Was that what they told you, David?'

There was a soft intake of breath in surprise. 'How do you know my name? And it is Daood.'

'I know. It means David in English. You are Daood Hassan, and you were brought up by a family who treated you as their own.'

'How do you know this?' Clearly puzzled, Hassan was trying to assimilate this new information.

Greville did not answer. Instead, he went on, 'You are far too late in your desire to kill me. Your father got there first . . . long before you.'

'My *father*? Are you mad? What are you talking about? My father is *dead*! You killed him!'

'Yes. He is dead. And he killed me on the same day that I killed him. It is just that it is taking me rather longer to die, you see.'

'So, you admit it!'

'Freely. He was doing his job, and I mine. And I did not shoot him in the back. You have been consistently lied to, by those who wished to use you for their own ends. Your father fired first, and hit me. I fired as I fell. Unfortunately, my aim was rather true. Your father behaved with courage and honour.'

Hassan paused for long moments. 'You are not lying,' he said after a while. There was surprise, as well as a question, in his voice. 'But if you are not lying—'

'It means, as I've said, that you have been lied to. You are also being used by those same people to kill Jens Müller, a police officer . . .'

'I am a professional. I honour my contracts.'

'This is no honour, David.'

'Do not talk to me in such a manner. You are not my father!'

'That is true enough.'

'And now, it is time for you to die . . .'

'I don't think so,' came Müller's voice from the bushes. 'If you fire that gun, Hassan, you will be dead an instant later. Put the gun down!'

'So, you were lying!' Hassan said savagely to Greville. 'You kept me talking, with your lies about what happened to my father! You in the bushes! Perhaps you *might* kill me. Perhaps not. But your friend *will* be dead. Will you risk his life?'

'Will you kill the man who has paid for your care since you were a boy?'

Hassan was shocked and did not want to believe it.

'That is another lie!'

'No lie. He arranged for the right family to be found; one that would care for you as one of their own. He calls you his detached son, because he kept that fact from you. He did it when he discovered that your father had been struggling to look after you since your mother died. If I am lying, can you explain how come I know this about you?'

'You could have read about it!'

'Where could I have? What public medium knows about the true circumstances of your father's death? You yourself don't even know. Your father was a guard, in a laboratory. That was the only job he could get. You were twelve when he died. I have the truth from the man you now hold at the point of your gun. How else can you explain how I came to know of it?'

Hassan seemed at a loss.

'The man before you,' Müller went on, pressing the advantage, 'did not want to kill your father. He was defending himself, just as your father was. Two people in the wrong place, at the wrong time. You intend to kill a man who is already dying; a man who gave you your life. Is this how you would repay him?'

'I did not ask him to do it! I did not ask him to kill my father!'

'If that makes you feel better.'

'Who are you to judge me?'

'I am not judging you, Hassan. You are judging yourself.'

'Can I move?' Greville asked suddenly.

'*No!*' Hassan told him sharply.

At that moment, the helicopter arrived overhead.

Startled, Hassan looked up. Greville, moving far swifter than Hassan would have expected, dived for cover. For brief moments, in which time appeared to stand still, Hassan was all by himself; and exposed.

Then something smashed into his chest, flinging him away from the car to fall heavily on to the track. The gun had arced out of his hand, to bounce loudly on the rough surface.

Hassan was not dead, and tried to pick himself up. He was flung back down as another thump was heard, again coming from his chest.

'*Greville!*' Müller called. 'Was that your doing?'

'No! You would have heard that cannon.'

'And you would have heard mine . . .'

'The helicopter!' they both said together.

It was still there, hovering in the golden sunset, low down below the tree tops. A bird of prey in the pre-twilight, on the hunt.

'*Get it!*' Müller shouted.

Greville had retrieved his gun and the magazine. Both he and Müller dashed out of cover at the same time. They pointed their weapons at the helicopter, which was well within range.

Both fired at the same time, in rapid bursts that matched each other. The helicopter was hit by an accurate barrage. The pilot was wounded and the machine seemed to stagger before wheeling in a sickening dive into the trees.

It exploded on impact.

They went to where Hassan was lying in a pool of his own blood.

Hassan's dying eyes looked up at Greville.

'Is . . . is it . . . true?'

Greville nodded slowly. 'Yes. It is.'

'My . . . my . . . father,' Hassan said, barely perceptibly. Then he seemed to pass out.

Müller squatted down and felt for a pulse. He shook his head slowly. 'Sorry.'

Greville took a deep breath, then took his time letting it out. 'Nothing to be sorry about. He was a cold-blooded murderer.'

Müller took a pair of cotton gloves out of a pocket, drew them on and began a swift search of Hassan's body. He found nothing; nothing at all with which to identify the dead man.

'Not really surprising,' Müller said as he got to his feet.

Müller went over to where Hassan's gun had fallen. He did not touch it.

'Makarov,' he commented. 'Interesting choice of weapon.'

'Good gun, that,' Greville said. 'Many of the Russians I met out in the Middle East, and quite a few members of the old DDR, favoured them.'

'I've come up against some who had the same choice. When he said "father",' Müller went on to Greville, 'did he mean you? Or his real father?'

'Who knows? I find no pleasure in it. I have done for the father and now, the son as well.'

'You did not kill him, Greville. The people in the helicopter did. Which raises some interesting questions.'

'I brought him here,' Greville insisted. 'To this place. To die.'

'He was here because he was a professional killer,' Müller corrected.

'To whom I gave life.'

'I'm sorry, Greville . . . but I can't let you take the blame for something that has nothing to do with you. You gave Hassan an opportunity to do what he wanted with his own life. He did with it what he chose.' Müller looked down at the body. 'Only one person truly brought him here.' Müller pointed. 'He did. Wrong place at the wrong time, as you would say.' He looked at the BMW. 'Did you touch it at all?'

Greville shook his head. 'I leaned against it, as you saw. But my hands were never on it.'

'Alright. I'll give it a quick search.'

Müller first went round the car warily, now and then lowering himself to the ground to check beneath it.

'Looking for booby traps?' Greville enquired.

'He did not expect to be killed,' Müller said, 'but you never know. Without a thorough check,' he continued as he straightened, 'hard to tell properly.'

With the gloves still on, he opened the driver's door cautiously.

'You should stand well away,' he warned Greville.

'My dear chap,' Greville said, 'in the first place, I fear not death. In the second, I'd hate to face Isolde by myself, if you should suddenly become a piece of toast.'

Müller looked at him. 'I certainly can't force you.'

'That you can't.'

'Your choice.'

With the door now open, Müller did a rapid search of the interior. The keys were still in the ignition. He left them. In the glove compartment, he found the usual car manual. He took it out, leafed through it, but there was nothing hidden between the pages. He returned it to the compartment.

He checked the back. There was a linen jacket lying across the seats; but that was all. He checked it. Nothing. He placed the jacket back on the seats.

He went to the passenger door and opened that. He checked that side of the car. Nothing. He decided to check the boot.

'If anything is going to blow,' he said, 'it could be triggered by the boot. Still don't want to move?'

'A rock is a reed in the wind by comparison,' Greville replied. 'Decades of living under the sentence radicalizes one's view of things.'

'As you wish.'

Müller went to the boot and opened it gingerly. It rose smoothly. He looked at the usual travel gear of suitcase and folding suiter; then his attention focused on the aluminium case.

'If you're going to be anywhere,' he said to it, 'it's in there.' He drew the case towards him. 'And if anything is booby-trapped, you are the likely candidate.'

With great care, he studied it closely. He could see nothing amiss; but that meant nothing.

He placed his hands on the sliding clasps. 'It's boom, or nothing.'

He snapped the catches and held his breath. There was no boom. He opened the case.

'Well, well, well.'

Foam padding, with cut-out spaces as with a camera case.

But there were no cameras or the usual accessories. Instead, the parts of a sniper rifle and its ammunition nestled there, plus two automatics with their spare magazines. An empty space showed where the Makarov belonged.

'No wonder you killed the officers near Münster,' Müller remarked softly. 'If they had seen this . . .'

'The result would have been the same.' Greville had come closer for a look. 'Elegant set of working tools. Your colleagues were dead the moment they decided to become curious.'

Müller nodded. 'I'm afraid you're right.'

He probed within the foam and felt a smallish rectangular shape beneath. He drew it out. A wallet. He opened it. Credit cards, a driving licence and an EU passport, all in the name of Emilio Garadini. Plenty of cash in a zipped compartment; hundred-Euro notes, all German.

'So, that's where you kept it,' Müller said.

He shut and replaced the wallet, closed the case and took it out of the boot, which he then shut.

Greville moved away to stand near Hassan's body. He looked down at it with an unfathomable expression.

Leaving Greville by the body, Müller, carrying the case, moved a short distance, got out his mobile and called Pappenheim.

'I've been calling the car,' Pappenheim said immediately. 'But it didn't answer.'

'That could be because we were busy shooting down helicopters.'

'Helicopters? *"We"?*'

Müller began to give him a quick rundown of events.

'You got him!' Pappenheim interrupted when Müller had got to the part about Hassan's death.

'Strictly speaking . . . no.'

'What does "no" mean? Exactly?'

'The helicopter did it. Then we got the helicopter.'

'So, the returnee still has the touch?'

'He's damned good, all things considered. No wonder he was so successful.'

'But why did they shoot their own man?' Pappenheim asked.

'Failure has a high price with these people. Hassan failed to get us, and they did not want him taken, under any circumstances.'

'He might have said too much.'

'Precisely.'

'Found anything?'

'Some.'

Pappenheim immediately understood Müller's reluctance to say more on the phone.

'I'll wait till you get back,' the *Oberkommissar* said quickly, 'for the rest of the news. Then you can also tell me all about racing on the Nordschleife. Anything I can do from here?'

'Yes – please. Sort things out with the locals. Hassan's body is lying by the car he was using, a new BMW 645 coupé . . .'

'Very nice. Ours to impound, I think. I have a feeling his former employers won't want to reclaim it, on the grounds that it might incriminate them. On the other hand . . .'

'They might,' Müller finished. 'Things in, or on it, that might incriminate them even more. We can do a proper check later. In the meantime, warn the locals to do a thorough booby-trap check before anyone attempts to move it, just in case.'

'Will do.'

'Sort out anything else, as you wish. We've been here long enough and I want to sneak out without having to talk with anybody. The helicopter will already have sent people swarming to the crash site. We don't need the publicity.'

'I'll get on to it as soon as we're done. I know someone . . .'

'Even out here. Why am I not surprised?'

'Dunno. So,' Pappenheim went on quickly before Müller

could respond, 'one takes it you're remaining in the area for the night?'

'One can take it as being so.'

'Nice rhythm of speech, that.'

'Pappi . . .'

'On my way,' Pappenheim said hastily.

When the conversation ended, Müller turned to see Greville still looking down at the body.

Müller went back to him. 'Come on, Greville,' he said gently. 'Let's leave this place.'

Müller kept the case as they went back down to the car. Greville started to hand over the Beretta and the spare magazine.

'Keep them with you tonight,' Müller said. 'Just in case.'

'You expect visitors?'

'I expect the expected . . . and the unexpected.'

'Nicely put.'

Müller put the aluminium case into the luggage compartment. He had to juggle with Greville's bag and his father's briefcase but, in the end, everything fitted snugly. Then he removed the gloves and put them back into his pocket.

From their position at the start of the Karussell, it was just three kilometres to their original point of entry.

A forensics team in their vehicles, accompanied by a patrol car, all flashing their lights, were already coming through as they got there. Another patrol car was stationed at the gate, on guard. The forensics convoy went off in the 'wrong' direction, the quickest way to get to Hassan's body.

The policemen at the gate, clearly forewarned, waved the Porsche through. They eyed it with both admiration and envy.

'I am glad I was not the one to shoot him,' Greville said as Müller turned on to the B412 in the direction of Döttingen. 'I think wiping out the male line like that would have been . . .' He let his words fade.

'If you discover that Hassan had children, would you do the same as you have done with him?'

Greville shook his head and said nothing. His eyes went back to the far distance that only he could see.

Over to the right, within the woods, the black pall from the crashed helicopter was a dark, billowing cloud on the backdrop of the sunset sky.

The house on the edge of Döttingen was substantial, beautifully appointed, and surrounded by its own gated and fenced grounds, bordered by tall trees.

Of classic two-storey design, the house sported a columned portico on adjacent pale cream walls, and looked out upon a beautiful panorama of the Eifel. On the top floor, a wide balcony was the most perfect of vantage points. There was garaging for three cars, plus a generous parking area.

A long drive snaked its way across the well-kept grounds to a small road which, a bare two kilometres later, fed itself on to the *Bundestrasse* 258, and into Döttingen itself. When Müller had said the house was close to the Nürburgring, he had not exaggerated.

The drive curved through the larger of the porticoes.

'My word,' Greville said as they pulled up before the main door, directly beneath the portico. 'This is a beautiful pile. It does not rival Isolde's place, of course. But it is still pleasant to look upon. Classic. Tasteful.'

'There's a large pond at the back too,' Müller informed him. 'Natural, and clean.'

'All the comforts of home.'

They climbed out, to find Frau Holz waiting. She had gone to the house to air it, and to ensure there were stocks of food and the beds were made; but she had done more than that.

A solid woman with abundant greying hair tied in a bun and a healthy, open face, she greeted them effusively, coming out of the house to meet them outside. She actually curtsied to Müller. Her small car was parked nearby.

177

'Herr Graf! So nice to see you again!'

They shook hands.

Müller introduced Greville. 'The Honourable Tim Greville.'

Frau Holz could not help it. She gave a brief little bob, and blushed as she shook hands with Greville.

'Did you hear about that helicopter?' she said to Müller, still blushing.

'We did. Yes.'

'Terrible! Those poor people in it.'

Müller did not look at Greville, who had moved a short distance to study the house with his usual hovering smile in place. Every so often, he would turn to admire the view, then back to continue his study of the building.

'I agree,' Müller said to Frau Holz. 'Quite terrible.'

She sighed. 'Terrible, terrible.' She paused, giving a few seconds to the memory of those in the crash. 'Well, everything's ready.' She handed him just the one key. 'As you know, all the main doors have a keypad. And you know about the alarm. The key is for the key cupboard, which holds all the other keys for the house. You know where it is.'

'I do,' Müller said, taking the key. 'Thank you, Frau Holz.'

'And,' she went on, 'I have prepared a little something. I hope you will like it.'

'Frau Holz, you really shouldn't have . . .'

'It was no problem at all. Some fish, and there is a nice Gewürztraminer in the fridge. I hope you both like fish?' She was looking at Greville.

Greville doffed his hat to her. 'My dear lady,' he said in German, 'I simply adore fish, and I am most grateful to you.'

Not quite certain how to react, Frau Holz blushed again. She looked at Müller, as if to hang on to him. 'Will . . . will you be able to manage, Herr Graf? I can—'

'No, no, Frau Holz. We'll be quite fine. You have done more than enough, for which, thank you. No need to trouble yourself. We'll simply enjoy your cooking, the sunset and this wonderful place.'

'Very well, sir. I have left the oven on low. Everything is quite ready. Oh . . . I still have the picture.'

'Picture?' Müller wondered what she was talking about.

'The picture of me with the baby, and with you, the godfather. It was a picture the *Gräfin* took on my birthday. They put it in the local papers.'

She smiled happily at the memory.

Müller remembered. A birthday celebration had been organized for Frau Holz by Jutta von Gersch, because it had been her fiftieth. Many shots had been taken. The one with Müller and the baby had made it into a few local papers.

'Of course,' Müller said to her. 'I do remember. I looked rather stern.'

'No, you did not, Herr Graf. My friends were jealous.' She smiled at him once more, pleased that her friends had been jealous of her. 'If you're sure everything will be alright . . .'

'No need to worry, Frau Holz. All will be fine.'

'Then I'll be going.'

'Yes. And thank you again.'

She gave another little bob. 'Herr Graf, Herr Honourable,' she added to Greville, and went to her car.

They followed, waiting until she had got in and, with a little wave to them, driven away.

'That's how they knew!' Müller said to Greville, watching as the car made its way down the drive. He explained about the birthday.

'Low-level intelligence,' Greville said. 'From my own experience, I can tell you that an amazing amount of information comes via that route. Sometimes it beats intel gathered by more . . . er . . . strenuous means, hands down. As in this case. The people who employed Hassan would have done their homework thoroughly. Every little item about you will have been collated.

'They assumed you would perhaps come to this house, and planned for the eventuality. If you didn't, too bad. But if you did . . . ah, well. Hassan, and the helicopter, found us. Good intelligence never overlooks anything. Never know what might be of use. These people are very, very good, old boy. Never underestimate them. Today's little setback will not be the end of it. They will keep trying; over months, years even. You must get them, or they will get you.'

Müller nodded. 'That's how I see it.' He continued to watch Frau Holz's car until it had disappeared. 'Let's get our bags.'

They entered the house, Greville with his bag, Müller carrying his father's briefcase, and Hassan's case.

Greville looked about him admiringly. 'Very well appointed. Don't wish to be ungracious, old man. The Derrenberg still takes my vote. But this is quite lovely.'

'No need to apologize. The Derrenberg is my home too.'

'So it is. So it is. And where are you putting me?'

'Let's go up. I'll show you. We've got adjoining suites, with Eifel views.'

'Suites!' Greville exclaimed. 'Of course,' he went on, as if he should have known. 'Only to be expected.'

Müller gave him a sideways glance, but said nothing.

They went up a wide, winding staircase to the top floor. A large, horseshoe landing led off to several rooms, one of which was a sitting room that looked out on to the balcony. The other rooms were bedroom suites.

When they got to the landing, Müller pointed to a pale-blue door. 'Blue door, yours. White door, mine. Green door over there is the balcony room. First, Frau Holz's dinner, then in there to relax and inspect Hassan's little treasure.'

'Five minutes to dinner?'

'Five it is.'

Frau Holz's roast fish drew a sound of delighted approval from Müller when he took it out of the oven.

'One of my favourites!' he said. 'Roast monkfish in a

180

provençal crust. The Gewürztraminer will most certainly go well with it. Greville? Do you like this?'

'Try and stop me, dear boy. Try and stop me.'

To have said they enjoyed Frau Holz's cooking would have been an understatement. They polished it off and taking the unfinished bottle to the balcony room, turned their attention to Hassan's case.

Müller, again wearing his cotton gloves, put it on a low wide table and opened it.

'Hello, my beauty,' he said to the gleaming sections within. 'Dragunov, but very specially made. Bespoke.'

Greville stared at the weapon, and the two Makarov pistols with it. 'Recognize it, do you? And he likes Makarovs as you do Berettas.'

'I recognize the type. We have got one of its cousins in Berlin, confiscated last year from the kind of person Hassan may never have met, but who almost certainly worked for the same people.'

'They have a taste for the champion – in my humble book – of sniper weapons. Nothing but the best. Are you going to put it together?'

Müller shook his head. 'No. But I am going to see if there are any identifying marks or numbers.'

Though the sun had gone down, the sky was still aflame with its passing. There was a bright kind of twilight; but, within the room itself, there was not enough light for a proper study of the weapon.

A mother-and-child lamp with a dimmer switch stood in a corner of the room. Müller brought it closer, then slid the dimmer switch to bright. The smaller lamp gave a bright spot that was perfect illumination for scrutiny of the rifle. He took out each section and checked it closely. He checked every piece, including the scope and its own accessories. None exhibited any distinguishing marks.

'*Nothing?*' Greville asked.

'Not even a disfiguring scratch.'

181

'Virginal sniper's rifle,' said Greville. 'A killer virgin.' He gave a tiny smile at his joke. 'And you are certainly correct. It is a bespoke weapon. David had the money, and the influence, to get something like that done.'

'Or he knew someone with the influence.'

'Indeed.'

'In your long experience, have you heard of anyone like that?'

'There are many practitioners of the art, of course. As in every form of human endeavour . . . almost. But this . . .' Greville paused, eyes partially closed, head slightly thrown back. He brought his head forward again. 'This is a piece of the master's art. There can't be many of those around. This means, to those who know, it is recognizable. Problem is, such a person would neither be residing in, nor known in the West. He could easily be living in a mountain village somewhere well east of the Caucasus. I recognize the work of a master, but not the master himself.'

Greville pursed his lips and looked at the beautiful weapon with something close to revulsion.

Müller noted the expression.

'Don't mind the way I look at the moment, old man,' Greville said. 'It's not the rifle making me squeamish. I've done some sniping in my time. It's the fact that I am responsible for—'

'I won't hear it,' Müller interrupted firmly. 'You, Greville, are *not* responsible. Daood Hassan, your detached son, chose his own road. You did not put him on it.'

'That's as may be. But I did deprive him of his father, and that sits badly. Line of duty, accident, twist of fate . . . call it what you will. I have reasoned this out over the years, and have used the same arguments you have. Makes it no easier.'

'I never said it did. But, as you have yourself said, his father gave you the sentence you now carry. And you have done all you can for the son. The son's choices have nothing to do with you.' Müller pointed to the sections of Dragunov. 'The man who went to the trouble of having this made took pride in his work. Hunting people.'

Müller now took out the wallet and began to probe beneath the foam padding. After a while, it lifted out cleanly to betray what was clearly a lid, the full internal width of the case. There was a small hole near one edge.

'Will you look at that,' Greville uttered softly. 'A false bottom.'

'If that hole is for a key, where is it?'

'Try the wallet. You never know.'

Müller took everything out. Nothing.

'False bottom,' he said to himself. 'Perhaps false lining?' He felt the empty wallet for unevenness. Something was definitely there. Closer inspection showed a barely perceptible slot in the back. He prised it open and turned the wallet so that the mouth of the slot pointed downwards. A tiny, hollow key fell out.

'Eureka!' Greville said.

Müller gently pushed the key through the hole. Something clicked and the lid sprang open for a few millimetres, giving sufficient room for leverage. He lifted it to discover neatly packed cleaning materials for the rifle.

He took those out and saw more neat packing; this time, it was large denomination Euro notes.

Greville whistled softly. 'Thousands?'

'Tens of. At the very least. Genuine too. He certainly had the money.'

Müller kept looking, and found the last item. A large envelope. He took it out slowly and placed it on the table.

'Photographs in there,' Greville said.

'I am almost afraid to look,' Müller said.

He stared at the envelope for long moments, then with a sudden movement opened the flap and shook out the contents.

They were indeed photographs. And they shocked him.

His own face stared back at him from the first. The next was of Greville, but taken somewhere in the Middle East. There were three more. One was of a well-known politician; well known because of his vociferous support for a united Europe, not because of his political stature. Another was of a sportswoman known to be against whaling.

The third was of Carey Bloomfield.

'*Carey!*' Müller exclaimed.

'*Captain Bloomfield!*' Greville said.

Both had spoken together.

Müller and Greville stared at each other.

'*You know her?*' both again said together.

'You first,' Müller said.

'As I told you earlier,' Greville began, 'I knew of her brother, though I never met him. After the rescue attempt, she was pointed out to me. We never actually met. I think she had something to do with it.'

'She did. She led the rescue attempt, against orders.'

'Guts.'

'She has plenty. She's a major now.'

'Promotion, despite a maverick streak. She must be good. And how did you two come to meet?'

Müller gave a rueful smile. 'Would you believe she was sent to shadow me? Posing as a journalist.'

'Always a good one. On account of?'

'Dahlberg. She came to me because those who sent her actually thought I could lead them to Dahlberg.'

'Ah. The cousin connection.'

'That and the fact—'

'That they knew about his involvement with what happened to your parents.'

Müller nodded, face now grim. 'Which, of course, I knew nothing about at the time . . . not even at the time we both shot him.'

'The help you mentioned,' Greville said, understanding.

'Yes. But she disobeyed orders again. She was under

184

orders to take him alive. She, however, wanted to kill him.'

'For her brother.'

'Exactly. I wanted to arrest him. In the end, he still finished up dead, with my bullets and hers in him. The irony of it is, it was he who got me involved, for his own reasons.'

'Reasons that go far beyond Dahlberg,' Greville said, 'as you now know.'

Müller began putting the photographs back into the envelope. He did this with great care; almost with reverence.

'As I do know,' he said, not looking up.

A silence descended.

'Strange being a target for one's own son,' Greville broke the stillness to say. His voice was hushed, as if in a church. 'Even a detached one.'

'How do you feel, now that you've seen this?'

Greville briefly stroked his nose. 'Sad. That's the best way I can find to describe it.'

Müller put everything back into the case, exactly as it had been, and shut it. He dimmed the lamp, and moved it back to its original place.

'But why Carey Bloomfield?' he now asked.

'The Dahlberg connection?' Greville suggested. 'You both got him. They would not have liked that. He was one of their best. They have other interests in you, of course. But for Miss Bloomfield . . .'

Müller shook his head. 'It has to be another reason. Dahlberg had become a privateer, short on scruples and allegiance.'

Greville gave that some thought for a moment. 'Quite possibly; but even people like Dahlberg like to wield power. Despite his outward disdain, he loved it, and would go where he would be most likely to attain it. Here's a wild guess. Does Miss Bloomfield happen to be the gel you're keen on?'

Müller shot him a glance. '"Keen on"?'

'Defensive, old man! Hit the button, I think. So, it is she. Then we do have a reason.'

'Which is?'

'Perhaps because they know it would hurt you.'

Greville was only partially wrong.

'There's more to it,' Müller said. 'I am certain. And, as with my parents, I will find out.'

Two people on the phone – one in Berlin, the other in another country. Theirs was a highly secure transmission.

'Hassan is down,' the first said. 'We had to do it. He had failed.'

'Fuck!' said the other. Those who thought they knew him would never have imagined that he would ever utter that word. 'What other damage?' He was the same man who had spoken to the man with the two rings.

'We also lost a helicopter, and the two people in it.'

'*Fuck!*'

'We're not very happy either.'

'How much do you really think he knows?'

'Hard to tell at this stage. He does not act as if he knows anything immediately inimical to our interests.'

'You said as much before. And in the long term?'

'He's a policeman. A good one. I also said that. He ferrets. Who knows what he might turn up?'

'So, you recommend a continuation?'

'There is no other way. We remove our presence in his life for a while. Give him time to relax, lower his guard. Then we hit him again. We keep up the procedure. He has many vulnerable points that can be attacked: people he cares for. Many to choose from. Of all ages.'

'It's becoming expensive.'

'Not as expensive as it will be . . . if he ever manages to find out. He will still be monitored, and we will still have our eyes and ears in his unit. He is not being let off the hook.'

'Then I'll abide by your advice.'

'It is good advice. It is also a matter of survival. One, versus the many. The outcome is not in question.'

There was a moment of silence.

'I agree. But this has not been a good day for us.'

'It's been a hot one.'

The conversation ended.

Pappenheim was in the rogues' gallery, looking through some old newspapers. Some were spread on the white-topped table, others were still in their drawers, in a cabinet directly opposite the one into which he had put the documents about Romeo Six, Neubauer and Hassan.

The papers went back several years. The one he was currently studying was about Aunt Isolde. There was a younger picture of her, standing by the then derelict shell of the Derrenberg. *Former activist Baroness inherits her ruin*, ran the headline of the article. The article itself was very detailed. It even mentioned that Aunt Isolde had brought up her nephew, due to the death of his parents when he was twelve.

'All there for anyone who wants to look,' Pappenheim murmured. 'And they certainly would. They would expect the place to be one of his havens.'

Another article, this time in a more contemporary, glossy magazine about a year old and in the same lifestyle vein, was about the von Gersch family and their country house in the Eifel. Excellent photographs showed their new baby and the distinctive house. There was also a picture of Müller, stating he was the child's godfather.

'So easy,' he said. 'So damned easy. Just a simple trawl and all you need to know is right there before your eyes. Everything with open access is a possible mine of information.'

He folded the paper, shut the magazine, and put them next to a pile he had already stacked. Each of them contained something about Müller, and the people around him. Even police magazines went into the selected pile. He worked at this assiduously. The pile continued to grow.

He looked at another pile he had previously selected. This one was more sensitive. Every magazine, broadsheet and tabloid in there had, as its main feature, one particular subject: the air crash that had killed Müller's parents.

Pappenheim was looking for anomalies that would have been missed, or ignored, all those years ago.

He opened a broadsheet at the centre spread. Directly opposite an article on Iran's demand for $150 billion war reparations from Iraq, and their pledge of continuing war until Hussein stood trial, there was a headline about the crash, followed by the article itself.

Tragedy in the High Alps
Society couple missing

One of Germany's most successful young couples may have lost their lives today in a tragic air accident when their private aircraft, piloted by themselves, crashed into a high rock wall near Grenoble. No reasons for the crash have as yet been given. Rescuers and air-accident investigators are on their way to the crash site, which is difficult to reach; but, unofficially, it is being admitted that there is little hope of finding survivors. They leave a young son, Jens, aged twelve.

Pappenheim read on silently, eyes gripped by the picture of the twelve-year-old Müller, taken before the tragedy, smiling into the camera. He imagined what had happened to that smile when the terrible news had come.

'Your world must have come apart then,' he said quietly to the picture.

The article went on to talk about a bishop, a family friend, who was on hand to give the boy spiritual guidance. There was a photograph of the bishop.

Pappenheim read on, but could find nothing to alert him.

188

He moved to another paper. This was dated a week after the crash and already the speculation had begun. Suicide was being hinted at.

In his contempt for the prurient slavering he could imagine had soon followed, Pappenheim skimmed through the remainder of the article, and almost missed it. He had to go back to double-check. And there it was.

Polizeikommissar Neubauer, who knew the couple, said it was the most terrible of tragedies, particularly so for the young son . . .'

'Yeah,' Pappenheim commented with a grim stare at the page. 'Bet you were sorry. Who would suspect a policeman? Even way back then, you were a shit.'

He took a yellow marker pen from a pocket, and highlighted the section on Neubauer. Then he decided to mark the bishop as well.

He continued with his search. It was not until three weeks after the crash that the flight recorders were found.

The flight recorders were found a great distance from the point of impact, Pappenheim read.

> *Experts suggest that the abnormal distance was quite likely due to the force of the explosion after impact, resulting in the wide scatter of pieces of the aircraft. As yet, no properly identifiable body parts have been found, though several pieces of charred remains have been collected. Investigators insist that it will take several weeks before any useful information can be extracted from the flight recorders.*

By now, the hints about marital problems had become certainties. The husband was known, it seemed, as a secret womanizer. People came out of the woodwork for their share of the limelight, and to make claims of having witnessed examples of the 'womanizing'. There was also a hint of drug-taking, for good measure.

It wasn't long before someone wrote a self-righteous article about the 'idle rich', and 'titled jet-setters with the morals of alley cats'.

It got considerably worse. Judgement had been passed. The betrayed wife had killed them both by deliberately crashing the aircraft.

'My God,' Pappenheim muttered, 'and all pouring into the ears of a grieving boy.'

It was in a tabloid from six months after the crash that Pappenheim found something that excited his interest. The flight recorders were still mysteriously unable to give up their secrets.

'Very strange,' he said as he marked the section. 'The extraction technology was not that bad in 1982.'

Two weeks later, in an aviation magazine, the flight recorders had suddenly begun to spill the beans. The voice of Müller's mother could be heard screaming the insults of a wronged woman at her husband, the journalist had written, as she held the aircraft in a steep dive, and she had somehow managed to prevent him from correcting in time.

Pappenheim shook his head slowly, as he again used the marker pen. In another aviation magazine, he found a photograph. This time it was of Neubauer, the bishop, and a man Pappenheim had so far never seen in any of the photographs about the incident. He marked a border around the man, for future reference.

'You seem not to want to be in the picture,' Pappenheim murmured. 'I wonder why.' He decided it was time to stop for now. 'I need a smoke.'

Ten

In Döttingen, Müller and Greville sat on the wide top-floor balcony, with its great view across the Eifel. They had watched the fading of the violent colours of a sunset that had seemed to have been painted across the sky, then had gone back into the balcony room.

Müller had made coffee, and had found some brandy to go with it.

'Can you handle brandy?' he now asked.

'I can handle anything,' Greville said. 'Any food I choose to eat. Any drink. That is the devilish beauty of that stuff inside of me. It reacts to nothing. It is so busy doing its foul work, it appears to have no time for anything else. So, yes, I can have as normal a life as can be had . . . with the single exception you know about. Strange feeling, knowing that. The last of your personal line. There's such a terrible finality about it.'

Greville looked into the golden fire of the brandy and seemed to see something in there.

Then he roused himself. 'I . . .'

He stopped. Müller had raised a warning finger.

'Our visitors,' he said in a low voice. 'Where's your gun?'

'Right here,' Greville replied just as quietly, picking it up from the chair next to him.

'Reloaded?'

'Absolutely.' Greville said that in a way that seemed to consider the question unnecessary.

191

'Sorry. Should have expected it.'

'Apology accepted, old boy.'

Müller's own Beretta was in its holster, which was hanging from the back of his chair. He drew it out in an unhurried movement.

'Are they inside? Or out?' Greville asked.

'They're coming in. Someone's feet crunched under the portico. I'll have to apologize later to Jutta, for the mess, and make good any breakages.' Müller smiled.

'I think you're enjoying this,' Greville said. 'I know I am.'

'I'm not sure "enjoy" is the right word. Pappi calls it blood on the tongue.'

'I've heard of that term. If he says that of you, you're a dangerous man, *Hauptkommissar* Müller.' Greville said that with his hovering smile. 'But it's necessary in your line of work.'

Then they made no further effort to be silent. Greville talked loudly, in a very English voice.

'So, tell me about that mysterious gel you would not talk about all evening, but about whom I know you're thinking.'

Müller pointed to a door. 'Nothing much to say.'

Greville nodded.

'Come now, old boy. There is *always* something to say about a fine young damsel. I used to wax lyrical about Isolde. Still do.'

Müller motioned to Greville to duck to one side when the door opened, while he went the other way.

Again, Greville nodded.

'I remember once, I was sitting in a tea house in the Port of Aden—'

The door was slammed open. Two men stood there, sub-machine guns pointing at the table.

But Müller and Greville had already moved well out of the line of fire. The men had to readjust their aim. It was already far too late. The two Berettas were unerringly zeroed on target.

'You have two options,' Müller told them in English. 'Put down your weapons, or take your chances. And don't make the mistake of misjudging the major over there, just in case you think he looks a little old for it.'

'Steady on, old boy,' Greville objected. 'Not so much of the old.'

The men understood. It was in their eyes. One was the baby-faced man, and the other his stocky companion, both of whom Kaltendorf had been so quick to release.

'You wanted to see me again so badly?' Müller said to the baby-face. 'Rorsch, isn't it? Or are you using another name for tonight's work?'

Time went into its bizarre stretch, as all four waited to see what would happen next.

It was the stocky one who moved first. He raised his weapon high in one hand, the other also went up.

'To hell with it,' he said in English with an accent neither English nor American, nor German. 'I'm not getting killed for this.'

Rorsch looked at him. '*What?*'

That was when the stocky man moved again. He dived to one side, grabbing at his weapon.

He had badly misjudged it.

Greville fired twice, catching him in mid-spring. He gave a strange grunt and fell heavily. The gun skidded away from his twitching hand. Greville kept his gun pointed at the man on the floor.

Rorsch froze.

Müller gave him a cold stare. 'What's it to be, Rorsch? Your friend made a bad mistake. He thought he had distracted us. This is your last chance.'

The man on the floor did not move.

'I won't talk,' Rorsch said with a tiny smile.

'Afraid?'

'Smart. As you should be. You can't win.'

'What can't I win?'

Rorsch suddenly rediscovered the joys of silence. He still held on to his gun.

'The gun,' Müller reminded him. 'On the floor.'

But Rorsch seemed to be weighing his chances.

'Don't be a fool, man,' Greville said. 'You won't stand a chance. Your partner is dead. I never miss. Never have.'

As if coming to a momentous decision, Rorsch turned the barrel of his gun upwards.

'Fine. But it won't get you anywhere.'

While Greville covered him, Müller went over to take the gun from Rorsch. It was another Calico. Müller handed the weapon to Greville.

Greville looked at it. 'Calico. Saw someone use one of these. What did you come here to do?' he asked of Rorsch. 'To kill? Or to make shepherd's pie?'

Rorsch made no reply, and obligingly put his hands behind his back to be cuffed. He kept his smile.

Müller pulled a chair a little way from the table, and indicated that Rorsch should sit down.

Rorsch did so, still smiling. 'You really have no idea what you're dealing with, do you?'

'I thought you were not going to talk.'

'Not to say anything that would be of much use to you. But advice is something different. You should listen.'

'We left the place wide open for you,' Müller said, 'and you walked right in. But thanks for the advice.' He looked at the man on the floor. 'Is he really dead?' he asked Greville.

'I'm afraid so. Never trained to wound, old boy. Every shot, killing shot.'

Müller nodded towards Rorsch. 'Watch him.'

'Like a hawk,' Greville said.

Carrying his gun, Müller went out of the room to call Pappenheim.

*   *   *

194

Pappenheim returned to his office. His self-appointed task, he reasoned, was an ongoing probe which would take some time; certainly weeks, at the very least. And besides, the smoke-free zone of the rogues' gallery had stretched his abstinence to the limit.

'But I'll do some more tonight,' he said to himself.

He had barely sat down and was in the process of lighting up his much-craved-for cigarette, when the phone rang. He completed the lighting of his habit stick, took a grateful draw, and picked up at the fourth ring.

'Pappi,' he heard. 'Do you ever leave that office?'

'Why, Miss Colonel! Glad to hear from you.'

'You might not be so pleased when you hear what I've got to say,' Carey Bloomfield said.

Pappenheim blew a rich cloud at the ceiling. 'You never know. Try me.'

'I can't make it.'

'But?'

'I have an idea.'

'I am always open to ideas.'

'I can make it in July. If you think about it,' she rushed on, as if fearing he would object, 'it's now nearly the end of May. I can come over in early July. Very early. Between now and then, it's only just over a month. And I'll have greater room to manoeuvre.'

'It sounds like a good idea to me.'

'That's a relief.'

'Am I that much of an ogre?'

'You are many things, Pappi . . . but never an ogre.'

'Such nice things, Colonel.'

'And Pappi . . . is . . . is he OK?'

'He's fine.'

'And the trouble?'

'When you come over.'

'Look after him, Pappi.'

'Your wish, as ever, is my command.'

They hung up together.

Pappenheim tapped the phone reflectively. 'Nice woman.' He smiled to himself. 'Who ever thought I would one day say that about Carey Bloomfield?'

He was still smiling when the phone Müller always called rang. This time Pappenheim grabbed it at the first ring.

'Let me guess,' he began. 'The Great White somehow found out where you are . . .'

'You're clairvoyant.'

'Now I know I'm not.'

'And why are you still in the office?'

'Why are you calling me then?'

'No answer to that. Talking of the Great White . . .'

'So, I am clairvoyant . . .'

'Only by indirect association.'

'"Indirect association"! Oh me, oh my . . .'

'We've got one dead fish, and one handcuffed.'

Pappenheim got serious. 'Who?'

'That's your indirect association. Two of those the GW let off earlier today.'

'As I know this is not a joke, which ones?'

'Rorsch, and his rock-like partner. The rock is the dead one.'

'What happened?'

Müller told him.

Pappenheim smoked furiously as he listened. This agitated smoking was one of the signs of a build-up of anger within him.

'The damned idiot!' Pappenheim said angrily when Müller had finished. 'He lets them out, and this happens. I am glad he is not here. Your cordial chat with him earlier would have been a prostitute's laughter by comparison. And here I am thinking he had discovered some decency, hiding deep somewhere. This is crass . . .'

'Pappi!'

'OK. OK. But that man is an idiot.' Pappenheim, unrepentant, took a brief pause. 'So? What would you like done?'

'Get the locals again, I'm afraid. Usual stuff, and a room for Rorsch for the night. Better yet, if you can get him and his dead pal shipped to Berlin immediately, even better. Hassan's body as well. Interesting to see if anyone decides to stake a claim to them.'

'I'd lay any bet no one will, despite the manic rush to get them out of here earlier.'

'You'll get no takers. Their usefulness is over.'

'Such nice people.'

'That's the brave new world they're planning.'

Pappenheim gave a worldly-wise sigh. 'Never learn, do they?'

'And never will. And tell our local colleagues, no fuss when they come to collect. No flashing lights, no noise . . .'

'Got it. I'll get our colleagues over as soon as possible.'

'Thanks, Pappi. What a day, eh?'

'It was something. Back tomorrow?'

'Tomorrow is another day.'

'So they tell me.'

'Break a leg.'

'You too.'

Pappenheim put the phone down and leaned back in his chair. He decided he would say nothing about Carey Bloomfield for now, nor mention the research he was carrying out in the rogues' gallery.

He blew a series of smoke rings at the ceiling, then picked up the phone to call his Eifel colleagues.

Berlin, local call.

'Bad news.'

'I'm waiting.'

'One down, one taken.'

'And their casualties?'

197

'None.'

A string of expletives followed. 'Who's down?'

'The short one.'

'Idiot!'

'Where are they taking them?'

'The local boys will be collecting; the live, and the dead.'

'Berlin might try to have them shipped tonight. There must be no risk of his talking. Are we able to mount an intercept at short notice?'

'It all depends on the timing, and the available intelligence. We need to know when they will be shipped.'

'Call back in five minutes.'

Berlin, five minutes later. Local call.

'What do you have?'

'You have thirty minutes to get a helicopter into the air for an intercept. They're moving them, including Hassan's body, by helicopter to Cologne/Bonn, for the flight to Berlin. I'll give you the route. Can you do it?'

'All I need to do is phone.'

'Here are the route co-ordinates.' The information was passed. 'Got that?'

'Got it.'

'Remember, they are not to make it to their destination. And it must be done before they can make an emergency call. You will have to be quick about it.'

'That won't be a problem. What about the flight recorders?'

'You leave that to us. Now, do it!'

Pappenheim had been as good as his word.

The local police arrived in record time, without fanfare, and spoke only when absolutely necessary. They were quick and efficient. Rorsch's dead companion was put in a standard scene-of-incident casket and taken out. Then it was Rorsch's turn to be led away.

As he was being taken out of the room, he turned to look at Müller. 'You're going to have a lot of grief.' His infuriating smile was still glued to his face.

The escorting policeman gave him an ungentle pull, and Rorsch stumbled. The smile remained.

The *Kommissar* in charge, Michael Hof, a tall, very thin man with cropped grey-streaked hair and eyes that looked softer than they really were, came up to Müller.

'Well, that seems to be it.' His voice was as soft as his eyes pretended to be. He glanced at Greville. 'I'd better not ask questions.' It was a statement, as well as a query.

Müller gave a fleeting smile. 'I'm certain what needs to be said . . .'

'Will be told to me by my boss if he feels I should know. I think I get the picture.' Hof took it in his stride.

'Sorry,' Müller said, 'but I can't tell you more.'

Hof nodded. 'I've been there.' He looked around the room. 'Very nice place. No damage, no bullet holes. Good shooting.' He gave Greville a fleeting glance.

Greville watched him with the hovering smile in place.

Hof looked at the two sub-machine guns that Rorsch and his partner had brought. They lay on the table.

'Are these staying?'

'Evidence,' Müller said.

Hof nodded again slowly, clearly wanting to say more; but he restrained himself.

He extended his hand to Müller. 'Try to enjoy the Eifel more quietly, sir.'

They shook hands.

'If I'm allowed to,' Müller said.

'I saw your picture in the papers last year. Taken here, in the garden. A baby, and Frau Holz.'

'Yes. My godson.'

'Never mentioned you were a policeman.'

'I try to keep that separate.'

Hof nodded for the third time. 'Wise. Different for me.

In an area like this, everyone knows. But I'm happy with that.'

'Each to his own,' Müller said.

'As always, sir. As always.' Hof, eyes full of questions, turned to Greville, hand outstretched. 'Sir.'

Greville shook the hand. 'Goodnight to you, *Kommissar* Hof,' he said in German.

Whatever he really wanted to say, Hof was astute enough not to give voice to it. The nod came once more, accompanied by a world-weary smile.

'We'll see you out,' Müller said.

They followed him down to the portico. In the soft glow of the overhead spotlights, his small, unmarked police BMW gleamed next to the Porsche.

'When we arrived,' he said, looking at the Turbo, 'I thought . . . *very, very nice*. They give nice toys to the Berlin police. But I bet it's yours.'

'It is.'

Hof looked at the house, then back at the car. He gave another of his nods, and went over to his BMW.

He paused. 'That BMW coupé involved in the earlier incident, *Oberkommissar* Pappenheim said it is to go to Berlin.'

'Yes,' Müller said. 'Important evidence.'

'Pity.'

Hof seemed to fold himself into his car, and drove off.

'He'll probably drive it there himself,' Greville said with dry humour.

'He'll be disappointed. Pappi will ensure that the locals leave it strictly alone, and will already have arranged for it to be collected. There is still the possibility that the people it belongs to may attempt to take it back. We can't risk putting our local colleagues in that kind of danger.'

'There is that point,' Greville agreed. 'And now what?' Greville continued as they went back inside. 'More visitors, do you think?'

Müller locked the door, properly this time, now that his trap had been sprung.

'For tonight, I very much doubt it. I want to take a look at the stuff in my father's briefcase.'

'Then I shall leave you to your privacy with your father's documents. If you need to talk to me about anything, do not hesitate.'

'I won't. Thank you, Greville.'

They went back upstairs. The balcony room seemed barely disturbed, despite what had occurred.

Greville went to his room, while Müller went into his own to get the brown briefcase. He returned to the balcony room and put the case on the table. He sat down and with the care he would probably have reserved for a holy relic, snapped the catch open.

He opened the briefcase and began to remove its contents. He put them all on the table. There were five thick files, three large envelopes that clearly held photographs, and two ordinary business-type envelopes which looked slightly yellowed. One of these appeared to have two solid objects inside.

He looked at the stacked files and the envelopes, and was almost afraid to start.

At last, he chose one of the smaller envelopes and turned it over. There was just the one word on it: *Jens*. He discovered that there was a slight tremor in his hands.

'I'm about to read for the first time,' he said to himself, 'a letter written to me when I was twelve. Of course my hands shake.'

He opened it and took out two sheets of high-quality paper, which he recognized as the kind his parents had often used, all those years ago. The handwriting upon the first was bold and flowing.

My son, he read,

> *if you are reading this, the worst that I have feared has happened. You are now a grown man, and will be able to*

cope with what you will find in this briefcase, which Isolde has kept in a very safe place for you. You must do likewise, for there are those who will kill to get at what is inside. Whatever you may have heard, know this: your mother and I love each other in a way that can never be destroyed. We both love you, and are proud of you, whatever you have become. I know that nothing you have decided to do with your life would have disappointed us.

You once astonished us by saying you wanted to become a policeman – a sort of special investigator who would only get the difficult and sometimes dangerous cases! Do you remember?

Müller nodded. 'Yes,' he said quietly. 'I do.'

Were those the dreams of a boy? he read on,

Or have you actually become one? If so, you may well be suited for what these documents might lead you to.

Your aunt will have taken care of you for us, as she would have done with a son of her own, and I know that you will have made her proud. I cannot imagine how you will react to the information you will now see. I have tried to serve our country to the very best of my abilities. Necessarily, this had to be done in the shadows, against shadowy people who are inimical to our way of life. The fact that you are reading this means they have found me out; but far worse is that your reading it also means they have not only taken their revenge upon me, but also upon your mother.

Use what you find in here to the best of your ability. But be careful. These are very dangerous people. I love you.

There was his father's signature, first name only. Then in parentheses: *Your mother wants to say a few words.*

On the second sheet, the handwriting was smaller, but with long elegant strokes.

Dear, dear Jens, it began,

> *your father has already spoken for both of us, but I just wanted to tell you in my own words how much I love you and wish I could have seen you grow into the man you have become. Whatever this might be, I know it would have pleased me. If you do read this, forgive us for leaving you so young. We love you, my son, so very, very much. God keep you safe. All my love, Mina.*

Mina had been Müller's childhood nickname for her.

He felt a great heat behind his eyes, and vision became slightly blurred as he noticed there were small splash stains on the paper.

'Oh God,' he said in a choked whisper. 'She'd been crying.' He put the letter down and wiped at his eyes. 'Oh God . . . oh God . . .'

He sat there, back to the door, staring through the large, open french windows to the balcony and beyond, and into the Eifel night. It had grown quite dark now, and even the fading stains in the evening sky had gone.

The tears ran, unheeded, down his cheeks.

He was quite unaware that Greville had entered the room, and had quietly backed out again.

After about a minute, Müller got to his feet and, wiping the tears away with the back of his hand, went out on to the balcony. He breathed deeply of the night air, cleared his throat and stood there, tightly gripping the top rail of the balcony with both hands. He remained quite still, for a full three minutes, before going back inside.

He switched on more lights and sat down again. He picked up the second of the small envelopes, opened it and turned it over. Two items fell out.

He stared. They were two rings.

He picked one up, studied it closely; then gave a quick intake of breath. It was of the same type and with exactly the same seal as the one Hedi Meyer had enlarged from Grogan's film. The second ring bore a seal he had never seen before in that exact form; though he recognized the Brandenburg eagle. He could not know it was similar to one the man who had addressed the eavesdroppers had worn.

'Never wear one of those, unless you are prepared to accept the consequences.'

Müller snapped his head round. Greville was standing at the door, eyes on the rings.

'I came in earlier,' he went on, 'but, as it was a rather . . . private moment, I withdrew.'

'You saw me. Sorry. Bit of a baby.'

'Nonsense, old man! You have every right. Weeping diminishes not the man. Far from it. I have done some of that in my time. May I come in? Or . . .'

'Of course. The personal stuff is over.'

Greville came further into the room, eyeing Müller warily. 'Are you . . . ?'

'I'm fine.' Müller pointed to each ring. 'Do you know these?'

'I have seen an example of each, on the fingers of people you would not want to meet in daylight, never mind on a dark night. One of them has no further use for it,' Greville added, with a finality that said much.

'Dead?'

'As the proverbial dodo.'

'You?'

'Me.'

'What happened?'

'We argued with guns. He lost.'

'And the ring?'

'Buried with him, in some unmarked hellhole that he deserved. Perhaps in a century or so, he'll be accidentally dug up, and the ring will become a source of much speculation. Meanwhile, his soul is holidaying in hell.'

Müller gave a weak smile. 'You clearly liked him. I have the uncomfortable feeling,' he went on, 'that these belonged to my father.'

Greville slowly took a seat opposite, eyes on Müller. 'What makes you say that?'

'Something he said in his letter to me. Something about serving the country in the shadows.'

'So, he did join them,' Greville said in a quiet voice. 'Courage indeed. Always difficult to go so deep, and avoid being infected. He must have managed to remain clean somehow, or they would not have taken their revenge.' He glanced at the pile of documents. 'You do realize, old man, that what these files may hold could shake your country to its very core. You now carry a great and extremely dangerous burden. This is an inheritance which in time you may well grow to curse.'

For a moment, Greville's almost flippant attitude to life became a very serious one.

'If I am frightening you, all to the good. It just may save your life one day.'

As he took this in, Müller studied Greville's expression. Greville's unworldly attitude seemed to have vanished. He appeared to have morphed into something very different. For a moment, Müller saw the tempered steel beneath the affable exterior: the Greville who had shot Rorsch's companion with such deadly accuracy. Then the hovering smile was back.

'Ah,' Greville said. 'Spotted the beast within. Sorry about that.'

'We all have one. Somewhere.'

'Yes, indeed. We do. If utilized responsibly, it can be quite useful. Most people do not do so. Hence the kind of world we have.'

'And the second ring?' Müller asked. 'Where did you see it?'

'On a man, not German, and with considerable clout in my line of work. These people never wear them in public. Only at very special occasions for the like-minded, or within their own company. I saw it by accident.'

'Do you know him?'

'No. But I will certainly recognize him, should I ever see him again.'

'And did he see you?'

'I very much doubt it. He did not know I was around.' Greville peered at the envelope. 'Something still in there.'

Müller looked, and saw a slip of paper. He took it out, recognizing his father's handwriting.

'"The variation of the ancient Templar seal,"' he read aloud. '"Always worn on the left hand. The Knights Bretheren. (The extra e is deliberate.) The variation of the 1253 seal – the Semper. Ownership of the first means membership of the most trusted, innermost circle. Ownership of two denotes exceedingly high rank within the trusted circle."'

Müller put the note down.

'I stand corrected,' Greville said. 'Your father did not simply infiltrate. He got into the very heart. Small wonder they became mightily enraged when he was discovered. To them, he would have been a traitor . . .'

Müller got to his feet and began to pace. '*They* are the traitors!'

'Indeed they are, old man,' Greville agreed calmly. 'But, from their maddened point of view, they see it quite differently. *You* must begin to see things differently. You will need to out-think them. You have the courage, Jens. You need more guile. You are your father's son . . .'

'I am my mother's son, too. She was a gentler person.'

'And you have that within you,' Greville said. 'All the better. These people . . . these . . . Knights, consider themselves an elite. They see themselves as bringing enlightenment to the lesser orders while they, of course, remain in control. They are planning for year zero. From what little I do know, they come from many different walks of life: politics, of course; the financial world, the commercial world, the military, the intelligence world, the religious . . .'

'The police?' Müller stopped pacing, thinking of Neubauer and, by implication, Kaltendorf.

'Naturally, dear boy. Highly essential if you wish to maintain order, and control your population. They do, of course, look after their own. As with all such organizations, they are cavalier with those who are outside their perceived "circle". But they save their true vitriol for those whom they deem to have betrayed the "faith".'

'Like my father.'

'In a way, yes. I am giving you a very rough overview. Your father must have gone so deep he was seen as one of them. Coming as he did from the *Adel* – noble – crowd, he would have been seen as a huge catch. All the more reason to spit blood when they eventually discovered that *he* was after *them*.'

'So, he wasn't really a spy in the ordinary sense, despite . . .'

'If you'll forgive the interruption, he was very much one of us, old man. Never met him, but heard of him, as I said at the Derrenberg. It's simply that the conditions must have been very favourable to have him inserted into that lot as well. He would have picked up a treasure chest of intelligence material. Never forget that, despite being what they are, these people also pursue normal, everyday interests, which they then put to use for the building of their insane utopia. And they are patient. They attach themselves to the backbone of the nation, over a long period of time, so that the takeover is imperceptible.'

Müller was pacing again. 'I have heard as much, from someone else.'

'Take it very seriously.' Greville paused to look at the three large envelopes. 'Photographs?'

Müller again stopped pacing. 'I don't dare look as yet.'

Greville picked up one of the envelopes. 'Do it, shall I?'

'Be my guest.'

Greville put a hand in and drew out the first photograph. He studied it for moments that seemed to stretch for years. He looked up at Müller, frowned slightly, then looked at the photograph again.

'Oh. My.'

He placed the photograph on the table, face up.

Müller paled, conflicting emotions raging through him. The photograph was of his father: in the full uniform of a Colonel of Police in the DDR. The rings on the table were on each little finger.

'The likeness is there for all to see,' Greville said. 'You are your father's son . . . and, indeed, your mother's. Your likeness to her is even more startling. I have seen the portrait on the wall, in Isolde's part of the Derrenberg.' He studied the photograph again. 'This man was more than a legend. I had no idea – just like many in the intelligence community – that he was involved in so many . . .' Greville paused, clearly full of admiration. 'In the Stasi, as well as the Bretheren, posing as a business with DDR sympathies, only to be finally betrayed . . . by his own side.'

'Someone from the Knights Bretheren?'

'Someone from his own side, who was also in the Knights,' Greville corrected. 'Vested interests to protect. As always. And the next one,' he added, probing into the envelope for another photograph.

He pulled it out. 'Well,' he said. 'Hello, Monsignor.' A robed bishop was smiling at him. 'Smug smile you've got there.'

The bishop wore the ring of the Knights Bretheren.

'Control the religion,' Greville remarked as he laid it down, 'and use the religion to control the masses. Always held the opinion the biggest mistake the Soviets made was to ban the opiate. They lost a vast control mechanism. See how quickly it returned once the old system had gone.' He stopped, noting Müller's expression. 'You *know* this man?'

'He came to our home once. He visited my parents. I remember him.' Müller's lips had drawn themselves tight.

Greville studied Müller critically. 'You would kill a bishop?'

Müller, teeth gritted, said nothing.

Greville gave a slight nod. 'In your current mood, you would kill this bishop.' He looked at the photograph again. 'Ah, Monsignor . . . betrayal is thy name.'

The next photograph drew a harsh sound from Müller. '*Neubauer!*'

Neubauer was in *Polizeidirektor*'s uniform, a single ring on the left finger.

'You would kill him too?' Greville asked.

'He's already dead.'

'You?'

'His driver, who then tried to escape. But Pappi had sent a team to trail Neubauer, so they were on hand when it happened. They challenged the driver, but he decided to argue the point—'

'With a gun. And, as with my own argument with one of the Knights, he lost.'

'Yes.'

Greville turned Neubauer's photograph face down. There was writing on the back, in the now recognizable hand of Müller's father. It identified the subject.

Greville looked at the back of the bishop's. He was identified as well.

'Thorough, your dad.'

The fourth photograph from the envelope was of a man in military uniform, a two-star general.

'Know him?' Greville asked.

'Never seen him before,' Müller said.

209

'Nor I.' Greville turned the photograph over. '"Major-General Kurt von Lützöwen,"' he read. '*Two* umlauts. Heard of him?'

'Never. But I'm certain Pappi will be able to find out.'

'Ah, yes. Pappi. The eternal guardian at the gate. What would you do without him?'

'I hope I never have to.'

One of Greville's hovering smiles lived briefly, but he made no comment. He returned the photographs to the envelope.

'That's all there is, in this one. I dare say he'll have made notes somewhere, about these three. Shall we do more? Or would you prefer . . . ?'

Müller sat down again. 'Let's continue.'

'Righto. You, or I?'

'You do it.'

'Then I shall.'

Greville pulled the second envelope towards him. The photograph he took out made him pause for what seemed an eternity.

'My word,' he began, voice gentleness itself. 'You were an angelic young thing. And your mother . . . quite, quite beautiful.'

'*What?*' Müller said.

Greville handed it over. It was a picture of Müller, his father and mother. They were in a large garden, mother and father holding their small son by each hand, him in the middle.

As Müller looked at the photograph, his hands shook slightly. He tightened his lips, controlling the emotions he felt rising within him. He turned the picture over. This time, the writing was his mother's.

'"Jens at three."'

'Has a beautiful smile, your mother,' Greville said.

'Had.'

'Has,' Greville insisted. 'She is alive in the photograph.

She is happy and radiant. Remember it. They put that picture in there for you. It was obviously one of their favourites.'

Still keeping a tight control of his emotions, Müller nodded slowly.

'Only one in there,' Greville said, peering into the envelope. 'They did not want it contaminated by any others, if you get my meaning. Next one?'

Continuing to look at the picture in his hands, Müller nodded again.

Greville turned to the third envelope. It was much bulkier. 'Quite a collection,' he said, peering in. 'All sizes.' He upended the envelope and a small pile fell out. He spread them out slightly. 'Some in colour, others not. Ah! Here's one you'll find of particular interest. Two familiar faces.'

He selected a longish photograph and passed it to Müller.

Müller gently put down the family photo and took the one Greville was passing to him. His eyes widened.

'Thought so,' Greville said.

It was a group shot of six, all in DDR police uniforms. Müller's father was one; as was a younger Dahlberg.

He turned the picture over. The names of the five others were written there, including the ranks at the time the picture was taken. Beneath the names was the caption: *The original Romeo Six group.*

'Recognize any more of them?'

Müller shook his head. 'No. But the names will help us find them, if they're still alive. I'll put Pappi on to it. He can find a needle in a haystack.'

They went through the entire pile of photographs. Most of the people on them were unknown to Müller, but he recognized some who were prominent in various professions. All the names had been written down. Not all were German.

'I've saved this one for last,' Greville said. 'I've read the back. The names are there. You'll find it interesting.' He passed it across.

Müller found himself staring at two young men in suits,

with a slightly older man he did not recognize, to whom they seemed to be deferring.

'Kaltendorf and Neubauer,' he said tightly.

'Indeed.'

Müller put the photograph down with something close to disgust. '*Kaltendorf.*'

'Don't jump to the wrong conclusions, old man,' Greville advised. 'I realize that your emotions are playing the giddy aunt with you at the moment. But always remember, you're a good policeman. Fall back on that. Your father left you the devil of a task. Do it well . . . with caution, with precision and, when the occasion demands, with ruthlessness. Never, never, *never* with the emotions clouded. Given what you have discovered so far, it will be difficult at times. But you will have to meet that hurdle, and cross over. You *must.*'

Eleven

With the sole exception of the family picture, all the other photographs were back in their respective envelopes.

Müller now pulled at a flat-spined file among the documents. 'It will take me weeks – most likely months – to go through all this; but this one . . . looks . . . like a diary of sorts.'

As it came free, he saw that it did seem to be a diary, about A4 in size. He opened it at random. His father's familiar script confirmed its ownership. It was not a narrative diary, but one into which day-to-day commentaries had been jotted down. In most cases dates, and even times, had been included.

Müller was staring at the page he had randomly selected.

Greville, noting the expression, asked in a soft voice, 'What have you seen?'

'I'll read it. "A strange whisper,"' Müller began, '"is making the rounds. News is of the accidental poisoning of a British agent by a new bio-weapon. No one seems to know whether this is true or not. The people to whom the weapon supposedly belongs deny all knowledge of this. They say it is a deliberate attempt to discredit their nation, and accuse the British. None of this is in the public domain. No details, and no identification of the supposed victim. Must find out more."' Müller stopped, and looked at Greville.

'Well, well,' Greville said. 'Confirmation from a most unexpected source. Do you see, old man? The intelligence

community can sometimes be like a sieve. Who floated that
"whisper", I wonder? Perhaps your father was indeed able to
find out more.'

'Perhaps. It may be in there somewhere.' Müller included
all the documents with a brief sweep of a hand.

'Or not, as the case may be.'

'Or not,' Müller agreed.

'Well. That's a relief.'

'What do you mean?'

'Come on, old man. As I've said, you're a rather good
policeman. I find it hard to believe that some part of you
has not been questioning my little tale about the bio-weapon.
After all, I appear suddenly, apparently from the dead, with a
tale to chill the bones. I am an oldish intelligence warhorse,
well versed in the art of dissimulation. You must have been
just a teeny bit sceptical.'

Müller looked awkward.

'There!' Greville said, triumphant. 'Knew it! Feel no
embarrassment, dear boy. Done exactly the same, in your
place.'

'Part of me also hoped it had really not happened, because . . .'

'Know what you're about to say. But there it is. I'm afraid
I have been truly nobbled. No escape whatsoever. The only
good thing about it is that the only stock went into me.
So it will die with me. And do me a great favour, if
you will. If you are in the vicinity when fate calls for
the bill, have me cremated, and the ashes scattered far
and wide. If buried, someone, somewhere, may try to dig
me up and attempt to extract the stuff from me. Can't
have that, old man. Take me for a last ride in the Healey
before you do the scattering. That would be rather fun.
Promise?'

'Promise,' Müller vowed.

'Good show. Now let's leave this morbid stuff and move
on. Find another page. Random, as before.'

Müller flicked the pages backwards and stopped again. He

214

studied an entry for such a long time that Greville was moved to speak.

'Well?'

Müller cleared his throat. '"Isolde and her Englishman came to dinner,"' he read. '"They are very taken with each other. I have no hesitation in saying that they would be a good family for Jens, should the worst happen."'

Müller looked up at Greville, who shrugged deprecatingly.

'He was being kind,' Greville commented with uncharacteristic gruffness.

'I don't think so.'

'And, as you see, I would not have been there.'

Müller nodded. 'He never suspected about you.'

'And I never suspected about *him*. In those days, Germany was overrun with spies of every hue; and not all are gone. Just a slight metamorphosis. Funny old thing, life.'

'I have another word,' Müller said, 'but funny will do.' He began thumbing through the diary again.

He stopped and began to read silently. Then he looked at Greville.

'Those photographs. The last pile. Could you take them out again?'

A question in his eyes, Greville did so.

Müller worked a hand through them, spreading them out like a pack of cards. He searched, picking one out, then rejecting it. At last, he stopped to stare at one – black and white – with four men and a woman. The background was a mountain landscape. All were in rambling gear, with solid boots on their feet. All had guns.

Müller showed the picture to Greville.

'They look like one's idea of partisans,' Greville commented.

'They are . . . sort of. There was an undeclared civil war going on at the time. Three of them belong to the country they're in.'

'And the fourth and fifth?'

'Two men. They do not.'

'How do you know?'

'Something my father wrote down; and something that was said to me, by Miss Bloomfield. Here's what he has written.' Müller looked down at the diary. '"Something about Grogan – as he currently calls himself – mystifies. Difficult to pin down which side he's on. As for 'Hackett' . . ."' Müller paused. 'He put that name in inverted commas, so Hackett is not the real name. "As for 'Hackett', who, like him, supported the anti-government forces, I would definitely not trust him."'

'In this picture,' Müller continued, 'the names of the two men are Wilson and Hackett. I have seen Grogan. So I know that "Wilson" is in fact Grogan, if younger.'

'And Hackett?'

'I'll quote you Miss Bloomfield's words: "He is one of ours. Fifteen years ago, when I was still a kid – just entering my teens – this guy was supposed to have died on a mission. When I was being trained, he was held up to us as a hero. But . . . but here he is . . . *alive* . . ." End of quote. She also added that Grogan knew. The man she pointed out was in Grogan's film. The same man standing next to Grogan in this photograph.'

'The past is never another country,' Greville said after a while. 'Just the same country, a little older.'

'And it catches up,' Müller said.

'That it does.'

Müller handed the photograph to Greville, who put it back into the envelope.

'One last selection,' Müller said, and began thumbing through once more. He stopped and went still. Then he began to read.

'"My controller is suspect. This leaves me exposed."' Müller stopped reading. 'My God. This is where it began.' He shut the diary and placed it with the other documents. 'I'm not going to read any more for the time being. I need to go through all of this, section by section, collate it with what I've already got, then look at the overall picture.'

'Weeks, or months, you said.'

'If that's what it takes.' Müller began to put everything back into the briefcase.

'I agree,' Greville said. 'Any help you may need . . . do not hesitate.'

'I won't. And thanks.'

'My total pleasure, old man.' Greville pointed to the briefcase. 'And put that thing somewhere very, very safe.'

'I have just the place for it,' Müller said, thinking of the rogues' gallery.

In Berlin, having refuelled on nicotine, Pappenheim had decided to return to the rogues' gallery.

The newspaper and magazine section had been created at Müller's instigation. One day, he had suggested what had then been to Pappenheim something quite bizarre: that all members of the unit bring in, from time to time, any piles of newspapers and magazines they had at home. After the initial disbelief, the material had started to arrive in such quantities that Pappenheim had begun to fear the rogues' gallery would fast become a paper dump.

Thinking about that early situation, Pappenheim gave a chuckle. 'Funny how the men never brought in a single girlie magazine.'

Müller and Pappenheim had then decided to restrict the type of journal that should be brought in; but some of the original arrivals had been retained.

Hedi Meyer had taken to the idea and in her spare time had scoured old repositories for newsprint dating back to the thirties. She had even found material from her old school and university.

The exercise had revealed an unexpected insight into the reading habits of the unit's personnel; some quite surprising,

217

some interests even merging. Müller's had displayed the expected vast eclecticism: from politics to history, to art, music in numerous forms, military, even cooking, within the huge range. Hedi Meyer also showed an expected selection that included a preponderance of scientific and electronic material, plus photography and, not so expectedly, lifestyle. Berger had lifestyle among her choices, travel, and diving, one of the subjects that also interested Müller. Reimer was a real surprise, with archaeology, plus architecture and the American wild west.

Klemp was true to type. His reading was basic in the extreme. While he had not turned in any girlie magazines, the newspapers included in his contributions invariably sported barely clothed women; plus sports magazines – mainly football – and the highly expected body-building.

Pappenheim was the most secretive. He wanted no one to know he contributed to a poetry journal. Not even Müller.

The scanning of the information into a database was an ongoing process, followed by getting rid of the newsprint to make room for more to come. It was a necessarily slow job, but it was working. Hedi Meyer did the scanning and cataloguing, which she appeared to enjoy.

The computer was on, and the appropriate page was onscreen. Pappenheim went to it and tapped in a search command.

The response was instant. It gave the cabinet designation, then: *Top drawer.* What he needed was not yet on the server database.

When Pappenheim had once asked Müller why not simply go to the libraries and newspaper offices, or even the Internet, Müller's response had been unequivocal.

'No,' he'd said. 'The Internet is wide open, and people post only what they want you to see; and, no matter how secure, you leave an address for those who are able to trace you. You have no sanction. Now we've got Hedi Meyer, we are very secure; but even so.

'The papers also only give you what they want you to read but sometimes little gems that no one's aware of can slip through. It's a matter of finding them. Libraries and other locations are good for what they are; but not for our purposes. Besides, we would need to allocate people to do this permanently. Other organizations already have such people. They have the resources. We don't. And, in any case, what we're doing is not official. The GW would never go for it.'

'That's true enough,' Pappenheim now said drily.

He looked up at the tall, wheeled ladder which hung from a solid rail with a two-ton breaking limit, and which could be slid to each cabinet in the room.

'Every time I look at you,' he said to it, 'I wonder if you'll drop me when I get on. I'm not as light of weight as Hedi Meyer.'

He moved it to the cabinet and began to climb. When he got to the top drawer, he tapped in the entry code, and pulled it open. He found two newspapers and one magazine that might have what he was looking for. Pushing the drawer shut but not far enough to lock it, he went back down with relief.

He took his finds to the white table and placed them on it. He opened up the first newspaper and began his search; taking his time about it.

Something had been nagging at him all day, and this had crystallized when he'd been searching for items about Müller. But it was not in the paper he was now study-ing. He put it aside, and picked up the second. If the item happened not to be in this, or the magazine, then he was stuck.

Everyone had brought in only what they were happy to do without, though once the scanning was done, contributed material could be returned if this were desired. And everyone throughout the building who had contributed, also read gun magazines; Hedi Meyer included.

219

The unusual thing about Pappenheim's current search was the avenue of his quest. He was studying Klemp's material: body-building.

He had been through the second newspaper, *The Body-builder's Healthcare*, without finding what he was looking for. He put the paper with the first, and turned to the magazine. It was his last hope.

A minute or so later, he found it.

'And there you are,' he uttered softly to a half-page black and white photograph.

The picture was of a group of people in a gym. All were on various exercise machines. One was pumping iron: the man who had called himself Rorsch.

'Well, well, well.' Pappenheim's voice was a whisper. 'This calls for a cigarette, but it can wait. Did you know someone had taken your picture, Herr Rorsch? Obviously not. I'll show it to you, in all its glory, when you get back. But there's something else I need.'

Pappenheim went to the computer, and with the awkward two-fingered tap of the keyboard novice, typed in another search command. The onscreen response was immediate.

'Oh good,' he said. 'I'll only have to go back up the ladder once after this.'

The requested document was on the database. He called it up and began to scroll through. The photograph that eventually came up was a video grab from a clandestinely taken film, and had come to him via one of his contacts. Vintage was two years before the fall of the Wall. There were two people in the photograph, both in uniform. One was a Russian major; the other the man called Rorsch. His uniform was neither Russian nor DDR.

'I need a print,' Pappenheim said. 'Where's "print"? Ah. There.' He hit the key. Nothing happened. He stared. 'What . . . ?' He stopped. 'The printer, Pappenheim! Turn it on!'

He turned on the printer and, when it had settled itself,

the printing began. When it was done, Pappenheim took the photograph and looked at it critically.

'Not bad, if I say so myself.'

He left the computer and went back to the table, to place the new print on the page of the magazine with Rorsch's other photograph. It had dried sufficiently, and he closed the magazine on it. Magazine and print went into the same cabinet that housed all the other sensitive information.

Pappenheim then went back up the ladder to replace the two newspapers, shut the drawer – this time allowing it to click home – then went back down. He turned off computer and printer and had a quick look about him to ensure everything had been put away.

'Alright, Rorsch,' he said. 'Let's see what you've got to say for yourself when you get here. And this time no one is going to let you off; not even the Great White. Because, if he does, I'll have his balls if Müller doesn't get there first. And hang the consequences.' Pappenheim smiled to himself. 'Sometimes, I really enjoy this job. Time for a celebratory cigarette, I think,' he added as he went out.

He hummed all the way to his office.

Above the Eifel, 23.50

The police Eurocopter EC155 was beating its way towards Cologne/Bonn airport. A medium-lift, twin-engine machine weighing in at five tonnes, it was a high-tech and modern piece of work. Its glass cockpit – multi-function displays instead of the usual plethora of dials – was greatly appreciated by its pilot, and co-pilot/observer. Depending on the mission, it could carry a variety of additional crew. Having main blades and a fenestron tail, designed to run quietly, it was a ghost flitting in the Eifel dark.

On this night, in addition to pilot and co-pilot, there were just two other officers on board. Both were armed escorts for Rorsch. The remainder of the helicopter's load were two

221

forensics caskets. In them were the bodies of Hassan and the stocky man Greville had killed.

For the EC155, this was a load with which it could easily cope. A machine with the capacity to carry twelve passengers, or six stretchers, plus a freight hold, there was more than enough room to spare. There was even a transparent, armoured partition – a special modification – that could be raised electronically to protect the crew from violent and unwilling passengers – armed, or unarmed – in the cabin. On this flight, the partition was lowered. The caskets travelled with passenger and escorts.

'I really hate flying with those two stiffs in the caskets,' the co-pilot said into his mike to the pilot in the right-hand seat. 'At night too.'

'Not superstitious, are you?' the pilot asked, meaning this as a joke.

'Nothing to do with superstition. I just don't like the feel of it.'

'Ah well. It's not around the world to the airport. We'll get there, land, dump them and be on our way back again to our nicely warm women.'

'Speak for yourself. My kids make sure we don't enjoy that side of life as often as we would like. They're still young enough to want to sleep with us.'

'Ah well,' the pilot repeated. 'Got to pay for your fun.' The pilot had no children.

'I thought you two were planning . . .'

The pilot grinned. 'We're still in the planning stage. Still plenty of fun to be had, and no patter of tiny feet running into the bedroom to interrupt.'

'Lucky bastard.'

'You made your own luck . . . or your own bed . . .' The pilot was grinning again.

The co-pilot was about to make a suitably pithy retort when he looked to his left and saw something moving on a parallel course.

'What the hell is that? Did you see it?' he asked the pilot.

The pilot, night-vision goggles snapped down, did a quick scan. 'Nothing.'

The co-pilot had snapped down his own goggles. Whatever he believed he had seen, was no longer there.

He snapped the goggles back up. 'I really don't like the idea of those caskets behind me.' He spoke loudly enough for those in the cabin to hear.

Rorsch, sitting with his feet on top of the casket of his recently deceased colleague, gave a short, soft laugh. 'Scared of the dark?'

'Shut up!' the co-pilot snapped, looking round briefly.

The escort sitting to Rorsch's left said, 'Yes. Shut the fuck up.'

'Happy people, aren't you? Wouldn't you be feeling better being with your wives or girlfriends . . . or boyfriends, if you're that way inclined . . .'

'Shut the fuck up!' all four policemen said together.

A little later, the co-pilot said, 'Definitely something out there!'

He again snapped down the night-vision kit. Again the shape vanished.

'Shit!' he said.

'Check with air traffic,' the pilot suggested.

The co-pilot identified their aircraft and flight plan and asked if there was any other traffic in their area. They were told none.

'I'm seeing things,' the co-pilot said.

'Get your eyes checked,' Rorsch suggested. His soft laugh came again. 'Have some sex.'

This time, they ignored him.

The dark shape kept station directly behind, and a little below, the EC155. So close was it, that on any watching radar the two would be like a single aircraft.

Then, at a precisely chosen moment, the second shape took up station abreast of the EC155.

'*There it is!*' the co-pilot shouted. 'I wasn't seeing things!'

Then the night lit up with the brief but fierce fire of a rocket-propelled grenade heading their way.

The round ended its flight explosively against the cockpit, killing both pilot and co-pilot instantly. The helicopter was pivoting about its vertical axis when the second round from the RPG launcher struck it at the base of its main rotor. Rotor and fuselage parted company in a flaming separation. Suddenly free of the weight, the still-whirling blades whooshed upwards, obeying the laws of aerodynamics before those of gravity would take over and bring it back to earth.

The decapitated helicopter, furiously rotated by its completely intact tail and fenestron rotor, described a fiery spiral as it plunged earthwards. Rorsch, and the two escorts, were still alive.

The escorts were screaming. They had released their straps and were frantically trying to get out, oblivious to the fact that they would hit the ground with a force that would immediately kill them. The spinning aircraft kept them trapped within its flame-wrapped embrace.

Rorsch sat in this raging hell, handcuffed and still strapped to his seat, a slightly mad smile fixed upon his face. He made no attempt to escape. It was as if he clearly understood the reason for the attack, and was resigned to it. There was no reproach in his eyes.

Then the engines caught fire and exploded.

As the blazing shards fell, the second helicopter, with no lights showing, matched the descent until, when low enough, it fled at ultra-low level to where it had come from.

To those watching on radar, it would appear as if something catastrophic had occurred to a single aircraft.

*   *   *

Scant minutes later, Berlin. Local call.

'Problem solved. Completely.'

'Excellent.' The man who had ordered the intercept was pleased. He knew that meant no survivors.

They did not talk further, and the connection ended.

The one who had received the call immediately called the secure number outside Germany.

'Yes?'

'Problem solved.'

'Completely?'

'Completely.'

'At least the day was not totally lost. Everything else continues.'

'That goes without question. Nothing, and no one, stands in our way.'

'Especially the son.'

'Particularly the son,' came the correction.

The Eifel, 23.55.

Müller and Greville were on the balcony, looking out over the peaceful Eifel nightscape, the dark pockmarked with the lights of towns, villages and isolated houses within their field of vision. Despite the location, it was a warm night.

Müller was relieved that the visit by Rorsch and his stocky companion had not caused the damage to the house that he had feared.

There were not even bullet holes, because there had not been exit wounds, close range notwithstanding. The stocky man's leap had caused both bullets fired by Grevillle to enter at an angle. They had decelerated quickly, causing massive trauma, and had remained within the body of their target, each having been stopped by bone.

'No damage to the house,' Greville now said. 'Lucky. You won't have to explain to your friends.'

225

'True enough.'

As before, Müller placed both hands upon the solid top rail of the balcony, and looked out on the night.

Greville looked across at him. 'Penny for them.'

'My thoughts? Not worth that much.'

'After what we've just seen from the briefcase? I rather think they're worth a bit more.'

'I was thinking of a twelve-year-old boy.'

'You? Or Hassan?'

'Both. Wrong place, at the wrong time.'

Greville turned back to the Eifel night. 'So peaceful. Do you think they know what is in the shadows? And would they care if they did? I remember sitting on some rocky escarpment reading weeks-old newspapers from the UK. Strikes, football skirmishes, all the sort of news you really do not want to read. And I used to think and wonder about the things that incensed the man in the street: someone cutting him up on a motorway; a nasty boy running a knife against the bodywork of his car; someone stealing his parking space; someone else bashing a child's head against a wall because it simply would not stop screaming. All in the news. I would sit there with havoc being wrought upon my genes and silently ask: what do you know?'

'I have often asked that question myself,' Müller said.

'All a matter of degree, is it not?'

Müller nodded, but said nothing.

Greville gave a sudden chuckle. 'Odd as it may sound, quite enjoyed the day . . . in a mad way. Not the best introduction to the Nordschleife. But all the same.'

'I'll have to take you back on a proper round or two.'

'I will hold you to that, old boy. Definitely. And don't forget the ashes, should my nemesis strike rather sooner than later.' Greville's eyes were hooded in the strange twilight of the balcony. 'Morbid as this may seem, I really would appreciate if you did that.'

'I have promised, and I will keep it. What will you do about Aunt Isolde?'

'Ah. That will be tricky. Shall have to tell her, of course.'

'As I've said,' Müller began, 'it is entirely up to you. I will not interfere.'

'Appreciate that, old man.' Greville paused. 'Must find me a bolt hole. As with you, those who want my head will not stop. Can't put Isolde in danger . . .'

'Why don't you let her decide for herself? It's only fair.'

'Quite right. All the same . . .'

'And if she finds it awkward, I have plenty of room, and my place is secure . . .'

'No, no, old chap. Much appreciated, but you've got enough on your plate.'

'You never know when I might need your help.'

'I'll be around,' Greville said. 'Never fear.'

Müller nodded. 'Whatever you decide.'

His eyes now accustomed to the night, and in the backglow from the security lighting in the grounds, Müller saw that Greville was again looking at him intently.

'They are stealing my country, Greville,' Müller said, voice low as he turned to stare into the dark of the Eifel. 'It has been stolen before . . . but not this time. *Not* . . . this time. It was Grogan's words that echoed when you spoke of the theft, by stealth, of a nation. One of the many little things he has sent me was a note. Very much to the point, and very close to what you have said. I know it by heart. "The ultimate objective," it said, "is to infiltrate the nation at all possible levels over a long-term period, so that the continuing shift of the country will be almost imperceptible. This is the slow drip of water on a stone. No one notices . . . until it is too late to reverse it. You have allies in the unlikeliest of places."'

'The planners of year zero,' Greville said, understanding only too well the meaning of Grogan's words. 'Perceptive man . . . or a man with impeccable inside knowledge; which does do wonders for the perception. He must have got himself into a similar position to your father. Let us hope he will continue to be fortunate.'

'I am still not certain he is on "our" side.'

'That, is a movable feast. For the moment, he appears to favour you, whatever his true agenda. And he is right. You do have allies in the unlikeliest of places. You've got me, for one . . . for as long as I have. You've got Miss Bloomfield, for another. Do not underestimate her importance. She is important enough to have been on David's hit list. She must have annoyed someone, somewhere.'

'That's an easy one to believe,' Müller said, unable to resist the dry comment.

Greville seemed to have tacked on his hovering smile. 'If you had any idea how those two words betray you, you would never have uttered them.'

'Meaning?'

'I think you follow my drift,' came the cryptic reply.

'Hmm,' Müller said.

'Quite. May I ask a question?'

'Ask it.'

'If you find it too painful, do not answer.'

Müller shot Greville an uncertain glance, and nodded.

'Have you kept any newspaper cuttings of your parents' crash?'

'That's an easy one too. No. I never wanted to see any photographs, or read about it. I could not avoid hearing, of course – radio, television; but I had no desire to keep such mementoes, even when I became an adult.'

'And as a policeman?'

'Especially then. I did not wish to be reminded. You could say I was in hiding. But do remember . . . the stories that came out at the time were not pleasant. People gorged themselves on innuendo. I did not want to save cuttings of the prurience that passed for the journalism of the period. Until last winter, I had no inkling of what the truth might be. Now, it is all very different. It is time to start digging. The newspaper archives will be just one point of entry.'

'Will that not alert the very people you wish to remain ignorant of the knowledge you are gathering?'

'We have our own archives,' Müller said, 'and I'm certain that what I can't find will be found via Pappi's network, somehow.'

'After seeing what your father has left you,' Greville said, 'there is no doubt in my mind that what I have left with Bill Jacques will be of great use to you. It will add to the sum of your knowledge.'

Like Müller, Greville now stood with both hands upon the balcony rail, and looked out upon the night.

'Do you realize,' Greville went on, 'that you were born in a most interesting year? You could say that was when the world finally came to understand just how truly vulnerable it was to the vagaries of the oil industry. Rhodesia, as was, rebelled against the Crown and tried its hand at its own brand of apartheid, giving itself a poisoned chalice out of which to drink to this day. De Gaulle popped it. So did Nasser, who was then succeeded by Sadat, thereby setting the scene for some things that continue to reverberate in my old stamping ground . . . and my own fate became entangled within it. *Sic transit gloria.*'

'Yet, as you've said, you would do it again . . . even knowing what you do.'

'Older and wiser? Possibly. But yes, I have thought about this for more years than I care to remember. I always come to the same point; and here I totally agree with your father. When people conspire to do things inimical to your way of life, you have no option but to fight them. So, yes . . . I would do so again; but perhaps, as I've said, a little more carefully. A little extra wariness would not have been amiss.'

'Wary of your enemies?'

'And of some of my so-called friends. Particularly so.'

They fell silent for a while.

'The Beatles disbanded,' Müller said. 'That had reverbera-tions that shook the world, I've been told . . .'

'It certainly did. And we actually had a golfing winner at the US Open.' Greville was smiling hugely. Then the smile went. 'And, sadly, Hendrix died.'

Müller stared at him. '*Jimi* Hendrix? You *like* Jimi Hendrix?'

'Steady on, old boy. You say that in shock. Do you think me such an old fogey? I still listen to "Purple Haze", I'll have you know.'

Müller could not restrain a laugh. 'Wonders.'

'Indeed. Some of my colleagues thought me quite mad. Certain some still do . . . those who know where I am.'

'I look at Kaltendorf, younger than you are, and his taste runs to *Volksmusik*. So,' Müller prodded, 'were you in a haze when you first listened to it?'

'Not the kind you're thinking. I'd met Isolde.' Greville spoke with a warmth that was revealing, as he stared out at the dark. 'Ah. Quite, quite taken I was, the first time we met. Taken to this day. Splendid, splendid woman. You do know what I'm talking about, don't you, old man?' There was a deliberate slyness in Greville's voice.

'Do I?'

'Of course you do. Miss Bloomfield has done rather the same to you, when you choose to admit it.'

Greville waited for a reaction, but Müller remained silent.

'You will find the killers of your parents, Jens,' Greville said quietly. 'The thieves who would steal your country. I know it. Fear not.' He paused. 'And now, I'm off to bed. Tomorrow is another day.'

A bemused Müller nodded. 'Goodnight, Greville.'

Greville gave him a pat on the arm and went back into the room.

Left with his thoughts, Müller found himself running over all that had happened during the day, commencing with his nightmare.

Greville's certainties were encouraging; but would he

really find the people behind the murder of his parents? They appeared to have so much power.

He was wealthy. He did not have to be a policeman.

Pappenheim had once jokingly said that he should take the money and run. Have a life of indolence, paid for by his money. It was what he would have done, Pappenheim had said.

But Müller knew differently. Were Pappenheim rich, he would still be doing what he did now. He would not have taken the money and run.

'And in my case,' Müller said to himself, 'I would be betraying my parents. My country too.'

No honour in that.

And there were the documents his father had left. Years of dangerously gathered intelligence. He would not allow that to go to waste. And Greville's notes, still to join the increasingly expanding database; and all the other little pieces that were coming in, drawing him closer to the killers, and the would-be thieves of a nation. There was Grogan, and there were Pappenheim's contacts. Plenty to do.

And, despite Kaltendorf, he liked working with the people around him. Nothing Kaltendorf could do would spoil that. And there was Kaltendorf himself; a former good policeman who seemed to have lost it all with high rank: lost his honour, lost his guts. Where did he fit in? Kaltendorf had known Neubauer; and Neubauer had known the thieves and killers.

And Carey Bloomfield. He would never have met someone like her if he had taken the money and run. He admitted to himself that he wanted to see her again.

'What would you say to that eh, Pappi?'

Probably too scandalized to comment, Müller thought. Which, for Pappenheim, would be something. He paused in his train of thought. The Eifel night seemed to swell around him.

'What do you know?' he said to the night softly.

*   *   *

Pappenheim stepped out of his office and locked it.

He walked down the corridor to the lifts and got in just as one was about to close. A uniformed sergeant he did not recognize was there. But the man seemed to know him.

'I don't believe it, sir,' the sergeant began. 'You're actually going home.' The man grinned at him.

Pappenheim frowned. 'Are you new here? I thought I knew everyone.'

'I'm one of *Kommissarin* Fohlmeister's team. New? Yes, sir. I'm due to see you tomorrow.'

'Ah. Yes.' Pappenheim paused, remembering. 'Hammersfeldt.'

'Yes, sir.'

'Word to the wise, Hammersfeldt.'

'Sir?'

'Don't be rude to your superiors before you get to know them properly.' Pappenheim grinned.

'Yes, sir.'

'And, as everyone will tell you, my bark is a lot worse than my bite.'

'I thought it was the other way round, sir.'

Pappenheim frowned at him. 'And you shouldn't get so smart so quickly.'

The lift arrived at street level. The sergeant got out with him and together they walked past the front desk.

The sergeant on duty looked up to see Pappenheim and Hammersfeldt.

'You're actually going home, sir?' the sergeant exclaimed in mock horror.

'What is this?' Pappenheim said. 'Don't you people think I've got a home to go to?'

Both sergeants grinned.

'Goodnight!' Pappenheim said to them, waving a dismissive hand as he left.

As he reached the pavement, he turned left. It was a

pleasantly warm night, and he wanted to walk. Berlin was his city. It held no terrors for him.

He stopped to light a cigarette.

Someone was running up behind him on silent feet. A single shot coughed into the night. The bullet from the silenced pistol struck Pappenheim in the back. Pappenheim fell forwards, cigarette and lighter flying in opposite directions.

Pappenheim did not move.

The silent runner sped away without looking back.

It was already another day.